Dear Reader:

Thanks for picking up a copy of *Recipe for Love*. Shamara Ray is an engaging and provocative new voice on the literary scene. Everyone is searching for that perfect love: someone who is their mirror image and complements them in every way. Sometimes, that person might have been in front of our eyes the entire time. Such is the case of the heroine in this story, who ends up falling in love with her greatest competitor. Of course they would have much in common; they share the same passion for food and everyone knows that cuisine can be the ultimate aphrodisiac.

In *Recipe for Love*, you get all of those elements but you also get to witness what happens when lovers have trouble letting go of the past. I am sure that most can relate to that; whether they have been on the giving or receiving end of the obsessed behavior. Shamara Ray does an excellent job developing her characters and making the lovely restaurants characters themselves. I wanted to pull up a chair to one of the tables myself and chow down.

Also included in the back of the book are several recipes to entice your palate after the novel has enticed your mind. I hope that you will enjoy *Recipe for Love* and, as always, I truly appreciate your support of Strebor Books, my epicenter that keeps me grounded in the middle of a storm. Please check out our other titles on Zanestore.com and make sure to join my online social network at PlanetZane.org.

Blessings,

Zane

Zane
Publisher
Strebor Books International
www.simonandschuster.com/streborbooks

ZANE PRESENTS

RECIPE FOR
LOVE

ZANE PRESENTS

RECIPE FOR LOVE

SHAMARA RAY

SBI

STREBOR BOOKS

NEW YORK LONDON TORONTO SYDNEY

SBI

Strebor Books
P.O. Box 6505
Largo, MD 20792
http://www.streborbooks.com

ISBN 978-1-59309-327-3
ISBN 978-1-4516-0804-5 (ebook)
LCCN 2010940488

First Strebor Books trade paperback edition February 2011

Cover design: www.mariondesigns.com
Cover photograph: © Keith Saunders/Marion Designs

10 9 8 7 6 5 4 3 2 1

Manufactured in the United States of America

For Aunt Dolly

ACKNOWLEDGMENTS

I would like to thank Denise, Joanne, Kelly, Linda, Mia, Olu, Selena, and Xalya for your eyes and ears. Mr. and Mrs. J, thank you for your deep well of encouragement.

Zane and Charmaine, many thanks to you both.

Words are not enough...a *special* thanks to my wonderful parents for their love and support.

It's been said that I have a problem admitting when I'm wrong. The main reason is because I never am.

Okay, that's not completely true. I was wrong once when I told my friend, Milan, it was all right for her to go to the beach on a first date, sans underwear, on a very breezy spring evening. You can imagine what happened. Now that I think about it, there was also the time I told an elderly gentleman to turn right at the next corner when he really should've made a left. I've always wondered if he made it to the emergency room before his chest pain got any worse. Either way, in both cases I had good intentions so it can't be held against me.

It has also been said I could stand a bit of humility. I don't necessarily agree, but Milan has told me this on numerous occasions. As one of my nearest and dearest, I entertain her criticism since I know it comes from a good place. But let it be known, I don't take kindly to being critiqued by just anyone.

Milan and I met at Minority Spring Weekend at Syracuse University. You know those special recruitment programs when universities bus in potential minority freshmen, show them all of the positive things their institutions have to offer, and then they arrive in the fall greeted by all the negative things that were carefully hidden during their visits? Well, if you don't know, now you know. It was during that visit that we hit it off immediately. Milan has been on my Diva Squad ever since. Born and raised in Philly, my girl was a trip. She was down to earth and could have you laughing for days with her crazy antics.

We registered for biology during our sophomore year, which neither one of us wanted to take but it was a requirement for graduation. Milan was adamant that there were certain things she wasn't willing to do in the name of science, dissection being one of them. She came up with the idea to pretend she was legally blind for an entire semester so she didn't have to splice, slice or dice frogs, pigs, or any other creature. The professor, convinced that her vision was impaired due to the coke bottle glasses she'd found at a thrift shop, actually went out of his way to describe each part of the specimen so she wouldn't feel excluded from the experience. Needless to say, she did exceptionally well in the course, much better than me and my 20/20 vision.

Milan reminded me a lot of myself. That's why we got along so well and still do.

NINE A.M. AND I WAS RUNNING LATE for our Saturday morning workout at the gym. I looked forward to our weekly stress-release-bitchfest to shake off all of the nonsense from the week. Since we'd started a year ago, Milan had lost about twenty pounds. At five-ten, she was never a big girl, but now she was a lean, mean brick house that turned so many heads when she passed, you would've thought men were auditioning for a remake of *The Exorcist*.

Men loved her Halle Berry short hair and cocoa butter brown skin. Milan was an unintentional flirt; it came across naturally. Her flirtatious nature usually resulted in some brother getting the wrong message and hurt feelings to go along with it.

By the time I arrived at the gym, fifteen minutes late, Milan was already on the elliptical trainer working up a sweat.

I tried to put on my best *I was rushing to get here* face. "Hey, Lan, sorry I'm late."

"Don't apologize to me," she panted. "You'd better say sorry to those flabby thighs of yours." She laughed at her own joke, lost her balance, then tried to get back into the zone before her rhythm was totally thrown off.

I climbed on the machine next to her and put my water bottle in the holder. "You wish your thighs looked half as good as mine do. There isn't one ounce of fat on my body. Don't forget you need to be here. I only come to keep you company, Porky."

We both laughed at that one. It never failed; as soon as we get together, the jokes started flowing. A petite, white woman on the elliptical on the other side of Milan laughed at our barbs as if she was a part of the discussion. I rolled my eyes upward at the intrusion and set my machine for thirty minutes. We'd grown accustomed to strangers butting into our conversations. It seemed like we were having such a good time that they wanted to join in the fun.

"So, what's the reason for today's hold-up?"

I hesitated. "I got a last-minute phone call."

"From?"

"Huh?"

"Jade, you know you heard me."

I increased the speed of my machine. "It was Nolan."

"Humph."

I braced myself for the pending storm; that grunt couldn't possibly be Milan's only response. We ran in silence for what seemed like the longest minute ever.

I eventually gave in. "We were only on the phone for about five minutes and I told him I had to meet you."

"Why are you still speaking to him?"

"Lan, if he calls me, I'm not going to be rude and you shouldn't expect me to."

"Well, I do."

"We were all friends at one time," I replied, trying to keep the conversation from taking a turn for the worse.

She blinked the sweat from her eyes. "Right. We were. That's past tense."

"Listen, you two chose to take things to the next level. It didn't work. However, Nolan and I are still friends. We've been friends since college and it's not right for you to expect me to cut him off because you did."

Milan clenched her teeth and the handrail on the elliptical simultaneously. I increased the speed on my machine again. Side by side we were running hard now, the humming of the machine magnifying the volume of our silence.

"Do you really think you're being fair right now?" I asked.

She stopped her machine and sighed. "No, I guess not. What happened between me and Nolan has nothing to do with you. You're right...as usual. Meet me downstairs at the pool when you're done here. I'm going to do a few laps to cool off."

"I'll be down in a minute."

The "as usual" was her attempt at a jab since I pushed her buttons, but I let it slide. I didn't want to ruin our day over a simple phone call.

As soon as we finished our workout, we drove back to my house. After a hot shower, I was invigorated. I put my shoulder-length hair up casually in a clip, leaving a playful tendril to fall on my neck. I searched my closet until I found what I was looking for—my strapless cream linen dress that stopped mid-thigh and hugged me in all the right places. The caramel accents down the sides of the dress matched my skin tone to perfection. Since you can't wear a short dress without some high-ass heels, my three-inch strappy brown sandals completed my outfit.

Just as I was spraying on my Ecstasy perfume, a favorite of mine from Carol's Daughter, Milan emerged from the bathroom; skin glowing.

"You have the best shower. The perfect amount of water pressure."

"I installed that showerhead this week."

She chuckled. "I might've enjoyed that shower more than I did our workout."

"Gross. You'd better not have been getting freaky in my shower."

"Stop trippin'. Nobody was violating your sacred bathroom. You're the only freak getting freaked up in here."

"And don't you forget it or else I'm going to start making you go home to get dressed after the gym."

"Girl, please. We'd never get to lunch if I had to go to Suffolk to get ready."

Milan lived further out on Long Island in Deer Park; forty minutes from my house in Baldwin Harbor if there was no traffic to contend with. It was easier for us to get ready at my place for our day of fitness, food, and fun since we did most of our hanging in Nassau County.

With the fitness portion taken care of, we typically had lunch at Rituals, the restaurant I co-owned with my childhood friend, Bria. Rituals was the realization of a shared dream that Bria and I had had since we were teens.

In high school, Bria and I had started a gourmet lunch business where we would charge our classmates to make their daily lunches. In place of awful cafeteria food, we offered specialty soups and sandwiches like grilled chicken with roasted red pepper and mozzarella on a baguette with basil mayonnaise. Unfortunately, most kids weren't willing to shell out six dollars for a sandwich when they could get a ham and cheese on rye for two bucks. The business was a flop, but considering we were high school students, it was the entrepreneurial spirit that counted.

I loved to cook—birthdays, showers, holidays, you name it; I created appetizing dishes for family and friends. My mother had the wisdom to start me in the kitchen at an early age and the desire to create culinary masterpieces blossomed. Back then, I'd put a new spin on regular dishes that would have my family reminiscing about it for days.

After high school, Bria attended the Culinary Institute of America in Hyde Park, New York. C.I.A. was one of the best culinary schools in the country. After C.I.A., she spent six years as head chef at some of the trendiest spots in Manhattan.

I received my degree in business administration from Syracuse, then followed in Bria's footsteps by going to C.I.A. Upon completing my culinary training, I delighted the clientele at Noir in Long Island with my specialties for two years before deciding it was time to turn my dreams into reality.

Despite our individual successes, Bria and I were obsessed with having our own restaurant. Four years ago, we'd opened Rituals.

Rituals served Southern cuisine with a neo-soul flair. We were known for making the most delectable seafood; one taste of our pan-seared salmon would make you forget that you'd had it any other way. We received stellar reviews in *Bon Appétit* magazine and in the *New York Times*, which helped to put us on the map. We stayed busy. As a result, we were currently in the process of expanding the restaurant.

"I don't think I want to eat at Rituals today," I said.

"Why not?" Milan asked. "I'm dying for some Grand Marnier pancakes or a crab omelet."

"I don't like going into the restaurant dressed so casually. I do have an image to maintain."

"Tell me, how is it that you don't fall off that high-horse you're riding?"

"Would you strut into Stowe, Black and Helms with those tight-ass pants you just painted on? I'm sure Wallace Black would love his attorneys looking like they're going to a party in the courtroom."

Milan was wearing a pair of dark blue, boot-cut, low-rise jeans that left nothing to the imagination, with a light-blue halter top with strings that crisscrossed her back and tied around her waist.

"Probably not, but that's only because I'm trying to make partner. After that, it's a free-for-all. I'm wearing what I want, when I want. I'll step in there with a bikini on if I so choose." Milan chuckled. "Now change your so-called casual clothes so I can eat."

I sucked my teeth. "Yeah, okay."

"I'm kidding." Milan checked her appearance in the mirror. "What's funny is that I probably could get away with this outfit. Wallace's daughter, Chanel, is doing her externship at the firm while she completes law school and you should see the skimpy skirts she wears to work."

"That's a perk to being the boss's daughter."

Milan grabbed her purse. "So I can't get brunch at Rituals today, huh?"

"Lan, it's called Sunday brunch for a reason. Today is Saturday. We don't serve brunch on Saturday. How come every week I tell you the same thing? Stop going into my restaurant asking my chefs to make you brunch on Saturday. Bring your ass down to Rituals on Sunday if you want Grand Marnier pancakes."

Milan cracked up. "What the hell is the point of having a best friend that owns a restaurant if I can't get any perks? And I didn't only want to go for the pancakes; I was hoping to get a look at that fine-ass brother of yours. Didn't you say he's been spending more time over there lately?"

My brother, Terrence, was an architect and he was drawing up designs for our expansion. He ran the firm my father started thirty-five years ago. He'd been at Rituals so much lately, and always with a plate in hand, that I was starting to think he was a part of the wait staff.

"You can flirt with Terrence some other time."

"Alright, we'll go somewhere else this time, but make sure you tell Terrence I have something for his fine ass."

I pushed Milan toward the door. "Take your hot-to-trot self downstairs so we can get out of here."

I backed my silver Lexus SC430 out of the garage and put the convertible top down. The sun was shining bright; a warm breeze was blowing; and we were too cool for words. Always one for some classic R&B, I turned on D'Angelo's first CD, pumped up the volume and started to groove to "Brown Sugar." I slid on my sunglasses, hit the gas, and we were on our way to the Hills for some eats.

WE PULLED UP TO VALET PARKING AT EDEN, hoping it wasn't too crowded inside for two hungry sistas to get their grub on. I liked to get there before all the people that partied on Friday night rolled out of the bed. Eden had a tendency to run out of dishes; especially the salmon croquettes that were a must-have with the garlic parmesan grits. I was always checking out the competition and I couldn't deny Eden served good food, but the menu at Rituals was a step above the rest and we had Eden beat hands down.

Milan went inside to get a table while I waited for my ticket from the parking attendant. She was engaged in conversation with the owner, Cain, when I walked up.

Cain greeted me with a kiss on the cheek. "Thank you for making my day."

"What are you talking about, Cain?" I noticed his slight grin and roving eyes. "Matter of fact, forget I asked." I turned to Milan. "Do we have a long wait?"

"He can seat us right now."

Cain cleared his throat. "Uh, yeah. I have a table out on the patio *especially* for you."

"Cain, when are you going to stop running those corny lines?" I asked.

He laughed. "When they start working."

I shook my head as he led us to the table. I could hear Milan giggling behind me. Cain and I went through this every time we came to Eden and she realized how much it irked me.

The table was accented with pink and pale yellow napkins atop a crisp white tablecloth. In the center of each table was a vase with an arrangement of pink and yellow tulips. I was admiring the ode to spring theme that Cain had going on. Things were always colorful at Eden. Cream walls with large murals reminiscent of enchanted gardens made you feel as if you were actually dining in the Garden of Eden. The table settings changed with the season, as did the lighting on the murals. In the fall, golden lights shine on the murals and pick up the copper and coral accents that aren't visible under the pink and blue lights used in the spring. I came to Eden expecting to see something new and creative.

Cain pulled out my chair, waited for me to get situated, then laid the cloth napkin across my lap—his eyes never leaving me. I quickly picked up the menu and buried my face in it.

"I suppose I'm chopped liver over here," Milan complained. "A sista can't get her chair pulled out, too?"

"I apologize. I was distracted by this rare…" Cain paused. "My bad. No more corny lines. Jade, you look beautiful today. Let me get that chair for you, Milan." He handed Milan a menu. "Enjoy your meal, ladies." Cain lingered for a moment before going back inside.

Milan looked from Cain to me. "Now that's a first."

"What is?"

"Cain trying to be sincere. He may really have a thing for you. At first I thought he was just being a flirt but now I don't know."

I glued my eyes to the menu, fumbled with it, then used it to fan myself. I sensed Milan observing my every move. I took a quick sip of my water. "Lan, please. That man probably drools over every halfway decent woman that comes through those doors."

Laying her menu on the table, Milan sat back in her chair. "Let me find out that you're attracted to Cain."

Cain was six feet three inches, weighing in with at least 240 pounds of muscle. A dark chocolate brother with perfectly straight, perfectly white teeth, he sported a bald head and a well-mani-cured goatee. Nice eyes and full, kissable lips…who wouldn't have found him attractive? Cain was dripping with sex appeal.

She started giggling again when I didn't immediately answer. "That's what I thought," she said.

"You thought wrong. I'm not thinking about Cain. Besides, I have a man, or did you forget?"

"No, but maybe you forgot. Didn't you two break up three weeks ago? Oh, let me guess, you got back together yesterday, right?"

"Nobody likes a smartass." I chuckled. "No, we didn't get back together and we probably won't this time. It's going to take a minute before I get used to the idea that I'm single."

"And the idea that you aren't getting any."

I snatched my menu from the table. "Whatever, Lan."

"Don't get sensitive on me." She leaned forward and lowered her voice, as if letting me in on a secret. "Seriously, you don't have to be single. You're a beautiful, young woman with a hell of a lot to offer. Any man would be lucky to have you. Maybe you should give Cain a chance. Nobody said you have to marry the man; just go out on a date with him."

"This sounds a bit familiar. Didn't I give you this same speech a couple of months ago?" I said, laughing.

She smirked at me. "Okay, so you give good advice. I figured that I'd return the favor."

The waitress arrived to take our orders, giving me a break from Ms. Love Connection. I ordered my usual, grits and croquettes, but decided to splurge and added the scrambled eggs with caramelized shallots. Milan had to satisfy her pancake-jones with the peach pancakes with vanilla syrup and homemade turkey sausage patties.

As soon as the waitress was out of earshot, Milan started going on about Cain again. "How could you not want to go out with a good-looking man like him?"

"It takes more than a nice body and a perfect smile."

"Oh, so you do notice him?"

"Of course I notice him, Milan. There's no way I could ignore all of that."

"Then give him a chance. Find out what he's all about."

"Lan, drop it."

"I will, but you need to get used to being single…quick."

Although we had begun to discuss what we wanted to get into after brunch, I was thinking about what Milan had said to me. She was right. I was single and I needed to act like it.

Plates of partially eaten food were all over the table. I had done as much damage as I could on my meal and was so full that I didn't want to taste another bite of croquette for at least a year.

"Eating that much food should be illegal," I complained.

"What was the purpose of going to the gym this morning?" Milan rubbed her stomach. "I think I just gained ten pounds."

"Let's get out of here and get to shopping. I need to walk this off ASAP."

We left the money for our meals, including a generous tip for the waitress, in the guest check holder on the table. I know, first-hand, how important tips are to the wait staff. As we made our way to the exit, I spotted Cain at the hostess station. I discreetly reached in my bag and pulled out my business card. Milan waved as she passed Cain; I looked at him, smiled, then pressed my card in his hand. Surprise washed over his face and he smiled back. I felt a flutter in my stomach. I continued to saunter toward the door, but turned my head and mouthed, "Call me."

He replied with a subtle nod. That simple gesture made my day.

2

M y street was quiet by the time I arrived home. The neighborhood kids had probably gone inside when the street lights came on, had dinner and baths, and were most likely dreaming of all the things they wanted to do tomorrow. I turned on the lamp in my bedroom and reclined on the chaise next to the window. I removed my sandals and began to massage my feet. Tired from walking store to store, the only thing I wanted to do was take a hot bath and climb into my bed.

I had done some serious damage on my credit card and would probably regret it in the morning. Milan and I'd had had to make three trips to the car during our shopping excursion to relieve ourselves of some of the packages. Don't get me wrong; I liked shopping as much as the next person, but Milan was in a league of her own. She would've shopped all day, every day, if she could have. She didn't see it, but the minute her feet stepped inside a store, she transformed into a plastic-money maniac who bought every third thing she touched. It was scary. She needed to seek professional help; my girl was definitely a shopaholic.

I'd intentionally left a few things in the car that I might've ended up returning. If you didn't bring it into the house, then you didn't form an attachment. It sounds silly, but it worked.

Forcing myself off the chaise, I dragged my sore feet to the kitchen for a glass of wine. Pinot Grigio, soft candlelight and the smooth sounds of Maxwell's *Embrya* CD were all I needed to end the perfect day. *Embrya* wasn't exactly new, but once I loved a CD, I was hooked, no matter how old it was.

I ran water into my whirlpool tub, added peppermint oil to soothe my tired feet and pinned up my hair. I stepped into the tub and turned on the jets. The pulsating action took me to another level of relaxation. I was at a private concert and Maxwell was singing his "Drowndeep: Hula" song. I used the remote to turn up the volume. The hypnotic bass and his smooth voice put me in a trance and I began to hum along. Now there was an enlightened brother. I wondered where I could find a man who wanted to drown deep in our relationship. I took a sip of my wine, slipped down further in the tub, and closed my eyes.

I was jolted by a vision of Cain's face.

I picked up my sponge, poured on my peppermint essence body gel, and began to caress my body. I tried to keep my mind from wandering to Cain, since he had no business in my bathroom, but all I could think about were those strong arms and his broad chest. Just as I was about to give in to my fantasies and let Cain wash my back, my telephone rang. I scrambled for the remote and pressed pause. My answering machine picked up and a familiar voice flooded my space.

Jade, are you there? Pick up. You there? Alright, peace.

The machine clicked off, snapping me out of my stupor. In a matter of seconds my entire mood had changed. Even though I was surrounded by warm swirling water, I felt chilled. I was not happy that my evening with Cain and Maxwell had come to such an abrupt end. What was Bryce calling me for, anyway? I guzzled down the rest of my drink, then showered the soap from my body.

I dried off, watching myself in the mirror, and thought about the advice that came back to me earlier that day like a boomerang. Why had I spent the last four years in an unhealthy relationship if I had so much to offer someone? I was intelligent, successful, and had a beautiful spirit and a face to match. I looked in the mirror long and hard at the one person I had to answer to. Neither one of us broke eye contact. I wanted answers. I wanted her to account for her actions. I wanted her to make me understand why she had let Bryce treat her the way he did. I didn't speak. She didn't speak. We weren't ready yet.

SUNDAY MORNING I HAD TO BE AT RITUALS EARLY. I typically arrived by six a.m. to make sure Sunday brunch would be problem-free. The quiet of the restaurant allowed me to work on the financial management of the business before the staff arrived at seven. It was difficult to work on budget and cost control issues once the first customer entered through the door and both staff and clientele needed your attention.

I unlocked the mahogany double doors and went inside. My shoes hitting against the hardwood floor echoed in the empty restaurant. The mahogany and black paneled walls, coupled with the six-foot-tall African statues that greeted you at the door, could have an intimidating effect if you weren't used to being alone in the dark and in the midst of a powerful tribal presence.

I turned on the recessed lighting above the bar and opened the blinds to let the rising sun pour through the windows and brighten the rest of the 15,000-square-foot dining room. This was the calm before the storm. Since we'd added the jazz band two months ago, the brunch crowd had nearly doubled and Sunday afternoons could be a bit hectic.

I made myself a cup of chamomile tea and read over the messages Bria had left for me.

The fishmonger has something new for you to try.

I'd call tomorrow morning to set up a presentation.

The linen service can't locate the gold and black silk shantung tablecloth.

If they knew like I knew, they had better find it in the quickness.

The band may be a half an hour late.

I'd have a talk with them to make sure they weren't starting any bad habits.

Cain called.

I read that one again.

Cain called.

As if on auto pilot, I picked up the phone and dialed the number on the paper.

After three rings, a husky, almost abrasive voice answered, "Mornin'."

"Good morning…this is…this is Jade," I stuttered, suddenly aware that I was calling this man at six in the morning.

"Believe me, I know who this is. I've been waiting for this call for a long time. How are you this morning, Ms. Jade?"

I immediately realized that it was a mistake to call him so early. I ran my fingers through my hair. Habit.

"Cain, I'm so sorry for calling you at this time of the morning. I can call you back later, if you want." I was dying to hang up the phone. *What was I thinking?*

"It's alright." He yawned. "I actually need to get up anyway."

"I'm so sorry," I repeated.

"Do me a favor."

"What?"

"Stop apologizing and have dinner with me tonight."

Damn. He didn't waste any time.

I thought about it. It wasn't as if I had plans for the evening and he had almost helped me bathe last night; well sort of.

I quickly concluded that I didn't have anything to lose. "That sounds good to me."

"Great. I'll speak to you a little later about the details. And thank you for the wake-up call, Jade."

"You're welcome, I guess. Talk to you later."

"I'm looking forward to it."

I placed the phone back in its cradle, walked over to the bar, and perched myself on a stool. I couldn't believe I'd agreed to go out with Cain. It had been a long time since I'd played the dating game, but like Milan had said, it was just a date—nothing more, nothing less.

Even though Milan was right, my nerves were already getting the best of me. Moving forward is the second step in leaving the past behind; the first step is your decision to make the present your past. I had officially taken steps away from my past. My father had once told me never to let the past interfere with my future. I didn't intend to.

As much as I would've loved to sit and ponder life, I had work to do. I hurriedly finished my tea and began to work on the menu for a private party booked for the following week.

I was startled when I heard the door opening; I thought I had locked it. No one arrived that early. I jumped off the barstool and tip-toed my way to the door. I was a few steps away when Terrence popped his head in.

"What's up, Lil' Sis?" He stopped where he stood. "What's wrong with you?"

I was stuck mid-tiptoe, feeling as crazy as I must've looked. "Boy, you scared me to death. What are you doing here at this hour?" I quickly straightened myself out before he had a chance to turn it into a huge joke at my expense. "Shouldn't you be under your covers with your curtains drawn like other vampires?"

Terrence came over and hugged me. "I should be but I left some blueprints here last night. I stopped by to pick them up."

"Stopped by? Where are you going to, or should I say coming from, at this time of the morning?"

His clothes were a bit disheveled but he smelled like he'd used some chick's Bath & Body Works products.

"Why are you all up in my business? Your young ears aren't mature enough to hear where I've been or what I've been doing."

"I'm two years younger than you and last time I checked, I was grown. But you know what? I don't want to know. Probably up to no good anyway."

"Now what kind of thing is that to say about your favorite brother?"

"You're my *only* brother."

"Yeah and that makes me your favorite by default."

"Whatever you say, fool. Oh, before I forget, I have a message for you."

"What did Milan have to say this time?" he asked, laughing.

"She said she has something for you."

"Well, tell her to drop it in the mail."

I tried not to encourage him, but the boy was funny. "You aren't wrapped too tight," I said. "For some strange reason, she's attracted to your tall, bowlegged self. If you ask me, I don't get what she sees in you."

"She sees that I'm the man; that's what."

"Why don't you take her out? It's not like you have to marry her; it would only be a date."

That line was really contagious. It kept going around and around, like the flu.

Terrence pointed his finger at me. "You know the rule."

"I know; I know. We don't date one another's friends. Although, I could make an exception for your boy, Malik. Now he's worth breaking the rule for." The look on my face must've told him that I was having impure thoughts about Malik.

"Don't make me sick so early in the morning." His playful smile intensified into a real one. "What happened? You finally kick that bum, Bryce, to the curb?"

Clearly there was no love lost between those two. My brother never did care for Bryce. Unlike Bria and me, they didn't play together as children. They belonged to separate crews, each crew thinking they were cooler than the other. Adding fuel to the fire, in high school they had dated a few of the same girls, not at the same time, but they were definitely snacking from the same box of Ho Hos. Once Bryce and I had become a couple, Terrence's dislike had escalated from bad to worse. However, he'd tolerated Bryce for me.

"Let's not talk about Bryce, unless you want to make *me* sick," I said.

"I'm not even going to ask."

"Good idea, Big Bro. This is grown folks' business." I assumed that he might continue with the questions, but he didn't. "While you're here, why don't you make yourself busy? Fold a napkin or something." I tossed a napkin at his head.

He ducked. "I don't think so. This is your place of business, not mine. I have some sleep to catch up on. I'm outta here. See you later, fool."

Before I could respond, he jetted out the door.

I was proud of Terrence. He was running our father's business and doing so with professionalism and skill. I could remember when he had no direction, no interest in taking over the family business. He'd never liked school and had done barely enough to get by. In high school, he'd loved to party and all of his friends had looked to him for a good time. When my parents had finally sat him down and quizzed him on his plans for the future, they were nonexistent. Terrence didn't know what he wanted to do. He hadn't applied to any colleges and seemed not to be concerned that his graduation was rapidly approaching. That's when my father had pulled rank and made the decision that my brother was going into the service. My father had been in the Army and now my brother would be a Marine.

After the recruiter left our home, I sat in my brother's room discussing the deal that had been sealed.

"Do you even want to go into the service?" I asked.

"Not really but *your* father made the choice for me."

"Then why didn't you apply for college?"

"I was going to. I have a few applications on my desk."

I looked at the desk full of wrinkled papers. "Then tell him you don't want to go."

"What's the point? He already decided."

That's where my brother and I differed. I'd always spoken up and voiced my opinion to my parents, even when they didn't want to hear it. I'd gotten in trouble many times for talking too much—or as my mother would say—not knowing when to shut up.

Terrence went into the service a teen, but when he came out, he was his own man. He had taken a few college courses in the service and decided he would enroll in NYU to complete his degree in architecture. He could finally relate to my father, man-to-man, and the respect between them was reciprocal. It was understood that my brother would work for my father after college. However, when he joined the firm, some old rifts began to resurface. Their work ethics were drastically different. My father was from the old school—my brother from the new—they clashed somewhere in the middle. If it wasn't my father's way, then it wasn't right. Terrence grew weary of being lectured and reprimanded day in and day out. Their relationship was tense. The time Terrence spent with my father at work was so stressful that he didn't want to be with him, if he didn't have to. Outside of work, Terrence steered clear of my father. He avoided family events, always saying he had other plans. It wasn't until my mother had had enough that the situation was resolved. She brought them both to the table to find out what was going on. Terrence explained to my father that he needed to have faith in his judgment and skills. He asked him to guide, not demand.

My father admitted it was difficult to relinquish the control he had held for so long. He had built the business from nothing and understood what it took to run it *his* way. He also realized that the business had to grow and evolve with Terrence since he wouldn't always be around. Bit by bit, my father had passed the torch to my brother.

That meeting was the catalyst for a new day at the company. Terrence finally felt free to submit his designs. My father saw both of his babies take off and soar.

Don't get me wrong, Terrence still loved a good time, and my brother sure could party, but he was committed to his career and to continuing my father's legacy.

I MANAGED TO COMPLETE THE PARTY MENU just as the staff began to trickle in. I went to the kitchen to discuss the brunch specials with the prep chefs. I wanted to use a fresh berry puree for the waffles instead of the apple nut compote we had the week before. There were fresh peaches to peel and slice, and the melon salad drizzled with raspberry-mint coulis had to stand for at least two hours before the refreshing flavors could be fully appreciated. I worked side by side with my chefs at the prep table, carving perfectly round balls from watermelons, cantaloupes, and honeydews.

Occasionally, I rolled up my sleeves and participated with the food prep. The chopping, mincing, and dicing could be tedious to most, but I enjoyed it—it kept me sharp. Spending time in the kitchen was a good way for me to bond with my kitchen crew. I could also observe their technique and offer advice, if necessary. What typically resulted from my working in the kitchen was a quick instructional on preparations. I didn't mind. I was willing to share my knowledge because it only benefited Rituals. There are some chefs who guard their techniques like they're the Holy Grail. None of our diners should've been able to decipher if I'd prepared something or if someone with less experience had. The taste had to remain consistent from one dining experience to the next. If I improved upon a dish, then all of my chefs *had to* know how to do the same.

With the berry puree and raspberry-mint coulis prepared, I went out front to inspect the dining room. The busboys bustled from table to table arranging the place settings while gossiping about who did what the night before. I asked someone to refill the salt shakers and pepper mills on each table. Call it a quirk, but I can't stand partially filled shakers.

Since the black-and-gold tablecloth was missing I had to use a crisp white one to drape over the buffet table. Only on Sundays did we set up a buffet, so I only needed the decorative cloth once a week. The cleaners losing that specific cloth was an unacceptable inconvenience. I'd purchased it during a trip to Africa from a small shop in Ghana where an elderly woman and her daughter made the most beautiful cloths and linens. The elderly woman had told me the cloth represented community and sharing. Every Sunday we'd arrange fresh fruit, home-baked breads, cakes, and muffins on the buffet. Our diners could either start or finish their meal at the buffet, and it was always available free of charge. It was one of our rituals—sharing our sweet bounty with our community.

I turned on the radio and tuned into smooth jazz—at least until the band arrived—then I headed to my office in the back to retrieve cash for the register from the safe. After performing a quick review of the previous day's receipts, I counted the cash for the drawer. When I emerged from the office, the dining room was ready and a few people were coming through the door. I fixed myself another cup of tea, then went to greet our steady stream of guests.

MY EYES WERE CONTINUOUSLY DRAWN TO MY WATCH. Brunch ended at two and it was only twelve-thirty. The day was crawling. Cain had called earlier to ask me if six p.m. was all right with my schedule. We started serving dinner at four on Sundays and we closed at ten. On most Sundays, I didn't leave Rituals until after midnight. I called my father to see if he would come down and work the evening shift at the restaurant. Since he'd retired in January, my father would fill in for Bria and me on occasion. He didn't like to be idle and he enjoyed the time he spent down at Rituals. My mother enjoyed it when he was out of the house for a few hours.

It wasn't absolutely necessary for my father to fill in for us; we had a restaurant manager, but Bria and I understood the importance of our presence. We did what we could to make everyone who entered Rituals feel like family during their dining experience. Even my father did his part. He was good at liaising with the patrons and his personal touch was just like getting mine. Rituals was in good hands when I left to get ready for my date.

3

I had given Cain directions to my house, but I asked him to pick me up at seven instead of six. He told me to dress comfortably; he was taking me to a concert in the park. I appreciated a man who could make plans and was considerate enough to tell you what to wear for the occasion.

As soon as I walked in the door, I went straight to the phone. I needed to tell Milan the scoop. Lord knows, she would've had a fit if I neglected to tell her what was brewing. Her phone rang a few times, then went to voicemail.

I'm not in or maybe I'm avoiding you, so cross your fingers and leave a message and I may call you back. Beep.

"Milan, it's me. You really need to change your ghetto-fied message. Anyway, I called to give you some juicy info, but since you're not home, or you're *avoiding* me, you'll have to wait until later. Peace, my sister."

I hung up. The phone instantly rang back.

I picked up and started running my mouth. "I should've known you were screening your calls, Milan."

"This isn't Milan."

No, it wasn't.

I sighed heavily before responding. "What's up, Bryce?" He caught me off guard. I didn't look at the caller ID before answering, which I always do.

"I left you a message last night…did you get it?"

"Actually I didn't," I lied. There weren't enough hours in a day for that conversation. I wasn't prepared for it; didn't want to have it. I plopped down on the sofa and turned on the television. "I was out all night and I just got home so if you don't mind, I—"

"You didn't come home last night? Where were you?"

"I don't see how that's any of your business, Bryce."

No response. I'd put him in his place.

He regrouped after a moment. "Jade, you'll always be my business. I was calling to see how you're doing."

"Really? Now that's funny. When we were together, you weren't too concerned about my well-being. Why the sudden interest, Bryce?"

Bryce wasn't a patient man. He was trying hard to mask his annoyance but I was pushing his buttons.

"Jade, I don't want to fight with you. I called you last night because I couldn't stop thinking about you. I wanted to hear your voice. I miss you. "

I lowered my defenses, told my inner bitch to chill. "I'm doing fine, Bryce. All is right with my world."

"I want to see you. Be honest; don't you want to see me, too? Wait, don't answer yet."

My doorbell rang.

"Bryce, that better not be you."

"What if it is? I miss you, Jade. I need to see your face."

My initial reaction was to pretend I wasn't home, but of course, that wouldn't work. Damn. I didn't have time for this. I reluctantly got up from the couch. I clicked off the phone and went to the front door. I looked out the peephole and there he was. I opened the door and stared blankly at Bryce, holding a bouquet of long-stemmed red roses. His hazel eyes sparkled when he saw me.

Hand on hip, I asked, "What are you doing here?"

"I needed to see you."

"So you show up at my door unannounced?"

"I brought a peace offering." He held out the roses and tried to ensnare me with his hypnotic gaze.

I looked away from his eyes for a second; I didn't want to get sucked into his emotions. I opened the storm door, took the roses, and let the door close.

We continued to glare at one another through the glass.

He rubbed his now empty hands together. "Can I come in or are you going to take my offering and leave me out in the cold?"

"It's over eighty degrees, Bryce."

"Come on, Jade."

I took a deep breath, then held the door open for him to enter. He stepped into the foyer, bent down, and kissed me on the cheek. I backed away from him.

"You can come in for a minute, but that's it."

"Fine. I'll take what I can get."

I closed the door, thought about making him stand in the foyer to talk, but didn't. He followed me into the living room and sat on the sofa. I went over to the loveseat. I didn't want to be close to him. I laid the roses down on the coffee table.

"You should put those in water," he said.

"I will, in a minute. As soon as you leave, I'll take care of it."

Bryce laughed as he stood up. "Is your vase still under the kitchen sink?"

"Yeah, why?"

He didn't answer but made his way to the kitchen with the roses. I heard the cabinet close and the water running. That was something I used to love about Bryce. He had a take-charge attitude that turned me on. He realized what he wanted and exactly how to get it; that's how we'd ended up together.

Bryce was Bria's twin brother. I'd known him for most of my

life. Back in the day, when we were nappy-headed rugrats, I'd never paid him any attention and he'd completely ignored me. You couldn't tell him he wasn't cute with his sandy brown hair and cleft in his chin. The girls would fall all over him but I wasn't interested; he was my best friend's brother. The Twins—that's what we called them in the neighborhood—are the same age as Terrence. Back then, Bryce pretty much viewed me as a little kid. Then I grew up and he began to take notice.

During the construction phase of Rituals, Bryce would come by to check out the progress. At first it was every couple of weeks, then once a week, eventually every day. We developed a friendship, became better acquainted with each other. At the time, I was dating a couple of brothers. Bryce aggressively inserted himself into the equation and subtracted out the weak.

Strolling the boardwalk in Long Beach at sunset, concerts in Central Park, intimate dinners at my place, street festivals in Brooklyn, midnight calls lasting until dawn turned into something special, something real. We'd become a couple. Inseparable. Insatiable. In love.

A COUPLE OF MINUTES LATER, BRYCE RETURNED with the roses beautifully arranged in my crystal Mikasa vase. He placed them in front of me on the coffee table.

"Now isn't this better?" A devilish smile crept across his golden face. "I wanted to see you appreciate them while I'm here."

"You're a piece of work."

"You're welcome."

"Bryce, the roses are nice but you shouldn't be here."

"I had to see you…I can't sleep…I can't even think straight. I didn't care if coming here was wrong—I had to see you today."

He sat down next to me, gazing at me like he used to when everything between us was solid. But things weren't like they used to be and I didn't want to see the longing in his eyes.

"Does your girlfriend know you're losing sleep over me? Does she know that you're here right now?"

"Jade, don't do this. I'm trying to reach out to you and salvage what we have."

"You want to salvage something that you destroyed?"

"Can you hear me out, for once? First of all, Noelle isn't my girlfriend. You may never understand why I behaved the way I did, but I want a chance to clarify a few things."

"Bryce, we've been through all of this and, right now, I don't have the time."

"You never did," he mumbled.

"What did you say?" I could see this was going nowhere fast. I should've slammed the door on him and his damn roses.

He repeated himself, only this time raising his voice. "I said, you never did."

"What is that supposed to mean?"

"It means I've done a lot of thinking about our relationship these past few weeks. I have to take responsibility for my actions, but you have to take accountability for your part in this situation as well."

"Let me get this straight. You decide you don't want to be in a relationship anymore. A week later, I see you out with your new woman; not just any woman, but a woman who works at my restaurant, and I'm responsible? Is that what you're saying?"

"What I'm saying is that I loved you…I still love you…but you weren't there for me. This problem started way before you saw me with Noelle. You spend so much time at Rituals with my sister and Milan that you didn't have time for me. I was unhappy with the way our relationship was heading. I needed attention and I wasn't getting it from you. I didn't feel like I was a priority in your life anymore and I had doubts about our future."

He was rambling, trying to make his point before I cut him off. He had already gone over his allotted minute and my patience was as thin as a sheet of phyllo dough.

I interrupted him. "Bryce—"

He ignored me. "I thought we'd be better off apart. I thought that I could be without you. I was wrong. That probably sounds insane to you, but I'm being honest."

He was speaking fast, like a salesman about to lose his commission. "Noelle and I only went out a few times and that was after you and I broke up. It meant nothing to me. I was trying to fill a void."

I looked down at my watch and thought how this could really mess up my evening.

Don't let the past interfere with your future.

I got up and went to sit on the sofa, facing Bryce, and then spoke slowly and steadily because I wanted him to catch every single word. "Bryce, I love you. I may always love you, but I want you to know something. I gave my heart to you and I expected you to take care of it; you didn't."

I needed to make him understand that he'd broken my heart and—because of him—I was in the process of putting all of the pieces back together. "The issue isn't whether or not Noelle is your girlfriend, or how many times you two went out; the issue is that you up and left. You made the decision to end our relationship on your own."

Bryce never came to me to tell me how he was feeling. We'd been looking at engagement rings a month before he left. He'd thrown me for a loop when he walked out of my life. We'd had problems in the past but I thought we were working out the kinks; that we were finally on the right path.

I looked directly into his pleading eyes. "Apparently it was better for you to be without me since you didn't waste any time before you started dating. At least Noelle had enough sense to resign after I saw you together. She saved me the time of having to fire her ass," I ranted. "I'm sure she'll have no problem finding work in a restaurant looking for fast waitresses. And I mean *fast* in every sense of the word."

Bryce put his head down, rubbed his hands over his sandy curls, and let out a stream of hot air. He was about to respond when the phone interrupted him.

I looked at the caller ID—it was Cain. "I need to take this call." I went into the kitchen and answered the phone.

"Jade, it's Cain."

"Hey, what's up?"

"I wanted to let you know that I may be a little late; no more than fifteen minutes, though. I need to stop by Eden to take care of a few things. I hope you don't mind."

If only he knew. I was going to need extra time to prepare after this unexpected drama. "No, I don't mind. Take your time, Cain; I'll see you when you get here." We said our goodbyes and I clicked off the phone. I turned around to return to the living room, only to find Bryce looming behind me.

"Who the hell was that?"

"Were you eavesdropping on my conversation?"

"I was coming to get something to drink." He moved directly in front of me and repeated, "Who were you talking to?"

My temper flared at his audacity. I let the bitch out, stepped to him like he had just stepped to me. "Who are you to question me? You and I are no longer together, per your request. As far as I'm concerned, it is none of your damn business."

"So are you sleeping with this guy? What's his name—Dane? Is that what you said?"

"That's it. I'm not doing this with you. It's time for you to leave, Bryce."

"Are you fucking this guy, Jade?"

"I don't owe you any explanations." I moved around him and marched toward the front door. Unfortunately, he was still standing in the kitchen. I yelled, "Let's go, Bryce! It's time for you to leave!"

I stood in the foyer, tapping my foot.

He took his time and strolled to where I was standing. "So it's like that? I come over here to bare my soul and you're waiting for the next man to come over."

"Next time you'll think twice before you pop up at my front door."

Nostrils flaring, he reached for the doorknob. "Have a good time on your date with Dane."

I motioned toward the door. He yanked it open and left. I shut the door behind him, then watched him through the peephole. He sat in my driveway for a few minutes before he drove off. Maybe he was waiting to catch a glimpse of *Dane*.

My hand was trembling. I was hoping he wasn't sitting in his car around the corner, watching to see who I was going out with.

I went back to the living room, contemplating my exchange with Bryce. This wasn't our first break-up, but this was the first time that he had bogarted my space. Bryce typically tried to wear me down over the phone with nonstop calls and messages. As arrogant as he was, he wouldn't step out on a limb if he thought he'd be rejected. He was surely stewing right then. He'd trekked over there, flowers in hand, only to get turned away. I'll admit that if Bryce hadn't tried that approach in the past, it may have worked, but not this time.

WHEN BRYCE HAD ASKED ME OUT ON OUR FIRST DATE, I was hesitant. I wasn't certain if it was a good idea to date my best friend's brother, but I was more concerned about the things I knew about him. Bryce had quite an interesting history.

He was the type of kid who saw a squirrel and, instead of thinking it was a cute, furry creature, he would hurl rocks at it. He was an angry child, always in fights. Always starting trouble. One summer day—when I was about ten or so—Bria, Bryce and I were walking to the store for ice cream and candy. Bryce dared Bria to steal a pack of Hubba Bubba Bubble Gum. This was no ordinary dare. Bryce's dares were full of taunts and threats. The kind of dare that you couldn't turn down or you'd be considered a punk. Bria reluctantly agreed as I kept repeating that she'd get caught. Well, we got to the store and sticky fingers nabbed the gum without a hitch. But as we approached the door to leave, Bryce said loud enough for the cashier to hear, "Bria, did you slip something in your pocket?" Bria froze. The cashier came over and patted Bria's pockets—they were empty. We went out to the parking lot and Bria was fuming. Bryce was laughing hysterically. He had set up his own sister. Bria didn't speak to him the entire walk home. When we reached their house, I took the bubble gum from my Jordache purse and threw it at Bryce. Bria had slipped the gum in my bag after she had clipped it from the rack. Bryce smirked at me, picked up the pack of gum, and ran off down the street to his boys with a wad of grape Hubba Bubba in his mouth.

The older Bryce got, the more trouble he'd caused. Taking his father's car without a license and crashing it into a telephone pole. Getting drunk on forty-ounces and passing out on his parents' doorstep. Sneaking into his many girlfriends' bedrooms. His parents received so many calls from angry parents that they made him come straight home from school and didn't let him out except for church on Sundays. Bryce was more than mischievous; he was downright devilish.

His parents shipped him off to military school for his sophomore year of high school. They promised if his behavior improved, he would only have to stay a year at the new school. He returned home for his junior and senior years and his parents bought him a new Nissan Sentra—a welcome home gift.

Bryce came back to school and he had indeed abandoned his fighting ways. He already had his rep and there was no thrill for him to be scrapping anymore. He found his excitement in watching all of his women catfight over him. Every day of the week Bryce had a different chick riding next to him in the front seat of his new car. On any given afternoon there were two chicks arguing over him as he cruised by with some other babe in his ride.

I didn't realize it when we'd started dating, but those early days had really played a large part in who he was today. Bryce was accustomed to having women at his disposal. I'd never fit the mold; that enticed him. I was the challenge of all challenges—his sister's friend, the sibling of an old nemesis, someone that had never fallen for his charms—until that cold, rainy winter day four years ago.

I had stopped by Rituals one evening to check out the progress at the work site. I pulled into the dirt lot and parked my car in front of the partially built structure. The crew was gone for the day and the site was empty. When I was backing out of the lot to leave, I heard a pop from my rear tire. As I stood in the rain, watching the air deflate from my tire, Bryce pulled up next to me. He rolled down his window and asked what I was doing alone in the lot at night. Once he saw my tire, he got out of his car, asked if I had a spare, and proceeded to change my flat. By now, the rain was pouring down and he insisted that I sit in his car to stay dry. I offered to hold my umbrella over him while he worked but he refused. I was surprised, yet grateful he came to my aid. He was dripping wet when he finished. I thanked him profusely and for the very first time, I saw Bryce exhibit signs of bashfulness. Bryce followed me to make sure that I arrived home safely. When I pulled into my driveway, he tooted his horn and proceeded down the street.

A couple of days later, Bria mentioned her brother was sick in bed with an extremely bad cold. Later that same day, I was ringing his doorbell with a container of homemade chicken soup. We sat and talked while he ate his soup. He was in sweats and a robe, his nose red from the nonstop blowing, looking like a cute, vulnerable little boy. Bryce got to me that day. I had never had the opportunity to be with Bryce, the man, up close and personal. The person I was sitting across from was not my best friend's obnoxious brother, but an engaging, insanely attractive man. Three hours of conversation later, I was putting on my coat to leave. Bryce stopped me at the door and told me he would pick me up for dinner the following night at eight. Just like that. No questions asked. Bryce had decided we were going on a date, and he knew as well as I did that I wouldn't say no.

The next night at dinner we laughed over the old days. I brought up how he used to speed by Bria and me as we walked home from school because he had some hoochie in the car.

He shook his head and confessed, "I was crazy back then. I don't know how anybody put up with me."

"It wasn't easy," I said, laughing. "What I couldn't understand was how you got away with all of that mess. You had those girls going nuts. Arguing and fighting all the time."

"I got away with it because I didn't care. Those girls were only something to do."

"Wow…"

"I'm keepin' it real. I was a different person back then. I didn't care about a lot of things."

"I always teased Bria that she was the good twin and you were the evil twin."

Bryce's expression changed. Although he was looking at me, he had a distant look in his eyes. "I probably was the evil one, but not because I was born that way. Not everyone had a happy home, like you, growing up."

"Bryce, I was at your house all the time as a kid and things seemed pretty peachy to me."

"Peachy?" Bryce snorted. "That's funny. My childhood was far from what *you* call *peachy*."

"What was so bad—"

"Trust me, Jade."

"So you're telling me all of the fighting, stealing, and let's not forget the girls, was due to some horrible life at home?"

"You were at my house all the time but what you saw through a child's naïve eyes wasn't an accurate picture. You missed a lot. Things you didn't know about or understand."

Bryce opened up to me and shared things about his family history that Bria had never told me. His parents had a less than perfect marriage. Although they had given the impression that they had a perfectly loving marriage, nothing had been further from the truth. They were always at war with one another and kept Bria and Bryce in the middle of their disputes. Bryce knew firsthand that his father was cheating on his mother; his father would take him along on his rendezvous. Bryce was always the alibi. His father was quite the ladies' man. Sometimes Bryce would wait out in the car while his father handled his business. Other times he'd go in the bar with his father and drink soda and eat pretzels while his father finessed a new prospect. One guarantee was that Bryce's mother would be waiting up at the door to usher him off to bed right before the battle began between his parents.

"Their fights would last for hours," he recollected.

"I had no idea."

"No one did. Except for me and Bria."

"But Bria seemed so happy."

"Bria shut a lot out. I'd tell her where I had been with our father and what I'd seen and we'd cry together. The next morning, she would get up and act as if I hadn't told her a thing. I'd wake up angry and withdrawn."

"So you lashed out at others…"

"Exactly. When most kids started their day watching cartoons before school, I was subjected to daily interrogations by my mother. She wanted to know where my father had been, what he had done, and who he had done it with."

"That's too much for a child to endure. Why didn't your mother take you and Bria and leave?"

"She had her own skeletons scratching on the closet door. Eventually they stayed together for my sister and me, and after a while, it didn't make sense for either one to leave. They were living separate lives anyway."

"I don't think I could've stayed in a loveless marriage. The cheating would've made me leave."

"I couldn't deal with the cheating either," he said.

I gave Bryce a puzzled look. "I don't mean any disrespect, but Bryce, you're the biggest cheater I know."

"Jade, that was high school; a long time ago. I've changed."

I GOT UP FROM THE COUCH AND LAUGHED OUT LOUD. Bryce had changed alright—for the worse. The things he'd put me through…

Tonight I'd be looking over my shoulder to make sure he wasn't following me around. I didn't believe that he'd do those things, but you never know when it comes to matters of the heart.

4

After four outfit changes, I finally decided to keep it simple and wear a pair of black cargo pants and a fitted white tank top. I blew my hair straight until it hung past my shoulder blades, parted it in the middle, and when it fell just right, I put on my black Kangol cap. I added a pair of large thin gold hoop earrings and put on my black Prada sandals and matching knapsack. I was ready to go. My doorbell rang as I was putting the finishing touches on my lips; you couldn't go wrong with MAC Lipglass in C-Thru with Chestnut lipliner. I blew myself a kiss, then rushed down the stairs to my date.

I opened the door to Cain, handsome and appealing, in a pair of tan linen pants and a cream linen shirt with a band collar.

I held the door open, taking him in from head to toe as he entered. His cologne was intoxicating. Made me want to bury my face in the crook of his neck and inhale his masculine scent.

He grabbed my hand. "As usual, you look gorgeous."

"Thank you. You don't look too shabby yourself."

"I can see you're not good at giving compliments." He pretended to straighten his clothes. "I thought I was looking pretty dapper, at least better than *not too shabby*. It's good that I don't suffer from low self-esteem, or I might be hurt right now."

I squeezed his hand. "I'm quite positive that you get your share of compliments, so stop fishing."

I continued to hold his hand and led him into the living room. "Would you like something to drink? I have wine, beer, juice, soda, water—"

"No, thank you," he said, looking around. "You have a very nice home. I see you have a thing for warm colors."

The living room was done in earth tones; a combination of browns, beiges and rusts. I'd paired a deep brown carpet with a cream sofa and honey-colored pillows.

Cain walked over to the fireplace. "Nice touch."

Large floor pillows surrounded the fireplace and were perfect for quiet, romantic evenings.

"Thanks. Have a seat. I'll grab my keys and then we can be off." I went into the kitchen to retrieve my house keys from the hook.

Cain called out from the living room, "Nice roses."

I didn't respond. I came back into the room and busied myself with closing the blinds.

"Do you always buy fresh flowers for your table?"

"Not always." I briefly looked in his direction and quickly changed the subject. "So, who's performing tonight?"

"Joe Sample. Do you know him?"

"Do *I* know Joe Sample? I love Joe Sample." I went over to my music collection and began pulling out proof. "I have every one of his CDs; even the ones from when he was with the Crusaders. 'Street Life' with Randy Crawford used to be my song."

"You mean to say we have the same taste in music? I knew there was a reason why I liked you. "

"Among other things," I joked.

"Oh, aren't we cocky? I like that."

"I like you."

He didn't expect that one. I didn't even expect it. I wasn't certain where it had come from, but suddenly, I was feeling bold. Rebellious. Flirtatious. My run-in with Bryce had made me yearn for a drama-free situation. Something new.

"Now that's a compliment," he said.

"Don't get a big head—I like a lot of people."

He stood up. "Just when I thought you were making progress. Don't worry; I'll squeeze another one out of you before the night is over."

"If you say so."

"We better get going before we miss the show."

Cain opened the door of his black Cadillac Escalade for me. Thank goodness for running boards; at five-two, I definitely needed it to get into his ride. Cain eased in behind the wheel and started the truck.

I sniffed. A hint of garlic scented the interior of the SUV. "Cain, what's smelling so good?"

"It's a surprise. I hope you didn't eat yet."

"Actually, I haven't eaten since this morning."

"That's good because you're in for a treat."

I could get used to that. I was a sucker for surprises.

He backed out of my driveway and navigated through the residential streets of Baldwin to the Southern State Parkway.

I turned around and tried to see where the heavenly aroma was coming from. "Is that garlic and basil I smell?"

Cain took his eyes off of the road. "You might want to stop being so nosey and put your seatbelt on before you get a ticket from the cop riding next to us."

I did as I was told but kept peeking over my shoulder. I could see a basket and a jacket, but that was it.

He studied my face for a moment, then said, "I was thrown off when you gave me your card yesterday."

I looked down at my pants and began to pick off lint that wasn't there. "Honestly, I surprised myself."

"How so?"

"We've known each other for what...two years?"

"A little more than two," he said.

"Well, then, for a little more than two years I never took you seriously."

"Why not?"

"For a couple of reasons, I guess."

"I feel like I'm pulling teeth here."

I looked over at him. "Okay. The truth is...I always got the feeling that you hit on every woman you see. I mean, I was flattered, but I didn't think you were being sincere." I tried to gauge his reaction, but was unable to read the expression on his face. "Then, yesterday, I received a slightly different vibe and a big-mouth friend spoke the right words at the right time."

He smiled. "Remind me to thank Milan."

"There was another reason." I hesitated. "I was in a relationship until recently."

I wasn't sure if he needed to know that information, but I figured it was better to put my cards on the table. Besides, that was then and this was now. I wanted to proceed with a clear conscience.

In a serious tone, he replied, "Well, now I have another person to thank." He looked in my eyes. "His loss is my gain."

I got chills from the way he'd said that.

He turned on the radio and started bobbing his head to the music. I settled back into my seat and enjoyed the ride.

We pulled into the parking lot at Heckscher Park. The sun had started its descent; the sky was a medley of golden and pink hues. As far as I could tell there were mostly couples in attendance, but I did see a few groups making their way over to the concert area. Cain walked around the front of the truck to open my door. He offered me his hand and helped me out. I stood waiting as he walked to the back of the truck and went into the trunk. Seizing the opportunity to see what was in the basket, I opened the rear passenger door. The basket was in full view. I leaned in the truck and reached for it. As soon as my hand touched the handle, the door across from me flew open. Cain winked at me, whisked the basket from the floor, and closed his door. I grabbed the jacket off the back seat, then shut my door. Cain came over to me with the basket as well as a blanket he had taken from the trunk.

Flashing a dazzling smile, he said, "Couldn't help yourself, huh? You gotta move faster than that."

"I only wanted to take a tiny peek in the basket. I'm dying to know what's in there."

"Sorry. You're going to have to wait."

I looked up at him and pouted my lips by MAC. I thought it might work in getting me a couple of answers.

"You look cute when you stick your bottom lip out like that. It's very attractive."

I could tell this was obviously amusing him. I finally conceded. "You win. We'll do things your way."

He handed me the blanket to carry, then took hold of my free hand. We followed our fellow jazz lovers across the grass. The band was warming up, giving us time to find a location to set up our picnic.

I pointed toward a tall oak that was close enough to see Joe Sample, but far enough for us to be able to talk without having to shout. I spread the blanket over the ground and kicked off my sandals. Cain placed the basket in the center of the blanket, then we both got comfortable.

There was a gentle breeze and the fragrance of freshly cut grass drifted through the air. The moon was vying for its position in the evening sky, the sun rapidly losing the battle as it faded into the horizon. Golden rays streaked through the trees and made delicate patterns on the blanket.

"It's supposed to be cool tonight," Cain said. "Let me know if you want to put on my jacket."

"No, it feels good. Spring is finally in full swing and I want to luxuriate in it. This past winter was brutal. I was beginning to think the warm weather wasn't coming."

Cain opened the flap on the basket, removed a bottle of Chardonnay and handed me two wineglasses. "How about a toast to spring and new beginnings?"

"Ahhh, the secret contents."

"Yes, one of them. This is why I was running late. I had to pick up the basket." He uncorked the wine and proceeded to fill our glasses.

I took the lead and made the toast. "To warm weather…and things to come."

He tapped my glass with his. "Things to come…"

We sipped the wine, watching each other over the rim of our glasses.

"So tell me about yourself," I said.

"Well, let's see. I own a restaurant called Eden—"

"So now you're a comedian? I meant tell me something I don't know, like where you're from. If you have siblings. About your parents. You know, stuff like that."

He swallowed a mouthful of the crisp white wine. "I was born in Brooklyn. I lived there until my father moved us to Long Island when I was ten. I have two brothers, one older and one younger. My father is a retired electrician with forty years on the job. My mother…" He paused and slowed down his flow. His voice softened. "My mother passed away from breast cancer when I was sixteen. She was the epitome of a beautiful, black woman… one of a kind. An original. The first woman I ever loved. Her name was Eve. She was my inspiration in finding the perfect name for the restaurant."

I reached over and touched his hand. Cain averted his eyes, put down his glass, then started clapping. Joe Sample was taking his seat at the piano. I joined in, hoping that my questions hadn't ruined the evening for him.

Joe started the set with "Mystery Child" from his *Did You Feel That?* CD. What a question. You can feel everything Joe Sample plays; his music touches the soul.

We listened to a few songs before we resumed our conversation. I wanted to get back to a more light-hearted atmosphere so I asked, "What else do you have in that basket or is a glass of wine all I'm getting?"

"You could use a refill, but yes, there's more in here."

Cain refreshed my drink, then pulled out plates, silverware, and cloth napkins from the basket. He set our blanket as if it were a table. I was impressed already. He arranged thick slices of toasted Tuscan bread on my plate, then his. He opened the lid on a small container, passed it over to me, then waited for my response.

I inhaled. "Mmmm, garlic."

He grinned. "Roasted garlic. I don't know how you smelled it through an air-tight container."

"Because I'm good, that's why."

"There you go being cocky again."

"I'm not cocky, just confident." I picked up the knife, spread the fragrant garlic on my slices, then took his plate and did the same.

He uncovered another container, this one filled with diced shrimp and tomato for the bruschetta. Cain spooned a generous portion over my bread.

"Your creation?"

"But of course."

I lifted the bruschetta, nibbled the corner, let the flavors roll around in my mouth, then took a real bite. The smoky sweet flavor of the garlic paired with the grilled shrimp and ripe tomatoes was exquisite. I'd had bruschetta on many occasions but never prepared quite that way.

"This is delicious."

"I know."

"Now who's being cocky?"

"You're rubbing off on me already."

"Don't go blaming me for your behavior."

"You have to admit, it did sound like something you would say."

"The only thing I'm admitting is that the bruschetta tastes good."

Cain laughed. "Well, if you think this tastes good, wait until you try the pasta salad with fresh herbs."

We ate, talked, and listened to Joe Sample stroke the piano keys. *So far so good*, I thought. Cain was charming, definitely skilled in the culinary arts, and a great conversationalist. I was interested in knowing why a man with all of this going for him was still single. Actually, I wanted to confirm if he was indeed single; I never asked, only assumed, his status and you know what they say about assuming.

A part of me didn't want to know if there was a special someone in his life. I was in the moment. Everything felt right. If he did have a significant other, it would mean I couldn't have him—if I wanted him.

My curiosity got the best of me. "Are you seeing anyone?" I didn't mean to blurt it out that way, but now it was out there.

"What took you so long?" he asked.

"Pardon me?"

"I thought you would've asked that question the minute I invited you to go out with me."

"Oh you did...and why is that?"

"You seem like the type of woman that doesn't stand for any nonsense. I don't see you being open to dating a man with a girlfriend; definitely not a wife. I figured you to be the kind of woman to ask that question before you ask anything else."

"I see. You think I'm the kind of woman that barely lets a man introduce himself to me before I start attacking him on whether or not he has a wife and kids at home?"

"Not my words, but more or less, yes."

I narrowed my eyes at Cain. He shifted on the blanket and appeared as if he regretted answering in the affirmative.

"Damn straight I am." I started laughing because Cain had me pegged. Any man that approached me should've been prepared for a grilling.

Cain wasn't sure what to do. He cautiously laughed with me, saying, "For a second, I thought I was in trouble." He lay back, propping himself up with his elbows.

I filled both of our glasses with the last of the wine.

He repeated his question for the second time. "So what took you so long to ask?"

"What's taking you so long to answer?"

We locked eyes. Verbally I was challenging him; silently I was inviting him.

Cain sat up and leaned over. He moved his face close to mine, invading my space. I lowered my eyelids, letting them close in anticipation of feeling his lips touching mine. Seconds passed. I opened my eyes. Cain was still hovering in my proximity. He smiled at me, then looked down at his glass I had just finished filling. He picked it up, took a long swallow, then moved back to his side of the blanket.

I grabbed my wineglass and downed half of its contents. I tried to hide the depth of my embarrassment by angling my body in the direction of the stage so Cain would be unable to see my face. Although it's rude to give someone your back, I needed a minute to regroup. I took off my hat and ran my fingers through my hair.

Joe Sample was playing "Summertime," a smooth composition on his CD *Invitation*. I focused on the music instead of Cain. My body was caught by the song's melody, swaying from side to side.

I heard the basket rustling, then felt Cain move up behind me. I didn't turn around. His chest barely touched my back but I could feel his body heat. He tenderly kissed me on the back of my neck. I turned my head to the side and rested my chin on my shoulder.

Cain brushed his lips against my ear and whispered, "I'm not seeing anyone, but I'd like to change that."

I turned around to face him. He rested his hand on the curve of my back, lowered his head, and kissed me on the lips. Cain's lips had an undeniable power and I was being swept up in his energy. I licked the sweetness of the wine from his lips; they were soft yet firm at the same time. Cain leaned in to kiss me deeper and our tongues danced like fire. He peppered my mouth with hot little kisses, gently sucking my bottom lip. His kisses moved me.

We slowly pulled away from each other when the song ended and the crowd began applauding. Joe Sample transitioned into a more upbeat number that had some people standing up to dance.

Cain spoke first. "I've been wanting to do that all night."

"I'm glad you did. That was nice."

He stroked my arms and felt the effect of the night air on my skin. "Do you want my jacket?"

I shook my head. "No, I'm all right."

"You sure? You feel cold to me."

"Thanks to the wine, I'm feeling no pain right now."

He maneuvered my body so that I was sitting in between his legs. He tried to warm me by rubbing his large hands up and down my arms. I scooted back and leaned against his chest. He wrapped his arms around me, resting his chin on the top of my head.

"I didn't ask if you had a girlfriend because a small part of me thought you would say yes. If you had one, then the possibility would be gone. Right now, I'm enjoying the possibilities."

"I've wanted to take you out for the longest time. There's something about you—"

"Oh no. You're not going to start with the lines again, are you?"

"Jade, I'm not running lines. You're a special woman. Being here with you tonight got a brother feeling things—" He stopped himself. "Let me chill. I don't want to scare you off...plus we know how cocky you can be." He kissed the side of my face. "I don't want your head to get any bigger or you may float off before the concert ends."

He laughed, turning his feelings into a joke. I laughed, too, even though I didn't think it was amusing. Cain was having an effect on me as well. I had no intention of telling him, but I knew where he was coming from.

ON THE WAY HOME WE RELIVED THE CONCERT, discussed our favorite songs and debated who qualified as the biggest fan. As we approached my street, I couldn't help but to think that I didn't want the night to end. Cain pulled into my driveway and cut the engine off. The radio was tuned to slow jams on WBLS.

I unfastened my seatbelt and shifted my body to face him. "Thank you for the show and the delicious food. I had a wonderful time."

"You're welcome." He reached out, placed his hand on the nape of my neck, and drew me to him. We picked up where we left off at the park—soft and sweet kisses. My mind raced. I wanted to invite him in but wondered if it was too soon. Technically we'd known each other for years; it wasn't like he was a stranger. While my thoughts wandered, he gave me a final peck and hopped out of the truck.

Cain went into the trunk, then came to my door. As I stepped from the truck, Cain presented me with a single rose.

"You probably can't see this in the dark, but this is a pink rose," he said. "Dark pink roses mean *thank you*, and I'm thanking you for accepting my invite."

That was cute; he got major points for creativity. I thanked Cain and then smelled the flower. While my head was bowed, a dozen roses materialized from behind his back.

"These are lavender roses," he said, handing me the arrangement. "Do you know what they symbolize?"

"No, tell me," I replied, barely above a whisper.

"Lavender roses mean love at first sight and enchantment."

My smile lit up the darkness. "They're beautiful, thank you."

His voice dropped an octave. "Jade, you have enchanted me."

Just when I thought this date couldn't get any better!

I was at a loss for words and searched for something appropriate to say. "How do you know so much about roses?"

"I asked the florist to help me select the colors to convey exactly what I was feeling."

It had been a long time since I'd been wooed and, right then, Cain had me in the palm of his hands.

"Do you want to come in?"

"I'd better not. It's late."

He kissed me on my forehead and escorted me to the front door. I inhaled the fragrance of the lavender roses, then tugged one from the arrangement. I offered it to him. He took the flower, kissed the tip, then touched my lips with it.

"Goodnight, Jade."

He walked to his truck and I floated inside of the house. Before I went to bed, I replaced the red roses from Bryce with the lavender ones.

5

"What exactly happened with you two yesterday?"

Here we go.

As soon as I walked into Rituals, Bria was all up in it—I hadn't even put my belongings down yet. Following me around the restaurant, she was looking every bit like her brother, with the exception of her natural locks. I had tried to prepare myself for the conversation; I was certain Bryce would run to his sister blabbing about our encounter. It never failed; whatever went on between him and me would re-run with Bria and me later on.

"All I'm saying is that your brother is out of control," I answered.

"He told me he came to your house and you were going out with some guy named Dane?"

I snickered at the misinformation. "Bria, your brother has a lot of nerve, dropping by my house in the first place."

"Forget him for a second. I left you a message on Saturday from that cat at Eden."

"Yes, I know; I can read."

"Then Bryce says you were going out with Dane." She raised her eyebrows. "I know you weren't hanging with Cain last night."

"Don't start this ride-or-die shit for your brother."

"I'm not. I'm just asking—"

"You're always *just* asking. Any time your brother and I have a beef, you start advocating for him. Let me deal with Bryce. I realize that's your brother and you love him, but he needs to stop putting you in the middle of our shit."

"What were you doing going out with Cain?"

Like brother, like sister.

"Bria, I don't plan to live like a nun simply because Bryce and I broke up. Cain's a nice guy and I don't see anything wrong with going out with him."

"You don't?"

"No, I don't."

"How about the fact that he's our competitor?"

"What does that have to do with anything?" I said, laughing. "It's not as if we were out swapping top secret information."

"I don't think it's a good idea, Jade."

"Duly noted. But for the record, you're trippin'."

When Bria and I had first announced our plans to open a restaurant, we hadn't received a positive response from friends and family. We were young, we were women, and in their eyes we didn't have a clue what we were doing. They were partially right. Neither of us had run our own business and we were taking a big leap. It was one thing to be responsible for what was on the menu, but to also be responsible for making sure that someone was sitting at the table, to read the menu, was an entirely different ball game. There were times when I felt that perhaps Bria and I had bitten off more than we could chew. Our lack of capital was the biggest hurdle we had to overcome. In addition to taking out a business loan, we had both refinanced our homes and appealed to our parents to invest in our dream. There were times when it had seemed like we wouldn't have enough money, as our expenses continued to climb from week to week. In spite of those fears, I had refused to compromise or settle on the workmanship or the quality of materials used—ranging from the lighting down to the flooring.

Once our families actually saw Rituals coming together, they

Recipe for Love 53

had begun to believe in our vision. They stopped telling us how hard it was to be successful in the restaurant business and started saying that we were on the road to success. But success always comes at a price. Bria and I were relating to each other on a foreign level. I had the opportunity to see her in a professional light and I wasn't sure if I liked it. In all of the years that we had discussed the type of food we would serve or how we wanted our restaurant to look, we had never seemed to disagree—until then. We couldn't agree on anything. Not the menu. The prices. The staff. Nothing. She had a dogmatic approach to everything. She didn't have to say it, but I could tell she thought her experience in the industry outweighed mine. She had questioned me over the minutest of details. Those questions evolved into debates, which escalated into arguments. When I felt that she had completely crossed the line, I had asserted my business acumen and reminded her that I was the one with the business degree. Not that it really mattered. We were both debutantes at the ball, trying to waltz through this venture together.

Fighting with Bria was new territory. We may have had an occasional disagreement in the past, as all friends do, but for the first time, I had seen things I didn't particularly care for in her. I didn't like the way she quizzed me on preparations and techniques, things we had always compared notes on and enjoyed chatting about. It seemed that she was now doubting my skills. As I watched our business get ready to take off, I had seen our friendship take a backseat.

Our opening night was magical. There had been a buzz for months about the new restaurant opening near the mall, but when we opened Rituals' doors at four o'clock sharp, we couldn't believe the line of people waiting to get inside. A few months later we had our regulars and, every once in a while, a celebrity would drop in for a bite. Celebrity sightings were more frequent, but our staff and clients were used to it. In fact, they had come to expect it.

I SAT AT THE TABLE AND HELPED BRIA insert the daily specials into the menus.

"So how was it?" she asked.

"How was what?" I liked to mess with her.

"Stop playing. I want details. Where did you two go last night?"

I toyed with her. "So now you want details? Two seconds ago you were concerned our date was a threat to national security."

"Jade…"

I couldn't hold out on Bria. We had been through way too much over the years and we'd managed to maintain our sister-friend relationship in the midst of many complicated situations. She tried her best to keep Bryce out of our friendship; I tried to keep her out of my relationship with her brother. Besides, girl talk superseded all of that.

I provided Bria with a play by play of the evening—leaving out the kiss and the roses, of course. That was my girl, but I was no fool. The last thing I needed was Bryce banging at my door because Bria let it slip that I was locking lips with another man.

"Cain, huh?" she said. "Well, take it slow. You don't want to rush into anything since you just got out of a relationship."

"Ride or die…" I teased.

"Make sure you've resolved your old shit before you start some new shit; that's all I was trying to say."

"Thank you, but I got this."

She sighed. "I guess I have to let go of the dream of you being my sister-in-law."

"Don't start," I warned.

I understood the twin connection—they were close—she wanted to protect her brother. What I didn't understand was why she seemed to think he was such an angel. No one knew better than Bria the things I had gone through with Bryce. Over the years, she had pried many stories out of me. She would listen to me complain for hours about some of his stunts, then recommend that Bryce and I try work it out. Sometimes I would wonder if she was even listening to a word I had said. The time that I told Bria that another woman had called my house for Bryce, saying that he'd never showed to pick her up for their date, Bria had ignored the fact that he had a date planned, instead focusing on the fact that he didn't go through with the date. Those were the moments I questioned whether she could give objective advice—she couldn't. It was bad enough being confused over my relationship; I didn't want to question my friendships, too.

Bria believed Bryce and I were meant to be together. It was strange, but sometimes I thought she believed that more than I did. If she wasn't telling me how he was really a good man and that there were just some things I didn't understand about him, then she was telling me how sorry he was for his transgressions. Bria insisted I was the first woman she'd ever heard Bryce say he loved. She reminded me how he used to be, how women he dated barely lasted a week. Bryce used to be a player, but bringing up his playeristic past was probably not the best approach for promoting a reconciliation. If you listened to Bria tell it, Bryce was a misunderstood soul that never knew love and had not begun to live until he started dating me. He seemed to be doing fine. It was hard enough, trying to be strong when Bryce launched a full-scale operation to get me back, but with Bria joining forces with him, it was almost impossible for me not to forgive him.

The irony was that Bria refused to be involved in serious relationships; she was convinced men couldn't be faithful. She was dating but whenever a guy got too attached, she would cut him loose. She'd said on many occasions that she wasn't giving a man the chance to cheat on her and refused to date only one man at a time. I had to give her credit; she was honest and told anyone that she was involved with her two golden rules—she was only dating and she wasn't looking for a commitment.

There was one guy a couple of years earlier that I'd thought had changed her mind. She had been seeing Rich for about a year, and although she said it wasn't exclusive, she hadn't mentioned going out with anyone else for at least six months. I could tell that she was feeling him. They were on the phone all of the time, went out a few nights a week, and he had met her parents—that's when the red flag went up.

Knowing Bria was opposed to marriage, Rich thought she might consider moving in with him. When she told me that he'd asked her to move in, I assumed she'd shut him down immediately, but Bria confessed that she was thinking about it. It was the happiest I had ever seen her about a man. It wasn't her nature to show emotion over a relationship.

Over the next few weeks I noticed a change in the way Bria would respond when I asked about Rich. Gone were the smile and the excitement that accompanied any mention of his name, replaced by cold indifference. I had to inquire what had caused such a drastic shift. Bria broke down and told me about her father's infidelities and how it affected her. In all of our years as friends, she had never told me any of this. I admitted that Bryce had already divulged a little bit about what had happened. Bria had confided that she had finally gotten to the point where she felt she could try to be with one person but her father had to mess that up. She'd overheard a conversation Rich was having with her father. Rich was telling him that he wanted Bria to move in with him and was hoping she would agree. Then, to Bria's surprise, she'd heard her father tell Rich that he should expect things to change between them once they live together. He said things always change for the worse but a man has to have a few back–up plans to get him through the hard times. He'd patted Rich on the shoulder and asked if he knew what he meant. Rich had laughed and nodded his head. That was enough for Bria to decide she wasn't moving in with Rich and she wasn't interested in a committed relationship. Yet it didn't stop her from trying to keep me from leaving her cheating ass brother. It was a tag team effort with them.

Bria was a lot like her brother. Possessive. During college, when Milan first came onto the scene, Bria was less than friendly; she was downright frosty. It had always been the two of us and I was bringing someone else into our world. It wasn't that she didn't like Milan; she didn't like the idea of having to share her best friend. If I went to Philly with Milan on my break, Bria wouldn't speak to me for weeks. All of sudden, she was too busy to talk. I'd give her space to work out her issues—I never could tolerate pettiness. When Milan would come home with me and we were all together, things were rocky at best. I was constantly in the middle of unnecessary debates, incited by Bria, which usually put a damper on the day. Milan was good for letting nonsense roll off her back; Bria stored everything as ammunition for the next round.

Eventually, when I was tired of the bickering, I pulled Bria to the side to put her in check. "What the fuck is your problem?"

Bria's neck started rolling before her mouth started moving. "Who the fuck are you cursing at?"

"I'm cursing at your ass. Now, like I said, what the fuck is your problem?"

"My problem is with that snooty bitch you keep dragging around with us every time you come home."

"Bria, grow up. Milan hasn't done anything for you to treat her the way you do. Now if something's really wrong, you need to tell me. Because right now, I'm not understanding your behavior."

"Maybe my problem isn't with Milan."

"Well, you just said that it was."

"Alright. I did say that, but now that I think about it, my problem's with you."

Bria went off on me. She felt that I was shoving my new friend down her throat. Bria explained that she had friends at culinary school, but she wasn't bringing them home and forcing them on me. And, from what she could see, I didn't even act the same. I'd changed and was just as snooty as my friend. She imitated how Milan and I would be snickering together about people from school, not caring whether she knew what we were talking about.

"Bria, half of the time we're telling you about those people because we think you could appreciate the humor of the situation."

"Well, I don't. I don't care about those people. I don't even know those people."

"Bria, I apologize if I've been inconsiderate in any way, but I'm not going to apologize for having friends other than you. I thought you'd like Milan, but if you're uncomfortable being around her, then I'll have to figure out a way to divide my time."

Bria sighed. "Milan's cool...and we can all hang together. I was being a little shady—"

"A *little*?"

She smirked. "Don't push it, Bitch. I was being shady because I miss hanging with my best friend. C.I.A. is full of fake bitches trying to backstab you when they can. The environment breeds competition. When I come home, that's the only time I get to be around people I really know and trust. I'm used to running with my homegirl and being able to talk about anything. Then here you come with Milan and I feel like I have to be on guard. It felt like I was back at school. Y'all had your little private jokes and I felt like I was some kind of outsider."

I hugged my oldest friend. "Girl, you *are* trippin'. If Milan wasn't good people, I never would've brought her into our circle. You and I will always be sisters, no matter where we go or who we meet. That'll never change."

The vicious words that flowed between us that day were the first and last time we'd spoken to each other in such a manner. Bria and Milan worked on getting to know each other better, and years later, when Milan moved to New York, it was Bria who had helped her find an apartment.

AROUND NOON, MILAN BOUNCED IN along with the lunch crowd. I was at the bar explaining to our hostess that she needed to keep the reservation book a bit more legible, when Milan captured me by the elbow and ushered me to an empty booth.

She gushed. "What's the 4-1-1?"

"Hello to you, too."

"What's the juicy info? You never called back last night and I was waiting for you to call me this morning."

"You're taking an early lunch today. What's the occasion?"

"Spill it, Jade; I have some news of my own to share."

"Okay. I was out last night…with Cain."

She let out a screech. A few people stopped eating and looked in the direction of our table.

I swatted Milan's hand. "Will you be quiet?"

She took it down a notch. "Sorry. I can't believe you did it. When did this come about?"

"I slipped him my card when we were at brunch on Saturday."

"Aren't you slick, acting like you weren't interested."

"Girl, we had such a good time. We saw Joe Sample in concert; had a picnic in the park. We talked, we laughed, we flirted and, damn, can he kiss."

We covered our mouths, laughing like two hyenas. We were trying to keep our noise level down, but obviously weren't doing a good job since the sisters at the next table were watching us.

"Look at you," Milan said. "There is life after Bryce."

"Bryce who?"

We cackled some more. Bria approached the table and sat next to Milan.

"What the hell are you two howling at over here?"

"Jade was filling me in on her date."

I kicked Milan under the table and her expression immediately registered her confusion.

Bria cut her eyes at me. "Jade, I must've gotten the G-rated version."

"Not at all. Lan was laughing because I tripped when Cain and I were looking for a spot to lay the blanket. I forgot to tell you that part."

One of the waiters signaled that they needed Bria in the kitchen. She left the table with a baffled look on her face.

"What was that lie about...and let's not forget the kick?" Milan asked.

"I shouldn't have lied but I don't want Bryce finding out about this. You know how he can be."

I told her about the incident with Bryce, explained how right after it occurred I was a little unnerved. However, I'd neglected to keep an eye open for him last night; I'd convinced myself it wasn't necessary. Hopefully he'd had better things to do with his time than to tail me all night.

"I have to admit, Cain impressed me. At the end of the date, he gave me lavender roses and told me that I enchanted him."

"What is this, a soap opera?"

"Telling you now it sounds corny, but last night it made my panties wet."

"That is way too much information."

We fell into another fit of laughter.

I composed myself and asked, "What news did you want to share?"

"Don't say anything, but I'm meeting Nolan here for lunch."

"I'm not saying a word…you're grown."

"You think I'm crazy, don't you?"

"Lan, I'm not even going there with you. The other day you wanted to bite my head off for speaking to Nolan and now you're having lunch with him."

"We'll have to talk about this later; he just came in." Milan waved Nolan over to where we were sitting.

I stood up, gave him a hug, and let him take my seat. They were a good-looking couple. Nolan wasn't much taller than Milan and, with his athletic physique, he could easily pass for a professional football player. His eyeglasses always gave him a smart, nice guy appeal—in actuality, he was both.

"You're not going to join us?" Nolan asked.

"No, I have to go call a few of our distributors but order what you want; it's on the house. I'll catch up with you later." I left them to their own soap opera, giving them the privacy they needed to air their dirty laundry.

MILAN AND NOLAN HAD SPLIT SIX MONTHS EARLIER when Nolan had discovered that oral arguments were merely one type of oral Milan was giving at the law firm. Milan had been spending long hours and late nights working closely with one of the partners at the firm on a big medical malpractice case.

Milan told me if anyone could give her direction on making partner it was Eriq. He had been with Stowe, Black & Helms for ten years, a partner for six, and was well-respected by Wallace Black. Milan knew Eriq in passing and had had only minimal conversation with him until they'd been paired together on the malpractice case. Milan said Wallace was known to assign an attorney that he'd slated as a future partner with an existing partner to get a firsthand account of whether he was making the right choice. It became routine for Milan and Eriq to have dinner or a couple of drinks during the week; eventually one thing led to another.

Apparently Milan wasn't the only woman this man was screwing; he had a history of infidelity. His wife had hired a private investigator to follow him since she didn't believe that he was spending his nights working on cases. Unfortunately, Milan was the chick on the side caught on film.

One evening his wife watched Milan leave work, followed her home, and then proceeded to confront Milan on her front doorstep. She probably wanted to know where to look for her husband in the future and didn't want to jeopardize his position by making a scene at his place of work.

Nolan had pulled up to the house to pick Milan up for dinner when the whole showdown was taking place; he'd seen the pictures of Milan and the woman's husband engaged in butt naked sex. Milan's version—it just happened. There was no rhyme or reason; she loved Nolan. Nolan's response—he needed time away from the relationship; time to get the images in the pictures out of his head.

I SPOTTED NOLAN BLAZING OUT OF THE RESTAURANT and diverted my attention to Milan at the table, dabbing her eyes. I let her get her emotions under control before I went to check on her.

"Are you alright?" I asked.

"Not yet, but I will be."

"You wanna talk about it?"

Milan choked back tears as she struggled to tell me what had happened. First off, she said Nolan didn't reciprocate when she mentioned it was good to see him. So she tried a different approach, acknowledging that he had every right to be upset with her. Nolan told her that *upset* didn't begin to characterize his feelings; that *irate*, *infuriated* and *disgusted* were more accurate.

Her voice cracked. "Jade, I can understand all of that but I told him that I need him to try and forgive me."

I continued to listen, not interrupting her. Milan rambled on, reciting Nolan's words. He said what she had done never left his mind; that he couldn't even escape it in his dreams. She said when he'd agreed to meet her, the first thing he'd thought about was that after lunch, she'd be going back to the office to what's-his-name. Milan made a mistake by commenting that his name is Eriq, not what's-his-name.

"That pissed Nolan off. He slammed his fist on the table and said he knew his fucking name." She dabbed her eyes again. "We sat in silence for a few minutes. I told him I was sorry. And explained that I ended it a long time ago." The tears she tried to hold back broke free. "I don't know how many times I can apologize. I made a mistake. I need him to forgive me. He told me he wasn't ready and for me not to call him again."

"Is there anything I can do?" I asked.

"Not now, Jade. I'm going to call the office and take the rest of the afternoon off. I'll holla at you later."

"Okay, Sweetie. If you need me, you know where to find me."

Milan hurried out of Rituals before the flood gates really opened. My heart went out to her. She'd never wanted to cause Nolan any pain; she'd only made a few bad choices.

Bria stood next to me on the outside steps, watching Milan get into her car. "They still haven't straightened out that mess?" she asked.

"Not yet."

"There must be something in the water because no one stays together these days."

We went back inside and sat at the bar. We chatted over virgin pina coladas about what was wrong with relationships today. On an ordinary day I could've discussed that subject for hours, but that day my heart wasn't in it. I wanted to concentrate on what was right with relationships, particularly new ones.

FOUR P.M.

"Bria, I'm on my way to meet with the fishmonger. I'll see you tomorrow morning."

"I won't be in until two. If you need me before then, hit me on my cell."

I was heading out the door when Taylor, our hostess, told me that I had a phone call.

"Ask who it is, Taylor. I'm running late as it is."

"He said his name is Cain," she replied.

"Tell him to call me on my cell!" I shouted as I rushed out to the parking lot.

My cell phone rang as I was backing out of my space. I put in my earpiece and merged with the traffic on Old Country Road.

I darted between two cars to make it over to the turning lane. "I was wondering if I was going to hear from you today."

"I wanted to call earlier but I didn't want you to think I was a desperate brother."

I could hear the smile on his face. "I'd never think that. In fact,

I was going to call and ask if you wanted to see a movie with me tonight; my treat."

There was no need to front. I liked the brother and wanted to get to know him better—much better.

"You want me to pick you up?" he asked.

"I'll come get you."

"Cool."

I memorized the directions to Cain's house. He lived over in Old Westbury, not far from the state university. "I'll be there around eight," I said.

"See you then."

I hit the gas pedal and sped up. I needed to get this meeting over with—there were a few things I had to tend to before I saw Cain.

6

I marveled at Cain's home as he guided me through each room. The place resembled a museum, with the multitude of artwork adorning the walls. The brother definitely had good taste. I was surprised to find out that he had painted the canvas that hung over the fireplace in his sunken living room. It was an abstract, in dark gray and black, that he had painted some years ago. There was something beautiful yet melancholy about it. I wanted to ask what had inspired it but he had already started toward the next room.

I looked out the sliding glass doors in the den into a massive backyard with acres of carpet-like green grass. Cain slid open the doors and we went out into the yard. He had an in-ground pool with a waterfall straight out of *Cribs* on MTV—rock formations with overflowing water, small caverns, and mini grottos.

I strolled the length of the pool, imagining how many wild parties must've taken place under the hot summer sun.

"The pool isn't ready yet; the water is still too cold," he said. "A couple of more weeks of warm weather and we should be set."

We. I liked that. Including me in future plans. I joined him on the patio. He was standing next to the Jacuzzi. It was covered up but it looked like it could easily fit eight people.

"Sometimes, after a crazy day at Eden, I'll come out back and unwind in the Jacuzzi. I do some of my best thinking in there. Even in the winter I'll grab a mug of steaming hot chocolate, get in here, and meditate."

"I must say, your home is amazing," I said, taking it all in.

"Make sure you invite me to your first pool party of the season."

"That goes without saying."

I followed him back into the den, taking a seat on the plush sectional.

"What time does the movie start?" he asked.

"The last show is at nine o'clock."

"It's already a quarter to nine. There's no way we'll get there in time."

"Is it that late? It seems like I just got here. Damn. I've been dying to see this movie for weeks."

"We can hurry and try to catch it. We'll probably only miss the coming attractions."

"No, you're right. We'd never make it."

"How about we order a pizza and a pay-per-view movie instead?" he asked.

"That could work."

A half-hour later we were eating spinach pizza, drinking a crisp Riesling, and watching a Samuel L. Jackson flick on pay-per-view. I was perched on the couch Indian-style with a plate on my lap. Cain was on the floor, his pizza on the couch next to my leg. We were doing more talking than paying attention to what was happening in the movie.

"How did you get involved in the restaurant business?" I asked.

"Interestingly enough, I sort of fell into it."

"How is that?" I replied, with a mouthful of food.

"I'm into real estate; that's how I really make my money. I own property in Brooklyn, Harlem, Long Island, and I have quite a few properties in Maryland, D.C., and Atlanta as well."

"Impressive."

"A few years ago I bought a piece of property, a restaurant that had closed a couple of months before. It was my intention to renovate it and make it into a full-service day spa, but after talking to my younger brother, who happens to be a chef, I decided to open Eden. He's the one with the formal training. I sort of learned things under his tutelage. Not to say that I can't burn, but he's the head chef at Eden."

"I didn't know that you were such a businessman."

"You've heard the one about judging a book by—"

"Yeah, yeah, yeah…"

"What about you? What inspired you to open Rituals?"

"Honestly?"

"Is there any other way?"

"Unlike you, I didn't fall into it. I have an inherent passion for cooking. I love it. I eat, sleep, and breathe it." I paused to consider how much of me I wanted to share; how close of a look inside I wanted him to have. "If I truly examined why I chose this career, it's also a desire for praise. I derive pleasure from creating dishes that leave a lasting impression on people, but I *thrive* off the attention and compliments that follow. Cooking has always been something that I could do well. Over the years, it evolved into something I was great at."

"Basically, you're saying you do this for adulation more than anything else?"

"Think about it. Through food, you can elicit a range of emotions. I can prepare a dish that can make you feel romantic…or sexy…or even melancholy. I might prepare a meal that reminds you of something your grandmother used to cook for you, or make you think of an old girlfriend, or a past experience. Of course I want my clientele to be extremely satisfied; however, I love the influence I have over a person through food."

Cain ate the last bit of his slice. "I need to have one of these emotion-inducing dinners…just you and me."

"Oh you will, when the time is right."

He cleared our plates and the pizza box and carried them to the kitchen. When he returned, he was holding a large bowl of popcorn in one hand and another bottle of wine in the other. Passing me the bowl and then the bottle, he went to dim the lights.

I filled our glasses with more Riesling. "Don't dim them; turn them all the way off. If we can't be at the theater, we can at least pretend we are."

"If we were at the movies, we would've been thrown out a long time ago, with all the yakking you were doing."

"Turn off the light and get over here; half the movie is already over."

Cain sat his six-foot frame next to me and took off his sneakers. He leaned back against the oversized pillows and put his hands behind his head. I snuggled up against him, resting my head on his bicep.

"I can't believe you made this popcorn after we ate a whole pizza," I said, tossing popcorn in my mouth.

"I noticed you over there hogging the bowl. I have to watch out around you; you can eat."

"Oh yeah, I can throw down. If you're used to those chicks who try to play all dainty when it comes to food, that ain't me. Did you want some of this?"

"Only if you can spare a kernel or two."

I took one kernel out of the bowl, leisurely brought it up to his mouth, and waited for him to take it. He bit his bottom lip and then opened up. I placed the popcorn on his tongue but, before I could move my hand away, he closed his mouth around the tip of my finger. He gently sucked as I pulled my finger from his lips.

"That was good. Can you spare another one?"

We continued in this manner, him asking for more and me

obliging, each time a different finger getting the attention. He took his hands from behind his head, placing an arm around my shoulders. Cain reached into the popcorn bowl, picked one out, and offered to feed it to me. I opened my mouth and let my tongue snake before accepting his offering. I heard a slight moan escape from his throat.

He inhaled deeply. "I can't believe that a woman like you is single."

"Well, I am. What I don't understand is why you aren't involved with anyone."

"It's been over three years since I've been in a relationship. My last one didn't end well. After it was over, I swore not to get caught up again."

"That bad, huh?"

"Emotionally draining." Cain dropped his handful of popcorn back into the bowl. "My ex-girlfriend, Chivon, was five months pregnant and she lost the baby."

"I'm sorry."

"It was rough for a while. No matter how much I tried to be there for her, she pushed me away. I kept thinking that we should've been able to help one another through it, but she didn't want that. I believe she blamed me. She was alone in our apartment in Harlem when she miscarried. I was traveling a lot at the time and was out of town on business. She couldn't get to the phone. Anyway, things went downhill after that happened. Everyone thinks the mother is the only one that suffers and that isn't true."

Cain went on to explain how losing the baby changed his life. He felt robbed. His joy was stolen away without a moment's notice. One day he was excited at the prospect of being a father, the next, he hurt to the depths of his soul. Emotionally, he completely shut down. "I never thought I could love anything or anyone as much as I loved that baby. Losing my mother...that was unbearable. Losing my unborn child...devastating."

I looked up at the pained expression on his face. "I can only imagine the pain you went through but know that your baby is in heaven right now with your mother."

He gave me a squeeze and smiled. "I know. I try to remember that every time I start to question why things like this happen."

"I've learned not to question certain things because we may never find an answer to satisfy us. No reason will ever be good enough. Through faith you find strength. And when you're blessed with another precious gift, you'll love and cherish that baby more than anything in the world."

"That's the one thing I learned from that experience; that love is not guaranteed. It shouldn't be taken for granted."

"Stay committed to your faith and you will be alright. Your pain will turn to joy."

"You're something else, you know that?"

"So I've been told."

"I knew it was too good to be true. Your cocky sidekick had to show up," he kidded.

I grabbed a small pillow and knocked him upside the head. Cain jumped off the couch and lifted me as if he was going to body slam me, but let me gently fall into the soft, fluffy cushions. He grabbed my right ankle and tickled my foot. I was laughing too hard to fight back. He lifted me again but this time he fell back onto the couch with me and I ended up lying across his lap. The bowl of popcorn toppled to the floor. The laughter stopped. We were out of breath and panting from our horseplay. Cain hungrily pressed his lips to mine. I wrapped my arms tightly around his shoulders and welcomed his kisses. As our breathing returned to a more normal state, we slowed the pace, savoring the heat of the moment. Cain nibbled my earlobes, my neck, my lips. I massaged his back, ran my tongue along his adams apple, kissed his chin.

In between kisses, he managed to ask, "What do you think about going in the Jacuzzi?"

"What about...the movie?"

"You're not watching that. Are you?"

I opened my eyes to find Cain peering at me. I turned my head toward the television only to discover the credits rolling. "I guess not."

Cain planted tiny kisses along my neck as he spoke. "We can take our drinks...and go out there...and chill."

"I don't have a suit with me."

"Who said you need one?"

He was smooth and I was open. I wouldn't mind a little Jacuzzi time with this fine, black man. "Okay. Let's get in."

I barely got the words out before he reached over me to the coffee table, his chest all in my face, to push a button on his universal remote. Outside the Jacuzzi turned on with a low rumble.

He sat back and looked down into my face. "You have beautiful almond-shaped eyes...and those lips..."

Cain brushed the side of my breasts with his hands, traced circles around my nipples and then began to unbutton my shirt. He eased my top from my shoulders, revealing my black lace demi bra. His eyes were glued to me as I sat up to take off my shirt. All I could say was thank goodness for Vickie's Secret. He bowed his head and kissed my cleavage, then placed a soft kiss on each nipple.

He stood up, pulling me off the couch with him. Cain put his hands on my waist, playing with the belt loops on my jeans. "So sexy..." he breathed out.

I pushed his T-shirt up, exposing his abs, and let my fingers become acquainted with each cut. I wasn't tall enough to lift the shirt past his shoulders so he pulled it over his head, tossing it on the couch. I observed how his chest flexed at the slightest movement, wondered how that hardness would feel against my softness. I unbuckled my belt and he nudged my hand out of the way. Cain unfastened my jeans and pushed them down my thighs. My matching black lace thong had him licking his lips. He bent down, sliding my jeans over my calves to the floor. I stepped out of them. He stuck his tongue in my belly button, gave it a little kiss. Hooking his pinky in the v-string of my thong, Cain started to lightly tug downward.

I put my hand on top of his. "I'm going to be needing these."

He stood up and took me in from head to toe. "Whatever makes you comfortable."

He unzipped his jeans and let them drop to his ankles. He was wearing a pair of charcoal Calvin Klein boxer briefs that clung to every muscle they covered; *every muscle*. Cain took me by the hand and led me outside. While he uncovered the Jacuzzi, I went back inside to get our bottle.

He was up to his chest in bubbling water when I returned. He stood and helped me in. I couldn't refrain from taking a peek at his wet boxers.

He saw me looking and asked, "You like what you see?"

I giggled and averted my eyes. "I'm definitely not complaining." I sank down to my shoulders in the warm water.

"Why are you way over there? I won't bite...unless you ask me to."

I smirked. "Bite me."

"Cute." Cain glided over to my side of the Jacuzzi.

I took the cork out of the wine and drank straight from the bottle. "Want some?"

Cain shook his head.

I took another swallow; some of the Riesling trickled down my chin to my neck. He followed the trail with his tongue. I let the bottle slip from my hand back to its resting place on the Jacuzzi, then faced Cain. Draping my arms around his neck, I rubbed my body against his; I wanted to feel what he had to offer. His hands were drawn to my waist and made a slow descent to my ass, where he filled each palm and then lightly squeezed. We were eye to eye, anticipating one another's next move. My hand left his neck, drifted down his chest, bumped over his rock-hard stomach, and landed on his upper thigh. His hands left my butt, glided around my hips and then gently slid between my thighs. Our eyes dared one another, both of us waiting to see who was going to be the boldest. Never one to resist a dare, I moved my hand from his thigh and touched his penis, let my hand get a firm grip and measured what he was working with. He moaned. Cain eased my thighs apart and rubbed my clit, tickling that oh-so-sensitive spot. I licked my lips. We watched each other for subtle hints of pleasure—lids closing, fleeting smiles, quick breaths barely above a whisper, heads slightly tilting back. He pulled me closer to him, allowing me to feel his excitement. We kissed and touched each other, taking sips of wine from time to time.

Cain worked his hands under my v-strings, attempting to remove my thong, but I stayed his hand. The Jacuzzi and the wine were definitely working but I needed to slow things down. If I didn't, tomorrow I'd be telling my friends *I don't know how it happened—I must've fallen on it.*

Sensing my retreat, Cain took his hands from my hips and nodded. He placed a single kiss on my shoulder and then took a drink of the wine. He passed the bottle to me and I took a sip, although I had had more than enough. I handed it back to Cain and he proceeded to take large swallows from the bottle, finishing off its contents.

"You ready to get out?" he asked.

"I am feeling a bit tipsy." And a lot tired. I wanted to lie down; my eyelids were drooping.

"Give me one second."

Cain got out of the water and went over to the pool house. He disappeared inside for a moment and then returned with two oversized white towels. He assisted me out of the Jacuzzi and wrapped the thick cotton towel around my body. I dried off, studying him the entire time. The way he wiped the water from his body almost made me grab his private parts again.

He wrapped the towel around his waist and then waited for me to finish. I tucked mine so it wouldn't fall off and followed him into the house. He hadn't said much since I put the brakes on our interlude. I didn't want him to think I was leading him on, but it is a woman's prerogative to take it fast or take it slow.

Cain closed the door behind us, locking it and drawing the vertical blinds. I didn't want to sit on the sofa with a damp towel, so I stood awkwardly with my arms folded across my chest, watching him turn on lights, pick up popcorn, and fix sofa cushions.

I moseyed over to pick up my clothes, trying to be as inconspicuous as possible. I stumbled into the glass coffee table, trying to step into my jeans. Cain stopped what he was doing and gave me a puzzled look.

"What are you doing?" he asked.

"I'm getting dressed so I can get home."

"You're not going anywhere. You've had too much to drink. Besides, you're putting your jeans on backwards. That's proof enough you don't need to be on the road."

"It won't take me long to get home from here," I said, through a loud yawn.

"Jade, you're not going anywhere. I'll give you something to sleep in. Come on upstairs."

I figured there was no purpose in arguing with him. I was tired and didn't need to be pulled over for driving under the influence.

The upstairs of Cain's home wasn't part of the tour earlier in the evening; perhaps it was the V.I.P. section of the house, reserved for moments like these. I walked into his bedroom and looked around—wine-colored carpet, dark mahogany furniture, a California king with a sprawling headboard and a burgundy comforter—definitely the room of a bachelor.

Cain pulled a T-shirt and a pair of New York Knicks basketball shorts out of his dresser drawer and passed them to me. "You can change in the bathroom. There's an extra toothbrush in the medicine cabinet and you'll find a towel and washcloth in the linen closet in there."

"Okay, I'll be right out."

I went into the bathroom and closed the door. Milan would've had an orgasm if she'd seen his walk-in shower. It looked so inviting, I had to jump in to take a quick one. I used Cain's Bvlgari shower gel and recognized it as the scent he'd been wearing the night before on our date. There was something about men's fragrances.

I came out of the bathroom, squeaky clean and smelling good, into an empty bedroom. I turned on the television and sat on the edge of the bed. An old episode of *The Cosby Show* was on Nick at Nite. I was cracking up at a very young Rudy screaming because she had shampoo in her eyes.

Cain entered with a black towel slung around his waist, his upper body wet. "I went to use the other bathroom, Ms. I'll Be Right Out," Cain said, laughing.

"I wasn't in there that long."

"I wasn't taking any chances. After five minutes, I got tired of waiting." Cain walked over to his dresser, opened the top drawer and then dropped his towel.

Nice ass. Something you can imagine yourself grabbing onto. He grinned at my blatant admiration of his nudity. He took a pair of boxer shorts out of the drawer and stepped into them.

"What are you cheesing for?" I asked, trying to play it off.

"Let's just say that your face tells everything you're thinking. Take a look in the mirror and you'll know exactly why I'm smiling."

"I *think* I'm ready to go to sleep. That's what I think."

"And so we shall."

I turned down the comforter and slipped in between the soft sheets while Cain cut off the light.

"Leave the TV on, please," I requested.

"You scared of the dark?"

"No, but I need the background noise to fall asleep. But if it bothers you, then turn it off. I don't want to disrupt your sleeping habits."

"I'll set the sleep timer. That way you can fall asleep and I can stay asleep."

"Thanks."

Compromise. Another point for Cain.

Cain joined me under the covers. He moved around until he got comfortable, which left us on opposite sides of the California king, no physical contact, no body parts touching. I felt like I was alone in his bed. When I was going to sleep or even just lounging on the couch, I liked to feel safe and warm. Plain and simple, I liked to snuggle. It was a comfort zone thing and, right then, I was comfortable with Cain.

I tossed from side to side to make sure I had his attention and then let out a few loud sighs.

"You alright over there?" he asked.

"Just trying to get comfortable."

Cain chuckled. "How can I help? You need me to fluff your pillows or something?" He was on to my antics.

I yanked the blanket up to my chin. "You think you are so funny."

"No, I don't. If you wanted me to come closer, you should've just asked," he said, moving over to me.

"Who said I wanted you over here?"

"I told you, your face says it all."

I rolled over into Cain's open arms and rested my head on his bare chest. He stroked my back, lulling me to sleep.

He kissed my forehead. "Good night."

"Sleep tight…and don't finish the rest."

I WOKE UP AT SUNRISE, MY BODY FEELING HEAVY from the bottle of wine I had the night before. Cain was lying on his side with his arm draped around my waist. I needed to get home and get ready for work. Slowly, I pried myself from under his arm without disturbing his sleep and slipped out of the bed. I stood beside the bed, gazing at him for a moment. I blew him a kiss before I left the room. I used the bathroom down the hall and then went downstairs to get dressed and to collect my things.

I left Cain's clothes in a neatly folded pile on the sectional, then went into the kitchen looking for a pen and paper to leave him a short note. I found a pen but no paper, so I scrawled a message, thanking him for a wonderful evening on a paper towel and left it on the counter.

I carried my shoes to the front door to avoid the click clacking of my heels on the tile. The door squeaked as I pulled it open just enough to squeeze through. I bent down to put on my shoes and caught a glimpse of the headline on the newspaper lying on the front steps. *Woman Hospitalized After High-Speed Chase on L.I.E. Leads to Serious Accident.*

I have to read that article later, I thought.

7

Terrence and I sat at the bar talking about the story in the paper. We were supposed to be discussing the expansion plans for Rituals, but last night's accident had taken place right in our own backyard.

"Have they said how the woman is doing?" I asked.

"She's still unconscious."

A witness to the accident said it appeared that the two cars were racing on the Long Island Expressway. The woman was going at least ninety miles per hour; the other car had to be doing over a hundred. Apparently, she sped around the eyewitness' car to catch up to the other one, clipped the back of the car she was chasing, and skidded into the guard rail. When they interviewed the eyewitness, he said the car must have flipped three times before it landed upside down.

I paged through Terrence's newspaper. "Did anyone see who was in the first car?"

"Nope. It was late. So far there is just the one eyewitness and he said he didn't notice because the car flew by him at top speed. You know how fast people drive on the L.I.E. It wasn't until the second car cut in front of him that he realized the cars must've been racing each other. The only thing he noticed about the first vehicle was that it was a dark sports car."

"That's why I stay off the L.I.E. at night."

"The police are searching for whoever was driving the sports car."

"Well, I hope they find him."

My cell phone rang. It was Milan calling. "Lan, what's up? You feeling better today?"

"Not really," she said. "Did you call here earlier?"

"No, I didn't call you."

"Oh. Chanel, our intern, said a woman called but didn't leave her name. I thought it was you." She sniffled between her words. "I have a meeting so I can't chat right now."

"Are you going to be alright?"

"I'll call you later, Jade."

The line went dead.

I turned to Terrence. "That was weird. Milan hung up on me."

"What's the matter with her?"

"She and Nolan got into it yesterday afternoon. She was really upset when she left here, but I thought she would've pulled herself together by now. Maybe I'll go check on her this evening."

"Yeah, make sure she isn't drowning her sorrows in a bottle of booze."

"Why don't you drop by to see her?" I chuckled as he started shaking his head emphatically. "Don't act like that, Big Bro. Be there for my girl in her time of need. It would lift her spirits."

"Keep dreaming. I ain't lifting nobody's nuthin. She better call her ex and seek comfort from him."

"Alright, alright. Stop making my girl the butt of your jokes."

"Can I help it if she always has some drama that I can make jokes about?"

"You're so insensitive. I can see why you don't have a girlfriend."

"You're right. I don't have *a* girlfriend. I have a *few* special friends."

"All that to say…you're hoin'."

"You don't think too highly of me, do you?"

"Terrence, let's just go over these plans. Okay?"

"Fine with me. That's what I'm here for, Baby Girl."

I laughed. "Save the *'baby girls'* for your *special* friends."

IT WAS AFTER TWO WHEN WE FINISHED reviewing the plans. Bria was coming in as Terrence was packing up. Bryce came trailing in behind her. A low groan emanated from within me.

Terrence smirked. "This is about to get good. I might have to stay a few extra minutes."

"I hate to disappoint you but there'll be nothing to see."

As Bria and Bryce reached the bar, I kissed my brother on the cheek and told him I would talk to him later. Terrence gave Bryce a pound. I said hello to Bria, nothing to Bryce, then jumped from the barstool and went to the kitchen. Bria was asking Terrence when she could see the plans. I looked back before walking through the swinging doors. Bryce was glaring at me. That was the last thing I wanted Terrence to see; Bryce giving me dirty looks. Men could get stupid sometimes and I didn't want my brother starting a fight because he presumed someone was treating his sister funny. I was a grown woman and he still thought he had to take up for me.

I peeped through the doors and Bryce's demeanor was cool and collected. He was chatting with Terrence as if he wasn't just ice grilling me. Hopefully, he wasn't planning to stay long.

If I was going to be holed up in the kitchen against my will, then I was going to make good use of my time. During my meeting yesterday, the fishmonger had promised he'd have a delivery of fresh fish to the restaurant by noon. I asked the kitchen manager if the shipment of seafood had arrived yet. I located the sea bass and went to work.

An hour later I was done. Sea bass, poached in a champagne

butter sauce garnished with fresh dill, arranged beautifully on a plate. I walked over to the door and peered out. Bria was alone at the bar. I grabbed two forks, picked up the dish, and went over to her.

"Hey, try this," I said, placing the plate down on the bar.

"I was wondering what you were doing back there."

"A little experimenting."

Bria flaked off a forkful. "Jade, that's good. I love the flavor of the sauce; it doesn't overpower the fish."

I sampled the meaty yet tender fish. "I'm adding this to the specials for tomorrow."

I felt a presence lurking behind me and whipped around in my seat.

"You didn't bring a fork for me?" Bryce asked.

"I thought you were gone," I snapped.

"Here, you can use mine," Bria said. "I have to check on something." She hopped off her stool and hustled over to the hostess stand.

There was that ride-or-die shit again. Bryce sat down next to me and picked up his sister's fork. I shoved the dish in front of him.

"What? We can't even break bread together?" he asked.

"Actually, I've had enough."

"I'll finish it then." He dived into the fish as if it was intended for him. "Pretty good. But I've always loved your cooking."

I started to get up from my seat. Bryce put his hand on my leg.

"Don't leave. Let me talk to you for a second."

I pushed his hand from my thigh and sat back down. "What now?"

Bryce put his fork down and then wiped his mouth with a cocktail napkin he had taken from the holder on the bar.

"I want to apologize for dropping by the other day. I was out of line."

"Yes, you were. Please don't do that again."

"I understand. You don't want me to run into your new man."

"Bryce, it has nothing to do with a man. You've lost your drop-by privileges and you need to respect our current situation."

"Our situation is that we love one another and we've hit a little bump in the road."

"No, we've hit a crater; that's our situation."

"What can I do to fix it, Jade?"

"Not a damn thing. Maybe in the future we can be friends, but right now, I need my space."

"We've always managed to work through our problems in the past. Why aren't you willing this time?"

"Because we've been here too many times before. We can't keep breaking up and making up. It's time for both of us to move on."

He balled up the napkin in his fist. "You must think I'm stupid. This has to do with you thinking that you can go on dates all of a sudden."

"Do you hear a word I'm saying?"

"Did you have a good time with Dane?"

"What is your problem?" I looked around for Bria. She needed to come get her brother. "You came here with your sister for a reason. I'm sure it wasn't to question me."

"I question you because I love you, but lately I feel like I'm the only one trying to save this relationship."

"What relationship? You wanted to test the waters and you did. Don't come running back to me now because you miss me all of a sudden. I deserve better than that."

I looked over my shoulder to see if anyone could hear us. Luckily, no one was paying attention so I gave him an earful. "When we were together, you didn't treat me like I was someone you had all of this love and affection for. You walked away like I meant nothing to you. I don't want to be in a relationship like that ever again. You've given me tons of food for thought. I now know what I want and what I don't want, and for the record, I have no intention of being alone. If I want to date, I will. I have a lot to give to the right man, but I need a man that will respect me. I need a man that will respect our relationship. I need a man that wants to *be* in a relationship."

"You don't need a man to make you whole. You should be content with yourself and not concentrate on finding a man to make you happy."

"No, Bryce, I don't need a man to make me whole or happy. I need a man to *complement* who I am. That was something you never seemed to grasp. A man and a woman should enrich each other's lives. They're supposed to complement one another. So, like I said, I need a man that's ready for me and all that I have to offer, a man that complements me with what he has to offer. And by the way, know that I recognize your attempt to discourage me from moving on with your little 'you don't need a man' comment."

"All I'm attempting to do is to get back together, where we belong. Think about it."

Bryce got up from his barstool, tossed the napkin down on the scraps in the plate, and left me alone with my thoughts.

One thing was for certain; this man still had the power to disrupt my day. I had to work on that. To love someone so much one minute and despise them the next didn't seem right. I had always felt that I didn't want to be without Bryce. I wanted to spend the rest of my life with him, to be his wife. No matter what type of problems we were experiencing, I convinced myself that we could work through it because I hated the pain I felt when we weren't together.

I dealt with his inconsiderate ways. I tolerated his selfishness. I had even forgiven him for cheating on me, a few times. I told myself our love was strong enough to overcome the bullshit. His bullshit. I forced myself to believe him when he said that he loved me more than anything in the world, despite his contradictory actions.

I was upset when he left, but a part of me felt relieved. This time had to be the last time; my heart was tired. My emotions were always up and down in our relationship, never steady. I grew so used to heartache that I was constantly waiting for the next problem to surface. I was always armed for battle, ready to fight for love.

Bryce once said to me that love was supposed to hurt. I found it hard to comprehend how or why he would believe something like that, but he did. I didn't though. I never did and I never would. It made it easier to stay away from him, knowing that he had committed himself to such an ideology, a belief that would no doubt affect my future happiness. Did I really want to be with a person who thought that you were supposed to hurt the one you love? I don't think so. I had done all of the hurting that I was going to do over Bryce.

I watched Bryce talk with his sister for a couple of minutes before I slipped back into the kitchen. I went out the back door, got in my car, and drove off. I didn't have a destination in mind—I needed some fresh air.

I pulled into a parking space in front of Eden. I checked my lipstick in the rearview mirror and then sprayed on a little Ecstasy. Outside of my car, I smoothed my skirt, unbuttoned another button on my blouse, and popped an Altoid.

Cain was standing in the dining room, conversing with two women seated at a table. One of the women had a long blond weave that flowed to her butt, and fingernails almost as long. Her breasts were about to pop out of her tight tank top. Somebody should've told her that she was a big girl and needed to stay out of the juniors section.

Her friend was a petite thing. Cute face. Short precision bob, tapered at the back. I kept my attention on her. She was wearing a short tennis skirt and a matching top, her flat stomach showing. Her tennis racquet was resting near her foot. The women were enthralled by whatever Cain was saying. The cute one kept touching his arm every time she laughed. I cleared my throat and busted up the party.

Cain saw me waiting and excused himself. He approached the hostess stand, grinning. Cutie Pie and Blondie seemed extremely disappointed that they had lost their company. They looked my way and then started whispering to one another. Once Cain reached me, I laid it on thick; I gave him a kiss on the cheek and a lingering hug. It was catty but Cutie Pie was doing a bit too much touching. As we embraced, I peeked over his shoulder to make sure the women were watching. If they wanted to whisper, I would give them something to talk about.

I pulled away from Cain and looked up into his face. "I was in the neighborhood…"

"I'm glad you were. I meant to call you earlier but it was busy in here. We had a private luncheon booked this afternoon. They finally cleared out about a half-hour ago."

"I hope I'm not imposing. I needed to get away from Rituals. Somehow I ended up here."

"Not at all; it's good to see you. Come sit outside with me."

Cain held my hand, leading me to the patio. I smiled and said hello as we passed Cutie Pie and Blondie's table. Blondie spoke, Cutie Pie didn't; she just rolled her eyes.

The patio was completely empty. We sat at a table in the far corner.

"Why didn't you wake me up before you left this morning?" Cain asked.

"You looked so peaceful, I didn't want to disturb you."

"You wouldn't have been disturbing me. It would've been nice to start my day seeing your face. What time did you sneak out?"

"A little after five."

"What was the hurry? Were you having regrets about last night?"

"Please, no. I don't regret a single thing. I thoroughly enjoyed last night."

"This morning, when I was getting dressed, I was thinking maybe I came on too strong and scared you off." He ran his hand over his bald head. "I have to tell you, when I see something I want, I go after it. I trust my feelings and have no problem showing them. I'm a passionate man. I want you to tell me if I need to tone it down."

"Everything that happened between us, I wanted to happen. If I didn't want you to see me in my drawers, then you wouldn't have seen me in my drawers."

He burst out laughing at me. "I would hardly call what you were wearing drawers. That was a sexy ensemble."

"Oh, so you liked it?"

"What kind of question is that? I'm catching flashbacks right now." He wiped his forehead with a napkin. "Is it getting hot out here?"

"I feel fine. It must be you."

He laughed. "Yeah, it is me. I need something to drink. Can I get you something?"

"Yes, but no alcohol. Two nights in a row is enough."

"Pellegrino?"

"Sure."

Cain went to get our drinks. I appreciated his concern about our activities last night. If only he knew. I had stopped at the mall after my meeting with the fish guy and picked up that little number from Victoria's Secret. A girl had to be prepared when she was going out on a date. You never knew when a little action might be jumping off and there was nothing worse than getting caught out there in some mismatched underwear.

I hate to admit it, but there had been occasions in the past when I wanted to have a little fun, but couldn't because I didn't want my date to see a pink bra clashing with rust panties or something equally as hideous. But that was long time ago when I was in college. Now I knew better.

I had an excessive lingerie collection at home but it didn't seem right to put on lingerie that I had worn to entice Bryce. I wanted to purchase something new. With a weakness for beautiful lingerie, it didn't take much to inspire me to add to the collection. I had picked up quite a few negligees, bras, and panties. Like I said— you had to be prepared.

Cain returned with our Pellegrino. "Since you're already here, would you like to stay and have dinner with me?"

"I can't tonight. I need to swing by Milan's house. We can have dinner tomorrow if you like."

"I'm going out of town tomorrow. I have to check out some property in Atlanta. I won't be back until late Friday night."

"Well, I guess we'll have to do it when you get back."

"Perhaps I can get you to make that special dinner for me on Saturday night."

"I might be able to do that, but right now, I need to get going." I got up from the table.

Cain stood in front of me. "Thanks for stopping by. It was a nice surprise."

He bent down and pressed his mouth against mine, giving me full kisses on the lips. His hands wandered to the curve of my back. We stood toe-to-toe, kissing each other in the late-day sun. We were interrupted by a couple being seated on the patio.

I straightened my blouse while Cain put his hand in his pocket to do a little adjusting. He spoke to his customers and then escorted me through the restaurant out to my car. Cutie Pie and Blondie were gone.

I kissed him on the cheek. "Have a safe trip."

"I'll call you when I get back."

He stood watching as I drove out of the parking lot.

TRAFFIC ON THE NORTHERN STATE PARKWAY was bumper to bumper. This was the wrong time of day to head out east to Milan's. I listened to the last hour of the Michael Baisden Show while creeping along to my exit. He was talking about dating. What women did wrong and how men had to put up with it. Michael was a trip. Listening to him instigate a battle between the sexes made the traffic seem not so bad.

By the time I cruised into Milan's cul-de-sac, it was almost seven p.m. and I needed to use the bathroom. Her car was in the driveway. I parked in front of her townhouse and hurried to the door. I rang the doorbell, dancing from side to side, waiting for her to let me in. No Milan. I pushed the bell again; the chime sang out, still no Milan. I came down the steps and leaned against her car. The hood was hot. I looked up toward her bedroom window and the curtains moved.

I took my cell phone out of my purse and dialed her number. No answer. I left her a message. "Milan, I don't know what's going on but I'm standing in your driveway watching you watch me. I drove all the way over here in traffic to check on your ass. You're not going to pick up the phone? Okay, I'm out."

I ended the call and walked back to my car. I turned around to see if she was looking out of the window but she wasn't. I jumped into my car and sped off to find the nearest gas station restroom.

8

My telephone startled me out of my sleep. I squinted at the clock; 1:32 in the morning.

I was becoming more like my parents; I immediately thought late-night calls were an emergency. There was a time when my friends and I had called one another, regardless of the hour, to discuss just about anything; a date, a television show, a silly dream. If my phone rang at ten p.m. or two a.m., it never crossed my mind that there may have been a problem.

"Jade, I need to come over."

"Milan? Where are you?"

"I'm driving down your street."

"What's wrong?"

"I'll talk to you when I get there."

"Alright. I'm getting up."

Now, I was worried. I flung the covers back and jumped out of the bed. I threw my robe over my tank top and boy shorts and ran downstairs.

Milan came into the house a ball of nervous energy. She went directly to the liquor cabinet in the living room.

I sat on the couch, observing her movements. Her hand was trembling as she poured Courvoisier in a glass. Milan wouldn't sit. She stood with her back to me, one hand holding onto the liquor cabinet for support.

"Milan, what's going on?" I waited a moment for an answer then shouted, "Milan!"

She barely turned to face me. "It was us."

"What are you talking about? What was us...I mean you...tell me what's going on."

She shouted, "It was us. The accident. Eriq and me."

Milan looked at me through wild eyes. I told her to sit, to try to calm down, and start from the beginning. She brought her glass to her lips, the contents swishing from side to side in her shaking hand.

"Put the drink down and talk to me, Lan."

"Eriq and I are responsible for the accident on the L.I.E."

"The woman whose car flipped?"

"Yes, it was us," she bellowed.

"Milan, you're scaring me. Are you sure?"

"Yes, damn it!" she yelled.

I matched her tone. "Calm down! What the hell happened?"

"It was an accident. It wasn't supposed to happen." Her eyes welled up.

I ran to the kitchen to grab a couple of napkins. I handed them to her and waited for her to speak.

"Milan, tell me what happened."

Her breathing was ragged. I sat down next to her and rubbed her back.

"The other day, when I got home from seeing Nolan, I was feeling pretty low. I said it was over with Eriq, but I called him up at the office. At first, we were just talking on the phone. I told him what had transpired with Nolan and he started complaining about his wife. He asked if he could come over. I said yes. I shouldn't have agreed to let him come by, but I didn't want to be alone."

Milan explained how she'd picked Eriq up from the office after work so that he could leave his car in the lot to make it seem as if he was still at the office working. They went back to her house, talked, had a little dinner and then fell asleep.

"We didn't even have sex," she said. "We both needed someone to talk to. Anyway, we woke up and it was two in the morning. Eriq was agitated because he hadn't planned to stay out until the wee hours of the morning."

According to Milan, Eriq knew his wife would be suspicious, just when he was finally working his way back into her good graces. Milan was too groggy to drive, so she let Eriq drive them back to the office to pick up his car, giving her time to fully wake up.

"A couple of blocks from my home, I thought there was a car following us. The roads were empty at that hour so I found it strange that every turn we made, the car made. I didn't say anything to Eriq until he had gone through a yellow light to get on the ramp to the L.I.E. and the car behind us blatantly ran the red."

"Oh, Milan…" I groaned.

"Eriq looked in the rearview mirror and said it was his wife's car behind us. He sped up and tried to outrun her, but the faster he went, the faster she went. Jade, we were doing at least ninety-five and she was keeping up with us. I begged him to slow down. I thought we were going to crash." The tears spilled from her eyes. "He wouldn't slow down. He kept rambling about how he couldn't get caught again, that his wife would divorce him and take everything he'd worked so hard for. I screamed at him to get off at the next exit or I was going to dial 9-1-1. We argued back and forth, him saying he could lose her and me screaming for him to get off at the next exit. Then he cut across from the left lane to the right and sped off the Hauppauge exit. His wife tried to follow. She was going too fast and must've lost control because her car spun into the guard rail. As we came off the ramp, I was screaming that she had crashed."

"Why didn't you go to the police?"

"I don't know…I was scared. Eriq told me to stop panicking, that he would handle it, that his wife was fine. He tried to convince me that it may not have been her car that hit the rail. Don't ask me why I listened to him." She wiped her eyes with her shirt sleeve. "He took the side streets to get back to the office. When he pulled up to his car in the lot, he said he was going back to the accident scene to make sure everything was fine. I went home and watched News12 for reports of the accident. It wasn't until the six a.m. broadcast that I saw the story. She's in critical condition; I haven't spoken to Eriq since last night in the parking lot. Today, at the office, everyone was talking about his wife's accident. I acted as surprised as everyone else." Heavy sobs shook her body.

I watched my friend having a breakdown. I hugged her because she needed it, but I wanted to slap her.

"Milan, you have to go to the police."

"I know I do, but I want to talk to Eriq first. Maybe he's already told them that he was involved."

"Are you serious? Why would he do that? He has an alibi; he was working late. His car was in the lot all night to prove it."

Milan howled, crying uncontrollably. I went to make her some tea to calm her nerves. We had to figure out what she should do. I left her on the couch, a sniveling mess.

I came back with two cups of hot chamomile tea on a serving tray. I set the tray in front of her and made her drink it.

"First thing in the morning, you call Eriq. Regardless of what he tells you, you need to call the police."

"I could lose my job over this."

"And someone may lose their life."

"I wasn't driving, Jade."

"No, you weren't, but it was your car. The witness said the woman was racing a dark sports car and she hit the back of it."

"That isn't true. She didn't hit us."

"Well, the police think it is. That means they think you left the scene of an accident. Did anyone at the law firm know you and Eriq were seeing one another? People may put two and two together."

"No one knew. We were extremely careful."

"You never can tell. How do you know someone didn't see you pick him up yesterday?"

"I guess I don't."

"Exactly. Go to the police."

"I need a lawyer." She scoffed at the irony. "I can't use anyone from the firm."

"We'll think of who you can use in a couple of hours. Right now you need to get some rest."

"I'm not tired."

"It's three a.m. Go to the guestroom and get in the bed. I know you feel like shit but you don't have to look like it."

"Now is not the time for jokes." Milan dabbed her puffy eyes. "But you're right."

MILAN CAME DOWNSTAIRS AT SEVEN. I was sitting at the kitchen table drinking a cup of tea and scanning the paper. There were dark circles under her eyes.

"Did you get any sleep?" I asked.

"No. I kept thinking about getting in touch with Eriq."

"Why don't you call him now?"

She put her hand on her stomach, exhaled and then went over to the phone. Milan pressed the speaker button and dialed. The phone rang a while before he answered.

His voice echoed in the kitchen. "This is Eriq."

Milan's voice quivered. "Eriq, it's Milan."

Eriq commented to someone in the background that he would be right back; he needed to talk to his sister for a minute.

"I can't speak to you right now," he whispered.

"We have to talk. I need to know what's going on."

"Now is not the time. I'm about to go to the hospital to see my wife."

"Eriq, I'm going to the police."

"Wait a minute," he said, in a strained voice. "Why would you do that?"

"You know we were involved in that accident and the police are conducting an investigation into the—"

"Don't you go to the police," he demanded. "Let's meet to talk about this before you do something stupid."

I sipped my tea and it went down the wrong way. I began coughing.

"Do you have me on the speaker?" he asked.

"Yeah, so what?"

"What number is this you're calling me from?"

"Eriq, calm down."

"Let's not forget you have a lot at stake here, Milan. I'll meet you at your house tonight around nine to make sure we're on the same page with this."

"Eriq—"

He hung up before she could finish.

"I can't believe this shit," she said. "He hasn't told the police a thing. This isn't happening."

"Milan, you're going to have to go to the police. I'll go with you. Let me get dressed."

"Wait, Jade." She paced the floor. "I'm going to go, but not yet."

"What are you waiting for?"

"Not yet, Jade."

"You're going to meet with this fool? Milan, you could be in a lot of trouble here. Eriq isn't thinking straight. He doesn't care if you take the fall for this. The longer you wait, the worse it will get."

"I know you're concerned, but you have to let me handle this my way."

I shrugged. "Fine. Handle it."

Milan sat down next to me. "Thank you for being there for me last night. It meant a lot to me."

"I'll always have your back," I said, without looking up from my paper.

"I'm going to get out of your way so you can get to Rituals."

She went into the living room to collect her things and I was on her heels.

"Are you going to work today?" I asked.

"No, I'm calling in sick."

"Where are you going?"

"To get my head right."

"Are you going to let Eriq come to your house tonight?"

"I don't know yet."

"I don't trust him. Are you sure you're going to be safe? I can come over, if you want me to."

"Jade, I said, let me handle this. I'm going to be fine. Eriq isn't dangerous. I'll call you later on. And stop worrying. I'm doing enough of that for both of us." She hugged me and then walked to the door.

"Call me," I said.

"I will."

My stomach was in knots. I was hoping she would head straight to the police station, but I knew my friend better than that.

9

I called Bria and let her know I would be taking the day off. I was in no mood to schmooze with anyone. I did, however, want to go for a run in Eisenhower Park. I needed to release some stress in the worst way. Most times I'd put on my iPod nano when running the trails, but today I wanted to be alone with my thoughts.

The pavement felt good underneath my feet. My muscles were all working together; none of them were having trouble getting into gear, which was rare when I hadn't run in a while. I regulated my breathing and let the wind help carry me around the trail. I ran past Safety Town—a place I'd visited as a kid to ride in little pedal cars through a mock town equipped with roadways and traffic signs—down toward the lake.

I couldn't get Milan out of my mind. It wasn't like her to be so reckless. I was shocked she had cheated on Nolan with Eriq in the first place. When she told me that she and Eriq had been flirting with one another, I thought it was innocent, that it wouldn't go any further than harmless flirtation, especially since he was a married man. How she got from point A to point B was still a mystery. Milan had always been the one to think cheating was an unforgivable act. The times I told her about Bryce's indiscretions and my decision not to leave him, she had lit into me. She was the poster girl for monogamy. She adored Nolan and he worshipped the ground she walked on. Their connection was deep.

Nolan and Milan were friends in college and didn't start dating until many years after graduation. We all hung out at Syracuse but Milan spent more time with Nolan than I did. The two of them would dawdle away the hours, watching movies, reading, going out to eat. It was easy to mistake them as boyfriend and girlfriend; they shared an undeniable closeness.

When they finally started dating, it wasn't a surprise to any of us who knew them. We were expecting it. We wanted to know why it had taken a decade for them to figure out they belonged together. I suppose they finally got tired of dating other people and fi..ding out that the person could never measure up to what they had in each other. Those two embodied what it meant to be friends before lovers.

After Milan had the affair with Eriq, Nolan cried on my shoulder. He said the reason it hurt him so deeply was because he couldn't fathom how Milan could betray a friend that way. A friend who was also her man, her lover. He was there through the rough times in her life, was there for her while she was in law school; even stayed up late helping her study for the bar. He was her biggest advocate in her quest for partnership at the firm. Over the years she was always there for him too, for all of his successes and failures. You didn't throw that away.

Nolan kept asking me what had led her to cheat on him. He wanted to know had she complained to me, had she confided something that he didn't know. As much as I wanted to ease his pain, I didn't know the answers to those questions any more than he did.

Now when Nolan called, he didn't ask about Milan, wouldn't even mention her name. I had tried, on occasion, to get him to forgive her, to work out their differences, but he told me that he couldn't relate to her blatant disregard of what they had shared. I hoped it was true, that time healed all wounds; in their case at least.

Bryce was another story. For four years, I had experienced the ups and downs that came with loving him. We loved hard and we fought even harder. When it was good, it was oh so good. But when it was bad, watch out. Nobody could get to me like Bryce could; he was the love of my life. There were times I would look into his eyes and would become overwhelmed by how much I loved him. Other times I would look into those very same eyes and want to scratch them out of their sockets. He was good for showing up late when we were supposed to go out or completely forgetting we had plans at all. He always wanted me to attend his family functions but would never come to mine, leaving me to go solo. He'd make up lame excuses, often times using his job as a reason. I'd never heard of a stockbroker who was on call twenty-four hours a day, even on weekends.

Bryce would infuriate me with his selfish tendencies, then make up for it by surprising me with jewelry or weekend get-aways. I would forgive him time and again because I loved him, didn't want to be without him. I thought it made sense for us to be together, even though we had to sift out the bad in order to keep the good. Who didn't have to do that sometimes? Relationships weren't easy; they took hard work and commitment. Somewhere along the way Bryce decided he wasn't interested in commitment any more. He told me he couldn't be with me, that he wasn't ready to settle down. This time, I didn't fight. I simply let go. I was tired of the crying, the yelling, the door slamming, hurt feelings and bruised egos. You couldn't keep a man where he didn't want to be.

Bryce left me to find something that was missing, only to find that it was me. Now he had to learn to live with his decision, the biggest mistake of his life.

After my five-mile run I was relaxing on the patio in my parents' backyard, drinking a tall glass of lemonade. I hadn't been to visit in three weeks and they were starting to wonder why they hadn't seen my face.

The cool breeze rustled the leaves on the trees. It felt like yesterday that I played away my summer days in this yard. When Terrence and I were kids, my father built us a clubhouse that all of our friends swarmed to get inside. It wasn't much of a house; it was really a large, ten-foot-high wooden rectangle painted brick red, with screen windows that ran its entire length. It had a squeaky screen door, with a simple latch and hook lock that slammed shut any time we went through it. There was a wooden bench affixed to the wall at the far end and if we had a lot of friends over to play, we set up beach chairs inside for additional seating. I loved that clubhouse and loved my father for building it. We spent many rainy days in that clubhouse with our friends, laughing and performing skits for one another. Sometimes I'd go in there to read or to have a little privacy.

My father didn't tear the clubhouse down until I was in college. After years of fall rains and winter snowstorms, it turned into a dilapidated eyesore that he could not stand to lay his eyes upon. The red paint had faded to a muted stain and the inside was used as a shed. I was sad to see it torn down and discarded; it was a piece of my childhood, a reminder of a more carefree time.

My father came out of the house with a tray of hamburgers and hotdogs and went over to fire up his gas grill. The minute I set foot in their house, my parents started trying to feed me. Even though I owned a restaurant they thought I didn't eat.

As he put the food on the grill, he couldn't resist engaging in our old debate. "My gas grill is ready for the burgers already. Now if we were at your house, we'd be waiting all day for the coals to die down," he said.

"If you were at my house, you would be eating real barbecue, not eating food cooked on an outdoor stove."

He turned to me and frowned. "Outdoor stove? The food that comes off my grill tastes barbecued to me."

"I'm not saying it isn't good. It just doesn't taste like real barbeque."

"Yeah? Well watch me eat up this good food from my outdoor stove."

My mother came outside and joined the conversation. "I tell your father that I like my food cooked with charcoal. I don't know why he always uses that gas grill."

"I don't see you cooking anything. You want to use the charcoal grill, then fire it up. I'll eat whatever you make," he snapped.

"Pay attention to what you're doing over there; I was talking to Jade. Next thing you know, you'll be burning up the food."

My father looked at me and shrugged his shoulders. I shook my head and laughed. They always carried on when I came over. They liked to act as if they really gave one another something to complain about. After thirty-seven years of marriage it must've gotten hard to find things to beef about; they had covered all the serious issues years ago.

My parents looked good to be in their early sixties. My mother didn't look a day over forty with her stylish cropped haircut. My dad's gray hair gave it away that he wasn't a spring chicken, but it also made him look very distinguished.

My mother poured herself a glass of lemonade. "How are things at the restaurant?"

"Everything is fine. You and Dad should come down for dinner soon."

My father chimed in. "You can't get your mother out of the house. All she wants to do is sit around watching her soap operas. I bet she has the DVR set to record them right now while she's out here talking to you."

"So what? I always record my soaps, in case I'm doing something and can't watch. If I record them, then I can watch them later and fast forward through the commercials," she said.

"See, I told you," my father said, waving his spatula in my mother's direction. "Your mother isn't thinking about coming down to Rituals. When was the last time you saw her down there?"

"Dad, I don't know," I said, chuckling. "I don't keep track."

"That's because you don't have to. Your father keeps track of everything. He could tell you how many times I go to the bathroom in a day," she said.

"Cute, real cute," he answered.

I interrupted their so-called argument. "Well, let me know when you want to come down and I'll tell Terrence to meet us there."

My mother asked, "Just Terrence? What about Bryce?"

"Uh…Bryce and I aren't together anymore, Mom."

"When did this happen?" she asked.

"About a month ago."

"Why, what happened?"

I never told my parents about Bryce's indiscretions. If there was one thing I knew, it was that you might've forgiven your man, but your parents didn't have to.

My father walked over with an aluminum pan filled with hot dogs. "Stop asking her all these questions. If they broke up then they broke up," he said.

I snatched one of the hot dogs and took a bite, grateful for the save.

My mother inspected the pan. "I don't know why your father cooks all of this food as if he's cooking for an army." She went back to harping on my father.

I wasn't ready to discuss my trouble with Bryce with my parents. They were expecting a wedding, not a breakup. My father kept hinting that he wished he had somewhere to wear his tuxedo. He wanted to get all dressed up to do the Electric Slide at somebody's wedding; he wouldn't come out and say *my* wedding but we all knew that's what he meant. I hated to disappoint them but we'd all be waiting a long time before I took that walk down the aisle.

We spent the rest of the afternoon, into the evening, talking, laughing, munching on snacks, and enjoying each other's company. I had come to love my parents on a new level. They had always been Mom and Dad to me, but now they were so much more. They were Bill and Barbara, my friends.

10

When I got home I checked in with Milan. I wanted to know what was up with the Eriq situation. She had agreed to speak with him before taking any action. I didn't think it was wise, but it wasn't my decision to make. I asked her to call me as soon as he left her house.

I should've called Bria at the restaurant to see if there were any messages for me but decided if there were, they could wait until tomorrow. Instead, I took a hot shower and then slipped on my terry cloth robe and lay across my bed. It was only eight o'clock and I was bored. I needed something to get into. If Cain wasn't in Atlanta, I would've invited him over.

I called my brother and asked if he was hanging out. He was going to a club in Manhattan with our cousin, Fitz. I told him to swing by to pick me up. Clubbing on a weeknight usually wasn't my style, but sometimes you had to live a little.

Black was the color for the night. I put on my black hipster pants and black shirt with the split sleeves and a pair of black stilettos. Black was my favorite color and when I wore it, I felt sleek and sexy, like a panther.

Terrence and Fitz pulled up at nine-thirty. I jumped in the back seat of Terrence's Yukon and we were on our way.

Terrence, Fitz, and I grew up together. Our parents made sure that our families spent time with one another. Weekend visits, picnics, holidays, birthdays, we were always together, ripping and running. Fitz and I were only nine months apart, but every year when my birthday arrived he would tease me about how old I was getting. I always remind him that I'd see him in nine months when we'd be the same age again.

"What's up, Cousin?" I asked.

"I haven't seen you in a minute. How you doing?"

"All is right with my world."

"What are you doing, coming out on a weeknight?"

"Every once in a while, I'll grace you two with my presence during the week." I laughed and then asked Terrence, "Where are we going?"

"Uptown to Club Blaze."

"We're going to Harlem? I thought we were going downtown to Elation."

"Not tonight. We've been to this spot a couple of times and it's hot."

I had to take his word for it. What did I know about what was hot in the middle of the week?

There was a line outside the club. The ladies were wearing all kinds of outfits, ranging from classy fitted dresses to short skirts that barely covered their asses, to tight jeans with the thongs sticking out the top. The men were sharp in slacks and suits, no jeans, no boots.

Terrence and Fitz headed to the front of the line and I followed. The dirty looks and teeth sucking moved up the line like a wave. Terrence and Fitz gave the goliath at the door a pound. To call him a big dude would be an understatement. His neck was as wide as his shoulders; he had to be at least 300 pounds. I thought he was the bouncer, but my brother introduced him as Ernest, the owner, and told me they had served in the Marines together. He kissed my hand and I winced. He was trying to be a gentleman but managed to crush my small hand with his big mitt in the process. I wriggled my hand free from Bonecrusher's sweaty palm and told him it was nice meeting him. Fitz saw my pained expression and nudged me in the back. I turned to him and mouthed "ouch" while opening and closing my hand.

Bonecrusher led us to the V.I.P. section and told the waitress to get us whatever we were drinking. The place was packed. The deejay was playing classic R&B, which was right up my alley. He was mixing Fonda Rae's "Over Like A Fat Rat" with Patrice Rushen's "Forget Me Nots." The waitress brought over my vanillatini and two Heinekens for my brother and cousin. Bonecrusher joined us with his drink. We were laid-back on oversized velvet sofas, warming up to the scene. He had a nice establishment and I told him so.

"I've been open about six months and so far, so good," he said.

Terrence piped in. "Yeah, this is a long way from Kuwait."

They both laughed. Fitz and I looked from one to the other, waiting to find out why they were so amused.

Terrence explained. "We used to be in our tents on Friday and Saturday nights, complaining that we were late for the party. Then someone would pump up the music on the boom box and we'd all sit around and talk about what we'd be doing if we were home."

"Your brother was always talking about some club and all the honeys that had to be missing him."

I cracked up; that was no lie. Any time Terrence wrote home, he asked about three or four of his chicks. I presumed that all of Long Island was writing to him.

"I give both of you credit. They wouldn't have gotten my ass over to Kuwait," Fitz said.

"No kidding. They don't enlist men who think they're too good looking to get dirty. You'd be in the trenches trying to fight in a designer suit," I said.

We all cracked up.

"What I hated most was the food. You want to talk about inedible." Those words came from the three-hundred pounder.

I looked Bonecrusher up and down. "You don't look like you were suffering too badly."

He grabbed his stomach. "I gained all my weight after Kuwait. I was so happy to be home, I couldn't stop eating. I was slim and trim when I went over there."

"Man, you are a lying ass," Terrence said, laughing.

Bonecrusher winked. "At least that's what I tell the ladies."

I left the guys to their "man talk" and went to look around. I stood next to the rail overlooking the dance floor and bounced to the beat. I surveyed the crowd on the lower level. At the bar below I spotted an attractive man watching me. I kept dancing to the music, occasionally glancing his way. He was talking to a short round guy next to him and pointed up at me. He raised his glass to me and I mimicked his gesture. He motioned for me to come down. Nothing was going on in the V.I.P. section and I felt like dancing. I put up one finger to tell him I'd be down in a moment.

I drank a bit more of my vanillatini and put the glass on the table in front of the guys. "I'll see you wallflowers later."

With raised brows they watched me head down the spiral stair-case to the main level. My hips did a gentle sway as I strolled over to the bar. Up close my admirer was a light brown brother with thick eyebrows and a smooth clean face; he didn't have a trace of facial hair. He had a freshly cut caesar and a diamond stud in his left ear. He looked like he had stepped off the cover of *GQ* with his tailored suit and gator shoes.

He smiled at me, showing off the deepest dimples. "How are you this evening?" he asked. "I'm Omar and this is my boy Kev."

"I'm Jade, nice to meet you." I smiled and shook hands with both of them.

His round friend moved from his space at the bar and motioned for me to take his place next to his boy. Kev wasn't a bad-looking brother either, but he could've used some work in the fashion department. His shirt was stretched to its limit around his stomach and his pants were so high they needed to be introduced to his shoes.

Kev told Omar he was going to see what was happening on the lower level and then left us at the bar.

"Would you like a drink?" Omar asked.

"A vanillatini, thank you."

Omar ordered my martini and another of whatever he was drinking.

The song changed to "Watching You" by Slave. "The deejay is playing all of the old school jams," I said.

"I saw you up there dancing. Your friends won't get upset you're down here with me?"

"No, they're fine."

"Jade, right?"

"Right."

"What do you do for a living, Jade?"

"I'm in the restaurant business. What do you do?"

"I'm a portfolio manager at an investment firm in midtown."

"That means you can give me some investment strategies," I kidded.

"Sure. I'll give you my card and you can call me when you're ready to get down to business."

The bartender put our drinks in front of us. I tasted mine; the vanillatinis in the V.I.P. were much better.

"This is my first time here," I said. "It's pretty cool. Mature crowd. Good music."

"Ernest, the owner, is one of my clients. I come here if I'm working late and want to blow off some steam. That means I'm usually here every week."

He laughed. His dimples were cute, gave him a baby face appeal.

"I may have to come back here myself," I said.

I found out Omar had played basketball for Georgetown during the time I was at Syracuse. He told me he was originally from the Bronx but lived in Harlem. He wanted to start his own investment management firm and was in the process of hunting down capital.

"What exactly do you do in the restaurant industry?" he asked.

"I own a restaurant on Long Island."

"Oh yeah, where?"

"Not far from the Roosevelt Field Mall. It's called Rituals. If you're ever in the area come try our food."

I should have brought a stack of business cards with me. I was always trying to expand our clientele so I gave him my sales pitch. I talked about our location, our delicious food, and our need for expansion in order to accommodate all of the people that had already fallen in love with us. The businesswoman in me was large and in charge. I let him know we catered events as well, in case he had any business meetings requiring refreshments.

He was grinning. "That's what I'm talking about. Black-owned businesses. I may take a trip out to Long Island to eat at Rituals. I believe in supporting my brothers and sisters."

"And when you get your investment firm up and running I'll give you my two dollars to invest."

"I'm sure a sharp sister like you has more than two dollars, but if that's all you have, I'll help you quadruple that."

I laughed and told him I would hold him to his offer. Omar and I chatted like a couple of old friends. The deejay put on "Just A Touch Of Love" and I started dancing.

"You've been wiggling all night. Come on; let's dance," Omar said.

He took my hand and maneuvered through the crowd. He

stopped in an open space near the middle of the dance floor and we started jamming to the music. He held onto my hand while we moved to the rhythm. He watched my style and then fell into the same groove as me. I liked his flow. He had an air about him—like he was too cool to break a sweat. He lifted my hand and twirled me around to the music. I did a slow turn, never missing a beat. He was probably looking at me shake my ass.

The music was pumping and I was feeling it. Omar was doing his thing, too. After the third song, he unbuttoned his jacket. He needed to be unrestricted to jam to "All Night Long" by the Mary Jane Girls. The bass was thumping and we were dancing close, singing along, making eye contact the entire time. Omar put his arm around my waist as our bodies moved in unison to the song.

I looked to my left and caught a glimpse of a familiar face leaving the dance floor. I tried to think of where I had seen it before but couldn't recall at the moment; Omar was keeping me preoccupied.

We danced to a few more songs before a Colonel Abrams cut came on. I never did care for him crying about being trapped. I suggested we take a break. On my way off the dance floor I passed Terrence grinding up with some girl. This time I was the one raising an eyebrow at him with his hand on her butt. He winked at me and kept dancing.

I leaned against the bar and ordered another round of drinks. I was a firm believer in women paying some of the time. I paid the bartender and then excused myself to go to the restroom. Standing on line I checked my hair in the mirror. That's when I saw her again. It was Cutie Pie. She was washing her hands at the sink. Blondie stepped out of one of the stalls and went to the sink next to her friend. They spotted me when I walked toward the open stall. Blondie said a peppy hello and Cutie Pie shot her a dirty look.

"Hi, ladies. Small world, isn't it?" I said.

"Too small," Cutie Pie replied.

I stopped in my tracks, looked Cutie Pie up and down, smirked and then went into the stall. I couldn't possibly imagine what her problem was and couldn't have cared less.

I heard Cutie Pie remark to Blondie, "Oh no, that bitch didn't."

Blondie said, "Let's go, girl. I came out to party, not to get into a fight."

They were leaving the bathroom when I exited the stall. *People are funny*, I thought. I washed and dried my hands, then went into the ladies lounge. I sat on the chair and took my cell phone from my purse. It was late but I dialed Milan's number anyway. She answered on the first ring.

"Lan, what happened with Eriq?"

"We agreed not to go to the police."

"You agreed or you were forced?"

"Jade, you may not think so, but this is for the best. It's his wife and he wants to deal with it in his own way."

"Milan, you need to check yourself. This isn't right."

The line went silent for a moment.

"I'm going to take a few days off from work and go to Philly to visit my mother. I'll give you a call in a day or so. This is all going to work out, you'll see."

I told my girl that I loved her and then ended the call. I ran my fingers through my hair and went back to join Omar at the bar.

"I thought you dipped out on me," he said.

"You know how the lines are for the ladies room."

"Before I forget, here's my business card. I wrote my home and cell number on the back."

I slipped his card in my bag. "Sorry, Omar, I don't have my card on me but you can reach me at the restaurant. That's where I spend the majority of my time."

He put the number to Rituals in his cell phone. "If I come all the way to Long Island to eat at your restaurant, will you join me?"

"Call me before you come and I'll let you know if I'll be able to have dinner with you."

"I'll definitely do that."

Frankie Beverly and Maze's "Before I Let Go" was playing. I was the one leading Omar onto the floor this time. We threw our hands up in the air with the rest of the crowd and sang along with Frankie. The crowd kept bumping Omar into me and he was taking full advantage of it. Cute as he was, I put a little space between us because a dance was just a dance. He was a nice guy and I wouldn't have minded developing a friendship, but as far as I was concerned, it was Cain that I wanted bumping up against me.

I saw Cutie Pie across the floor dancing with Kev and I chuckled. She watched me and Omar for a minute before she left Kev dancing by himself with no partner. There was something wrong with that girl. Kev pushed his way through the crowd to where Omar and I were and then tapped his friend on the shoulder. Omar turned around and Kev tapped his watch.

Omar nodded. "I'll be ready in a minute."

"I'll be at the bar," Kev said, walking away.

"I guess the party's over," I said.

"After this song. He can wait a few more minutes."

"I need to be leaving, too."

"Is someone waiting for you at home?"

"No, I just meant if I don't get home, I won't want to get up tomorrow."

"Jade, I had a good time with you tonight."

"Me, too."

"Do you have a man?"

I paused for a moment. "I think so…"

"You think so? You're not sure if you have a man?"

"Well, I recently started seeing someone."

"So it's not serious?"

"Not yet."

"In that case, I'm going to put it out there. I'd like to get to know you better, but the ball is in your court. I'll leave it at that."

"Either way you're still welcome to dine at Rituals."

"Oh, no doubt. That hasn't changed."

Omar and I hugged and then we headed off the dance floor. He met up with Kev and I returned to the V.I.P. section.

Fitz was sitting on one of the couches, vibing to the music. "The dancing machine is back," he said, chuckling. "You finally got tired of doing the robot out there?"

"Fitz, don't quit your day job. Leave the jokes to the professionals."

"I'm one of the funniest people you know."

I rolled my eyes. "Have you been up here all night watching the party from the sidelines?"

"I was up here talking to the beautiful ladies. I may have to make this place one of my regular hangouts."

"Where's Terrence?"

"He was right over there. He said he's ready to leave whenever we are."

"I'm ready."

"That makes two of us. Let's find him and bounce."

11

B ria sat at her desk, staring at the computer screen, while I stood with my back to her, looking out of our office window. She was reviewing my projections for Rituals, post-renovations.

"So we're going to see twice the revenue by the end of a two-year period starting in January?" she asked.

"We're looking at double-digit growth within the next six to eight months."

"What about our operational expenses?"

"A slight increase. Remember we're increasing our seating capacity by thirty-five percent. And with an additional bar in the back of the restaurant, we'll also need additional staff. Those things do add up, but you have to factor in the increase in daily seatings; that offsets the increase in expenses."

"What do you have in mind in terms of advertising?"

"Well, it doesn't hurt that you have your connection at WBLS. We need to partner with the station and promote a weekly event at Rituals. That's guaranteed mentions on the air. I already contacted Johnnie Walker and Hennessy to host tasting parties and they were interested."

"I'll call Cyrus at the station first thing in the morning. I want to get the ball rolling with him so we can kick this off as soon as the expansion is completed."

I laid out my entire plan for making sure all of those extra seats would be filled. We were going to run fifteen-second spots on two of the local cable channels and have a featured ad shown on the screen prior to the movie previews at the Roosevelt Field and Raceway theaters.

Bria nodded. "We have to grow our catering services, too."

"I know. Cain was telling me that Eden caters at least five events a week. I told him we were looking to bump up that aspect of our business."

Bria rolled her eyes. "Why are you telling that man our plans?"

"I would hardly consider that a plan. That is a goal we have for Rituals, not a step-by-step plan of action."

"You running your mouth to Cain would be like Bill Gates sharing his strategies with Michael Dell."

"That's a little extreme. Cain and I both own restaurants. It's only natural that occasionally our conversation is about work."

"Damn. Are these even your ideas for advertising or did Cain tell you what we should do?"

The expression on my face told Bria I wouldn't dignify that stupid question with a response.

"Leave it up to you two and before you know it Rituals and Eden will have the same menu." The phone rang and Bria snatched it up. "Okay, transfer him to me," she said.

I knew by the way she was talking that it was her brother.

"No, I'm not busy…just looking at a few projections…huh… where's Jade?"

I mouthed, "Tell him I'm not here."

"She said to tell you she's not here."

I shot Bria a look of death. This was the type of shit that made me want to knock her head off.

"Bryce said he wants to take you to dinner," she obediently reported.

"I can't. I have plans."

"Jade, I didn't tell you when."

"I'm never available."

Bria frowned. "Bryce, let me hit you back."

I immediately pounced. "Bria, why did you do that?"

"Do what? Tell you that my brother wants to take you to dinner?"

"Don't play stupid. You thought it was necessary to tell him I was here when I asked you not to."

"Jade, what's the big deal? He wanted to take you to dinner. I don't see the harm in that."

Bria amazed me. Her brother could do no wrong in her eyes. "One word. Noelle."

"Noelle is old news."

"Old news, new news, newsflash, breaking news, hot off the presses…I don't give a damn. It shouldn't have happened. And in case you forgot, he left me."

"And now he wants you back. That should mean something."

"It does. It means he's lost his mind."

I was starting to think that Bria had lost hers, too. Why she was pushing so hard for me to be with her brother, when he had clearly violated everything we had shared, made absolutely no sense. I was certain of one thing—those days of double teaming me were over. There was nothing Bria could say that would make me consider going back to Bryce.

"Jade, he hasn't lost his mind. Bryce loves you. He's made a few mistakes. Who hasn't?"

I laughed at her simplistic assessment of Bryce's antics. "You're right. It was a mistake when I called him at home and I heard a woman giggling in the background. It was also a mistake when he was supposed to go with me to my father's retirement party and chose not to call or show up. It was even a mistake when he promised to marry me and didn't. The biggest mistake of all was how he'd come down here and flirt with Noelle while I was in the damn kitchen."

"Calm down, Jade."

"No, I won't calm down. I don't expect you to sit here and trash your brother or dog him out, but I do expect you to at least be objective."

"Let's drop it."

"You have nerve. You want to talk about your brother and put a positive spin on things but when I keep it real and rattle off the negative stuff, the real deal, you don't want to hear it."

"You're getting riled up, and I don't believe you're thinking clearly."

Unbelievable. It had to be the twin thing because those two were identical—even though they were fraternal. I returned to the window and gazed out while Bria ran her mouth about how I was being too hard on Bryce. Lectured about love having ups and downs and taking the good with the bad. She believed Bryce had come a long way. He never was the type of man to commit to one woman. Bryce spoke to her about getting married and starting a family with me. He was excited about his future as a husband and father. If I had to listen to her say that her brother was a good man one more time, I was going to scream.

"Jade, you just don't stop loving someone."

"Weren't you the one that said 'drop it'?"

"He wants to propose to you."

I spun around to face her. "What did you tell him?"

"I said he has to follow his heart."

"Bria, I swear, if you don't discourage your brother from pro-posing, he *will* get his feelings hurt."

"Why don't you think about it?"

"I thought about it the four years we were together, when it didn't happen."

"Bryce is his happiest when he's with you."

"What about my happiness? I wasn't happy with Bryce."

"Jade, don't stand there and front like you weren't happy with my brother. I've seen you together over the years. Now you're conveniently forgetting the good times."

I sat down on the chair next to the desk. I admitted times were not always bad with Bryce, and yes, I did love him. But I finally arrived at the conclusion that love wasn't enough. Bryce being a *good man* wasn't enough—not when there were times that his behavior contradicted his love for me.

Bryce and I were intrigued with each other when we initially started dating. Everything with us was like a new discovery. I knew him and he knew me, but only on the surface. We plunged below the surface with curious fervor. I could truly say I learned that man. Inside and out. He was my world and I became lost in him. My feelings, wants, needs and desires became secondary to his. I accepted his shortcomings, his excuses, his disregard for my feelings—because I loved him.

I shrugged my shoulders. "Regardless of what may have been, I'm moving on."

Bria scowled at me. "Yeah, with the competition."

"With my life," I shot back.

12

Saturday morning I opened my eyes to a dreary, gray sky. I burrowed underneath the warmth of my goose down comforter. It had been a long week. Since Milan was out of town I'd skip the gym and watch a little television.

I turned to BET to watch videos. There was booty shaking everywhere. They didn't make a video unless it had at least ten booties flying across the screen. It was too early for all that butt jumping. I changed the channel to the Food Network and watched the Neelys make various desserts.

I was supposed to cook for Cain that evening and didn't have a clue as to what I was preparing. I made a mental to-do list. If I wanted to accomplish everything I couldn't afford to lounge around in the bed all day. I got up and stripped the linen off the bed. I misted the mattress and pillows with vanilla linen spray and then put on fresh thousand-thread-count Egyptian cotton sheets. I took a quick shower and then threw a load of laundry in the washing machine before I set out on my tasks.

It was a nasty day to be out running errands. My first stop was the supermarket. The parking lot was jam packed. I hated it when the shopping carts were dripping wet from sitting out in the rain in the parking lot. I wheeled one inside the store and then took a tissue from my knapsack to dry my hands and the cart handle. There were long lines at the registers already. Ironically, bad weather brought people out to the market in droves; on a rainy day there was nothing better than staying home and eating good food. I raced through the aisles dodging the other shoppers, tossing groceries in the cart.

The shortest line was eight people deep. I rolled my cart to the end of the line and then watched the cashier move in slow motion. It never failed; I always chose the slowest line. Twenty minutes later, after piling my bags into the trunk of my car, I was driving to the fish market on the Nautical Mile over in Freeport.

My strategy was to go in, inspect the fish, and buy whatever jumped out at me. Once inside, my plan crumbled. Everything was so fresh. I considered getting red snapper, but then the swordfish caught my eye. Tony, the proprietor, called me over to the counter when he saw me wandering from fish to fish. I was a regular in his store and he typically gave me recommendations on what was good on a particular day. He told me a shipment of jumbo prawns had arrived and suggested I take some of them home. If there was one thing Tony realized about me, it was that I loved fresh shrimp. Shrimp were versatile—they would be perfect for dinner. I could determine how I would prepare them once I got them home. I purchased the jumbo prawns then high-tailed it back home to drop off the groceries.

I was putting the food away when the telephone rang. I looked at the caller ID and then picked up.

"How was your trip?" I asked.

"I'm glad to be home. Ten meetings in three days...I'm exhausted," Cain said.

"Not too tired for dinner, I hope."

"I could never be that tired. Do you want me to bring anything?"

"Just yourself."

"I can do that. What time should I be there?"

"Is eight o'clock too late?"

"No, that's perfect. It gives me time to go by Eden and then get a little rest."

"Make sure you get a lot of rest."

"Why, do you have some special activities planned for me?"

I could hear the smile on his face. "Activities? No. I just don't want to be sitting across the table from someone that's half asleep."

"I'll be wide awake. I've had you on my mind all week."

"You crossed my mind a time or two." I chuckled at my blatant lie. I had thought about Cain more times than I wanted to admit.

"Well, it's always nice to know that someone is thinking about you…even if it's only a time or two. You know something?"

"What?"

"We're going to have to work on you expressing your feelings."

"What does that mean?"

"It means if we could get your mouth to express things as good as your face does, then we'll be alright."

"Oh, be quiet. Listen, I have a few appointments to get to. I'll see you at eight."

"Alright. I won't make you late. See you tonight."

He sure could put a smile on my face. I quickly cleaned the prawns and then whipped up a marinade to pour over them. I set them in the fridge and took the garbage out; I didn't want shrimp shells smelling up the house.

I needed to get to Farmingdale in ten minutes, which was highly unlikely on a rainy Saturday afternoon. I called the hair salon to let Andie, my stylist, know I was running a bit late. Andie told clients that they missed their appointment if they showed up a few minutes late without calling first. I didn't want to deal with any part of that, especially not that day.

I was thankful the rain had temporarily subsided and people weren't driving like idiots like they usually did in such weather. I drove down Broadhollow Road to Shades of Essence and found a space in front of the shop just as someone was pulling out. I rushed inside the salon, arriving only five minutes late. I spoke to all the ladies and then went over to Andie. She looked up at the clock on the wall.

"Don't start," I said.

"I'm checking to see how late you are."

"Five minutes. I know you aren't going to complain about that?"

"Who said I was going to complain."

"I know you, Andie. You're ready to complain about me being five minutes late and if I were here five minutes ago, I would still be sitting on the couch waiting, like I'm about to do now."

She laughed; that was the absolute truth. I'd probably be on the couch for an hour before I was called to the sink to get my hair washed.

"Did you come in here to argue or to get your hair done? You don't have to answer that. I can see your hair is a mess."

"I said, don't start."

I sat up front to wait for my turn to be washed. I was thumbing through a few magazines while the girls in the shop were talking about the usual…men. One girl was saying she had been with her man for seven years and they had two children. She had been telling him that they needed to get married to set a good example for the children. He told her that their kids were too young to know whether they were married or not so what was the rush. The women were yelling back and forth what they thought she should do about the situation. There was a woman with short curly hair screaming at the top of her lungs that the girl should give him an ultimatum, either marry her or kiss his kids goodbye. She could barely complete her sentence before everyone attacked her. The only male in the salon, Francois—it was really Frank but he had changed his name to match his flamboyant style—scolded her for giving out the milk for free. Everyone shouted for him to be quiet and wanted his loud pink hot pants to do the same.

An older woman with beautiful salt and pepper hair spoke up. Out of respect for an elder, all the women stopped shouting and listened to what she had to say. She asked the girl if she loved her man. The girl told her she did. The older woman said if she loved her man, then she needed to weigh how much being married mattered to her; was it absolutely necessary for her happiness. She also told her to consider why her boyfriend didn't deem it necessary to get married. She explained that, most likely, there were underlying issues that needed to come to light. If after she discussed with her man her wants and needs and he was still unable to meet them, then she should think about what it would take to make her happy and move forward to achieve that end.

What the older woman said made sense and I hoped the girl would get what she wanted, but I seriously doubted it. After seven years and two kids he didn't want to be *rushed* for a reason…he just didn't want to get married. I had to remember to follow up with Andie the next time I came in to find out what happened.

I was coming from under the dryer, fanning myself.

"You better be dry," Andie said. "You're always getting out too soon."

"I've been under there an hour and a half and I want to get out of here sometime today."

"Keep getting smart and I'll do you last."

"I'll flat iron my own hair if I have to."

"Girl, sit your ass in this chair so I can get you out of here."

She nudged me in the head as I sat down. Andie had been doing my hair since my senior year in high school; that was a lot of beauty shop banter between the two of us, but I wouldn't have had it any other way. She parted my hair in the center and flat-ironed it from the roots to the tips. When she was done, my hair was straight yet bouncy, hanging nicely to my shoulder blades. I kissed her on the cheek, stuffed her tip in her jacket pocket and then went up front to pay my bill. I yelled for everyone to enjoy the rest of their weekend on my way out the door.

Next stop, manicure and pedicure. The nail salon was on the adjoining block. I left my car where it was and walked down the street. The place was empty when I got there and I managed to get in and out in no time.

As I was walking back to my car, it started to drizzle again. I hurried home, eager to start dinner. I waved to my neighbor across the street before pulling into the garage, leaving the drive-way open for Cain's truck.

I STOOD AT THE ISLAND IN THE KITCHEN, working on dinner. I skewered the prawns and prepared a spiced coconut sauce. I planned to serve the shrimp with mango rice, plantains, and salad. I sau-téed the rice and the mango pulp together. The aromatic spices took over the kitchen. I added the remaining ingredients and left the pot simmering on the stove.

I took out a bottle of wine from the refrigerator and then poured myself a glass. I walked to the living room and located Bilal's *1st Born Second* CD, put it in the player, turned the volume up, and went back to my preparations. I checked the rice, low-ered the flame on the burner and then went out to the backyard. Dragging a bag of charcoal from the shed over to the grill, I stacked the coals but didn't light them. I would wait until Cain arrived. My black hands signaled it was time to take my shower and I didn't have much time left.

I sprinted up the stairs to my bathroom and turned on the shower. I didn't make it too hot because the steam would cause my hair to lose its body. I disrobed, put on my shower cap, and stepped into the warm water. The water streamed down my body, relaxing my muscles. I soaped and rinsed my body. I wanted to take a long, lingering shower but forced myself to turn off the water. I dried myself, smoothed on my lotion, slipped into my robe, then went to search my closet for the perfect outfit for the evening.

13

When I opened the door for Cain, I stood before him in a kimono sleeve top with a pair of vintage wash stretch denim jeans.

"Aren't you looking handsome," I said.

He was wearing a camel-colored crew knit shirt and khaki pants.

"Thanks. You're getting better with the compliments."

He bent down and kissed me on the lips. I closed the door behind him.

"What's that?" I asked.

"I bought you a bottle of Moët to go with dinner."

"I told you that you didn't have to bring anything."

"My mama always taught me not to go to someone's home empty handed."

"She taught you well. Come on into the kitchen. Dinner will be ready soon."

"I can't wait. It smells good in here."

Cain followed me into the kitchen and sat down on a stool at the counter.

"So what's for dinner?"

"You'll have to wait and see. Does that sound familiar?"

"Vaguely."

"I thought it would."

"Is there anything I can do to help?"

"As a matter of fact, there is. Would you mind going out back to light the grill?"

"Where do you keep the matches?"

"I have a propane lighter out there on the table."

I watched Cain's swagger as he went out to the backyard. If only I could've given him the time of day years ago. I cleared my sinful thoughts and began making the salad.

Cain came up behind me and rested his hands on the counter on both sides of me. "The fire is lit. You want me to help you cut up the vegetables?"

"No, you're my guest. I want you to have a seat and relax."

"I like where I am right now."

"But if you expect to eat some time this evening, then I'm going to need my space to get around and finish dinner."

He moved my hair to the side and kissed the back of my neck. "In that case I'll have a seat."

My lips curved upward at his flirtation. Cain was open with his feelings and comfortable with showing affection. He was sending a message that he was digging me and I was receiving it loud and clear.

"I'm sure you were busy in Atlanta but did you squeeze in any fun?"

"I was down there scouting possible locations for another Eden."

My brows furrowed. "Really?"

"Why do you seem so surprised?"

"I'm not surprised. Well, maybe a little bit. I didn't realize you were interested in opening another Eden."

"I figure why not. Eden has been doing well here and Atlanta has a lot of potential. I'd need to make changes to the menu, probably add more Southern dishes, like your restaurant."

"Did you find a spot?"

"I saw a couple of places that may work but I have to go back in a couple of weeks."

"I've considered opening a Rituals in Brooklyn, but I hadn't thought about out of state."

"Atlanta would be a good look for Rituals. Your restaurant would fit right in down in the South."

"You think so?"

"Definitely. There are a lot of up-and-coming brothas and sistas down there and the caliber of our establishments complements their lifestyles. Have you ever been to Atlanta?"

"No, but I have a few friends that live there. I've been telling them for the longest time that I'd come to visit. I've yet to make it."

"I like it in Atlanta. I used to want to live there, but it made more sense for me to stay in New York with the majority of my business endeavors. If I go forward with this Eden in Atlanta plan I may build a house down there."

He was thinking about moving. I didn't know how to feel about that.

I tossed the salad in a bowl and then took the prawns from the refrigerator and carried them out to the grill. The fire was just right; the charcoals had a soft orange glow. I laid the shrimp on the grill and then went inside to slice and fry the plantains.

I handed a small bowl of the spiced coconut sauce to Cain and asked him to baste the shrimp. While he tended to the shrimp, I set the table. I used my good china, the stuff that usually collected dust in the china cabinet. I placed the salad in the middle of the table and set a platter loaded with the plantains next to it. I filled a bowl with the aromatic rice, put it on the table and then joined Cain at the grill with a platter for the shrimp. He used the tongs to layer the skewers on the plate and we went inside to eat. I drizzled a bit more of the coconut sauce over the prawns and added the dish to the table.

Cain stood over the table, surveying the spread. "This looks *good*."

"Well, have a seat and let's eat."

We sat at the table and I picked up my fork.

"Let's say grace first," he said.

"Oh, okay." I put my fork down. "You do the honors."

He bowed his head and I closed my eyes.

"We give thanks for this meal that we're about to receive. Please bless the hands that prepared it and those who are to receive it. I ask that this meal strengthen and fortify us. Thank you for your blessings. Amen."

"Amen," I repeated. I opened my eyes and smiled at Cain. "Well done."

"We need to remember to give thanks. We have a lot to be thankful for."

"You're right."

"Alright. Now pass me the rice and those plantains. I'm ready to get my grub on."

"Hand me your plate." I fixed Cain's plate and passed it back to him.

Cain used his fork to slide the prawns from the skewer. He cut one in half and put it in his mouth. His eyes closed briefly. "Oh man, that's good." He sampled the rest of the food on his plate. "This is delicious. Jade; I have to give you your props. This reminds me of being in Jamaica."

"I'm glad you like it." I chuckled, then commenced eating my own food. Everything was perfect. The prawns were spicy but not so much that you couldn't taste the flavor of the food. The plantains were sweet and the rice, light and delicate.

Cain grabbed another shrimp skewer. "I could get used to this."

"Used to what?"

"Eating this good every night."

"You own the best restaurant in North Hills. You mean to tell me that you can't get a good meal?"

"There's a difference between grabbing a bite to eat while I'm working and having a beautiful woman cook dinner especially for me."

"I would think that you have a lot of women making you dinner."

"Actually it's the complete opposite. Most women expect me to cook dinner for them since I own a restaurant. When they start *expecting* me to cook, I send them right over to Eden to pay for a meal. I only break out the pots and pans if I want to do something special for a woman."

"I guess that's why I got pizza, huh?"

"No, you got pizza because I hadn't been food shopping in about a month."

"Yeah right. Tell me anything."

"Jade, I told you before, I have no problem putting my cards on the table. I would've made you dinner, breakfast, and lunch if you would've stayed long enough."

I cleared my throat. "Thank goodness your fridge was empty or I would've left your house twenty pounds heavier." I giggled, but ended up laughing alone.

Cain put his fork down. "You still don't take me seriously, do you?"

"It's not that."

"Then what is it?"

"Men don't value relationships these days."

"Now you're generalizing."

"Even you haven't been in a relationship for years," I said.

Cain rebutted that he hadn't been in a relationship for good reason. That he had literally shut down. It wasn't because he didn't value what he had or the situation he was in. "Most *women* don't know what they want. They place too much emphasis on superficial things like what a man's driving or whether he can have her laced in jewels," he said.

"I don't disagree with that."

"And then women look past the good brothas for some joe knucklehead."

"Men don't know what they want."

"Neither do women."

I challenged him. "Respect, honesty, security, love and trust..."

"That's all? You got it."

I blushed. "It's not that easy. Men can't be trusted."

"Whoa...*some* men; not *all* men."

"What about you? Can you be trusted?"

"Implicitly."

"We'll see."

"Judge me by my actions, not someone else's. We both know how I feel about you. I make it extremely obvious. I don't want there to be any mistake about my intentions. I haven't felt this way about someone in a long time."

"That's just it. I'm feeling things and I keep trying to tell myself it's too soon to feel this way. I find myself thinking about you more than I want to say. Do you know how many times I almost called you while you were away? I sort of feel like we should take things slow, but then I get around you and I throw caution to the wind."

"It's not as if we just met, Jade. We've known each other for years. I'm the kind of man that doesn't let an opportunity pass me by, but I also don't want to make you uncomfortable with my directness."

"Believe me. You're not making me uncomfortable. The truth is, I'm feeling you, too, and it scares me a little."

"Why is that?"

"It scares me because I'm moving on so quickly after a break up. I start to think about the whole rebound relationship thing."

"Do you feel like this is a rebound situation?"

"I don't think so. I feel like what's happening between you and me right now is much more than bouncing back from a messed up relationship."

"Are you finished with your ex?"

"We were finished a long time ago."

"Then that's all that matters. You and I have nothing to do with you and him. The way I see it, you're embarking on something new because that's where your heart is leading you."

I reached across the table and stroked the top of his hand. "Good advice that I'll be sure to follow…along with my heart."

I assessed all of the leftovers sitting on the table. I wanted to eat a few more prawns but my stomach wouldn't let me; I was stuffed.

"Have you had enough to eat?" I asked Cain.

"More than enough."

I pushed back from the table and started clearing the dishes.

"Let me help you with the dishes," he said.

"I'll wash, you can dry."

I armed Cain with a dishtowel and we proceeded to clean the kitchen together. A half-hour later the kitchen was spotless and the leftovers were packed into plastic containers.

"Do you want to take any of this food home?" I asked.

"I'd much rather come back tomorrow to eat leftovers with you."

"You're more than welcome to do so." I reached for the dishtowel to dry my hands but Cain wouldn't release his grip on it.

He lured me to him, placing his arms around my waist. "Are you going to leave your arms dangling at your sides? You can't think of a better place for them?"

"I didn't want to wet the back of your shirt."

He lifted my arms and draped them around his waist. "I don't care about my shirt getting wet."

We stood in the kitchen, arms around one another, staring into each other's eyes.

"Thank you for my special dinner."

"You're welcome."

"Next time I cook for you."

"Are you going to wear a little apron?"

He squeezed me. "If that's what turns you on."

"It might. You'll have to wear one and see." I pulled away from him. "Do you want to watch a movie?"

"I want to do whatever you want to do."

"Come on. Let's go to the TV room."

"You want to bring the Moët?"

"No, it'll make me tired."

I PUT *Love Jones* INTO THE DVD PLAYER. I was in the mood for black romance and *Love Jones* was one of my favorite movies.

"You're taking it way back with this one," he said.

"You sound like my brother. He always makes jokes about my taste in old music and movies. We can watch something else." I started to get up from the couch. Cain pulled me back down.

"Leave it on; I like this movie. I haven't seen it in years."

I told him to take off his shoes and get comfortable. He was looking a little uptight. He kicked off his shoes and settled into the corner of the sofa. I positioned myself in the opposite corner and stretched my legs out. Cain captured my foot and began to massage my pressure points. I tried to focus on Nia and Larenz chatting at the bar, but Cain wasn't having that. His strong hands were working their magic as he kneaded up to my calves.

Cain had my attention; not the movie. *Love Jones* had faded into the background. He slid his hand up my thigh. I inched over to his side of the sofa and wedged myself between his body and pillows, throwing my legs over his lap. He brushed his hand across my cheek. I placed my hand on the back of his neck and gently pulled his face to mine. I kissed his lips, his cheek. I nudged his face to the side and kissed along his jawline. He put his hand on the nape of my neck and tangled his fingers in my hair.

I gently sucked on his neck—his scent aroused me. I bit and licked my way up his neck to his ear. I flicked my tongue on his earlobe and he moaned. Cain tried to nudge me away from his ear but I persisted in nibbling on his lobe. His breath quickened. Cain ran his fingers through my hair and grabbed the back of my head. I moved away from his ear and looked into his face. His eyes were closed and he was licking his lips.

I leaned over and pressed my lips against his. Cain granted me access and let my tongue slip inside. The tip of my tongue probed his mouth. We exchanged tiny kisses, each kiss leaving me wanting yet another. I nibbled his bottom lip and he responded by sucking mine. I yearned for more. He watched me with questioning eyes as I moved my legs from his lap.

"Where are you going?" he asked.

I sat up and straddled him; his eyes widened. I reached for the bottom of his shirt and he leaned forward so I could pull it over his head. I tossed it aside. Cain sat bare-chested, watching me tentatively. I ran my hands across his shoulders, over his pecs, and down to his abs.

I kissed his collarbone and then licked my way down to his chest. When I flicked my tongue across his nipple, his body tensed. His arms were resting at his sides, hands clenched in fists.

A naughty smile played on my lips. "You can't think of anything better to do with your hands?" I asked.

"Tell me what you want me to do with them."

I took his hands in mine and placed them on my ass. I held them there and made little squeezing motions. When I felt him take over with his firm grip, I went back to exploring his body. My lips were all over his skin, from his shoulders to his navel.

Cain's hands were underneath the back of my shirt, unhooking my bra. His hands eased around to my breasts. He lifted my shirt just enough to admire them. He had one in each hand, softly squeezing them. Bringing his mouth to my breasts, he gently sucked one nipple and then gave the other his attention.

I pushed Cain back against the pillows and pressed my naked breasts to his chest. I rubbed up against him until he moaned his appreciation.

He folded his arms around me and whispered in my ear, "I want you, Jade. Can I have you?"

I eased from his lap, stood in front of him, and extended my hand. He arose from the couch and let me lead him upstairs to my bedroom.

A flash of lightning lit up the room. Thunder followed close behind, rumbling in the distance. There was a storm brewing. I left Cain standing in the middle of the floor as I lit a candle on my dresser and retrieved a condom from my nightstand. I slipped the protection under my pillow for easy access and went back over to him.

I didn't take my eyes from his while I unbuckled his belt. The tip of his penis was protruding from the top of his pants. I opened his button and carefully unzipped his pants. I pushed them downward and backed him over to the bed. He sat on the edge while I pulled off his pants and his socks.

Cain stood up and removed my shirt in one fluid motion. He finished what he had started downstairs and slid my bra straps down my arms, freeing my breasts. He kissed my shoulders, drawing me close to his warm body. I felt his hardness against me. I stepped out of my pants as he focused on my breasts touching his body. There was nothing but skimpy panties and fitted boxers between us.

I crawled onto the bed and struck a pose, letting Cain take in my glory. He was captivated.

"You know you're sexy, don't you?" He pointed to his erection. "Look at what you do to me."

"Come show me."

Cain climbed on the bed and positioned his body over mine. I wrapped my arms around his neck and pulled him into a kiss. He rolled us over so I was lying on top of him. I gyrated my hips in slow motion, my clit rubbing against his penis. He began to move with me, hands cupping my ass, pulling me into him. Cain licked, sucked, and nibbled my neck and shoulders, squeezing me tighter as my hip roll intensified.

His hand strayed from my ass to the crotch of my panties. Cain felt my wetness and moaned. He rolled us back over and took control. He caressed my breasts, filling his mouth with their tender flesh. Cain licked down my stomach, planting ravenous kisses along the way. I quivered. He slowed the pace and lingeringly kissed the area covered by my panties. Cain slid his hands underneath my ass, raised my nani to his face, and inhaled.

"You smell so good," he whispered.

Cain stood and yanked off his briefs—he was at full attention. An involuntary smile spread across my face. He was packing. Cain slipped my panties down my legs and let them fall to the floor. He dropped to his knees and then gently tugged me by my waist toward the edge of the bed. He spread my legs and buried his face between them. Cain tickled my clit with his tongue, darting it back and forth across my sensitive spot. A quiet purr escaped me. Cain moaned in reply. He sucked my clit into his mouth. I grabbed the top of his head and pulled it into my center. He plunged his tongue into my wetness, tasting my juices. My hips responded rhythmically to his flow.

He watched me as I bit my bottom lip and tried to squirm away from his grasp. He held my hips tighter as he twirled his tongue inside. I gasped and moaned, unable to endure much more.

Cain joined me on the bed. My leg was shaking as he lay on top of me. I held on to him tightly as I kissed him long and hard. I wanted to feel him inside. I couldn't hold back anymore. I reached for the condom and tore the packet open with my teeth. I handed it to Cain to put on.

He rubbed his penis in my wetness and then slid inside. We moaned in harmony. Cain took his time and moved nice and slow. I looked down and watched as he would disappear inside of me and then reappear glistening with my essence. I brought my hips up to meet his every thrust; our pace quickened, matching the tempo of the falling rain.

I wrapped my legs around his waist and pulled him in deeper. There was no space between us. We rocked our hips back and forth. He growled as I contracted my vaginal muscles around him. I was on the verge of exploding. My four-poster bed shook hard and fast from our movements. My legs locked and I cried out as I felt my juices flowing all over Cain's penis. I rode the wave of pleasure, putting an extra twist in my hips to help him get to the level of ecstasy I was experiencing.

"I can't hold it!" Cain yelled, burying his face in the curve my neck as he exploded.

He offered a few more pumps before lying still, his full weight on top of me. I wiggled until his semi-hard penis slipped out of me. He rose up on his elbows, peering into my face and then kissed me on the forehead.

"That was amazing," he said.

"Yes, it was," I purred. "Can we do it again?"

He raised his eyebrows. "Just give me a minute to recuperate and—"

"I'm kidding."

"Thank goodness. You scared me for a second. I thought I didn't bring my A game."

"You brought your A through Z game."

LISTENING TO THE RAIN HIT THE WINDOW, we shared soft and sweet kisses. Cain caressed my shoulders and I rubbed his back. He played in my hair while my fingertips stroked the smoothness of his head. He whispered in my ear, the kinds of things that men and women whisper to one another in the dark.

"I know, I could get used to you, too," I said.

14

I woke up in Cain's arms, our bodies spooning. I pushed my backside up against the front of his body. He tightened his arm around my waist and moaned. I turned around and faced him. Cain opened one eye. "Good morning, beautiful."

"Morning, sexy."

"Oh, now I'm sexy?"

"Yes, you are a sexy, strong, black man."

"I'm all that?"

"Yup."

"Now I know what it takes to get a compliment out of you."

I pinched his nipple. He knocked my hand away and then pulled me to his chest. We lay quietly together, the sun streaming through the blinds onto the bed. A few minutes later Cain was snoring.

I managed to free myself from his arms and went in the bathroom to pee, wash my face, and brush my teeth. I gathered my hair up into a ponytail and then put on my silk robe. I came out of the bathroom and began picking our clothes up from the floor. I bent over to retrieve Cain's pants, my short robe exposing my ass.

"Why don't you get back in here?"

I jumped. Cain was propped up against the pillows watching me, his hands behind his head.

"I thought you were asleep."

"I was but something told me to wake up."

"Well, now that you're awake, do you want some breakfast?"

"Not yet. I'm going to use the bathroom and then I want to curl up with you in this bed."

Cain went into the bathroom, leaving the door wide open. He called out, "Is this toothbrush on the counter for me?"

"Uh-huh."

I hopped back under the covers, fluffed the pillows behind my head, and turned on the television. I didn't expect to find anything good to watch on a Sunday morning, but once in a while I stumbled across a gem on TBS or TNT.

Cain walked across the carpet, his manhood hanging. In the morning light, I looked over his dark chocolate body—it was simply beautiful—from his broad chest down to his muscular calves. He had the kind of body to make you forget what you were thinking. I lifted the covers for him to get under the sheets with me. He slid in and entangled his body with mine.

I flipped through the channels, searching for something to watch—I ended up passing the remote to Cain. He turned directly to ESPN. We watched the recap of the previous day's sports. I wasn't a big sports fan, but I was certainly all for pretending if it meant that I could spend quality time with someone special.

"What's on your agenda for today?" he asked.

"Not too much. I'm going to the restaurant this afternoon and I'll probably stay until eight or so. Then I'm coming back home."

"I was thinking about hanging with my dad today. I haven't been to see him in a few weeks. Maybe I'll take him to play a few rounds of golf over at the course in Douglaston."

"Sounds nice. Are you and your dad close?"

"We are now. After my mother passed, we fought a lot. I carried anger and hurt inside. I had just turned sixteen and thought I was a man. I wasn't going to school like I was supposed to. I was coming home late. My father had to show me the hard way that he was the only man in the house. He had to rough me up a bit on more than one occasion. I was grounded so many times my brothers used to call me the inmate. He was tough, but he always showed his love for me. He helped me come to terms with the fact that my mother was gone; that he'd be raising us alone. It took a while, but things got better once I understood that I had a long way to go before I would ever be half the man that he was. So yeah, we're close. That's my main man."

I sniffled. It didn't take much to make me start crying and my eyes were welling up.

Cain craned his neck and looked at my face. "I know you're not crying," he said.

I shook my head and whispered, "No, I'm not crying."

He kissed me on the forehead. "My dad would love you. Beautiful, can cook your ass off, and sensitive. You would remind him of my mother."

That did it. I couldn't hold back the tears. The thought of losing someone you love so much, so early, hurt my heart. I cried for the husband and sons that lost their beautiful black queen. Cain held me in his arms, trying to console me. I felt sort of silly, crying all over his chest when he was doing perfectly fine.

"I'm sorry," I said, my voice quivering. I sat up and plucked a tissue from the box on the night stand. I dabbed at my eyes and blew my nose. "I don't know where that came from. I don't want to upset you with my silliness."

Cain rubbed my back. "I'm touched."

I looked over my shoulder at him. "You think I'm crazy now, don't you? I don't even know your family and I'm sitting here crying like a baby."

He sat up beside me. "I don't think you're crazy. You have a big heart and it's hard to keep everything inside sometimes."

Cain kissed the side of my face and grabbed my hand. He got out of the bed, pulling me with him. "How about that breakfast now?"

"I'll try not to cry into your eggs."

"If you do, make sure you don't add any salt."

I cracked a smile. I was relieved that he was making light of my teary performance. Cain put on his boxers and followed me down to the kitchen.

"The paper should be out on the front porch, if you want to get it. But be careful because I have nosey neighbors. If you don't want them catching you in your drawers, you better move fast."

"If they catch me, I'll give them a show," he said, doing a nasty dance like he was a male stripper.

I popped him with the dishtowel and he scurried off to the front door. I went to the fridge to survey the contents.

Cain came into the kitchen with the newspaper under his arm. "The police may be arriving in a minute."

"Why?"

"The old lady across the street didn't appreciate my talent." Again, he did his exotic dance.

I rolled my eyes at him. He sat at the table, unfolded the paper, and perused the headlines.

"What would you like to eat?" I asked.

"Toast and coffee is fine. I'm not a big breakfast eater."

I smirked. "We have a big problem then."

He lowered the paper. "What kind of problem?"

"Breakfast is my favorite meal of the day and I make breakfast consisting of more than toast and coffee."

"Baby, I'll eat whatever you want to make."

With that said, he raised his paper and resumed reading as I went about the task of whipping up a big breakfast.

15

Early afternoon I breezed into Rituals. Mello 4.5 was jamming. I said hello to a few of our Sunday brunch regulars and then danced over to the hostess stand to check my messages. I waved to Bria over by the server station; she was talking to one of the waiters.

I went to the bar for a mimosa. Bria two-stepped her way up to me.

"Girl, the band is hot today," she said.

"I could tell as soon as I came through the door. Was everything alright yesterday?"

"Yeah, it was cool. I only stayed for about three hours. It was a little slow because of the rain."

"How long you been here today?"

"An hour. We pay Winston a lot of damn money to manage the place, so we need to let him do his job."

"I hear you."

"And you know when the weather's warm, I like to spend my time in the sun."

"Well, take off then. I'll be here for the rest of the day."

"Believe me, I'm out of here in a little while. So what did you do yesterday?"

"Ran some errands during the day and then had dinner with Cain." I was real nonchalant when telling her that.

I didn't like being so evasive with her but the breakup with her brother played a major role in my behavior. I feared that lately

Bria and I may have been growing apart. Before we opened Rituals, Bria and I hung out and posted up on the phone nonstop. Now that we saw each other almost daily we did most of our conversing at the restaurant. Relationships evolve and that's what may have been happening with us, but I missed how things used to be. We had changed the dynamics of our relationship—we had gone from friends to business partners. Sometimes we interacted as one Diva Squad member to another and other times we were strictly business. Bria would always be my sister, but I missed the closeness we had shared in the past.

"Where did you go for dinner?" she asked.

"Actually, I made dinner for him at my place."

"Is it safe to assume that Cain is the reason for the spring in your step lately?"

"I didn't realize I was dragging before."

She paused to scrutinize me. "Your skin is even glowing today."

I didn't want her making any connections as to where my glow originated, so I redirected the conversation. "Do we have any private parties this week?"

"We had an engagement party booked for Thursday night but the woman called yesterday to cancel."

"What happened?"

"I didn't ask but I could tell she'd been crying."

"Did we keep the deposit?"

"No, I told her we'd be happy to refund it if she didn't want to reschedule. I wouldn't have done that in any other situation, but since she was canceling her engagement party..."

"She probably called off the engagement as well."

"That's what I figured."

"You made the right decision."

A deliveryman entered the restaurant, carrying a floral arrangement. He handed the flowers to our hostess, Taylor, then stood at the door for a moment to listen to the music.

My stomach turned as I watched Taylor look for a card to see who the flowers were for. She made her way over to Bria and me. Bria looked at me and I gave her a weak smile. Shit. Here we go…

"Jade, it looks like these are for you," Taylor said.

"Wow, really?" I said, with lukewarm enthusiasm. If only he could have sent them to my house. I took the arrangement from Taylor and sat the flowers on the bar.

Taylor and Bria stared at me, waiting for me to tear the paper off.

"Aren't you going to open them?" Bria asked.

"Oh yeah," I replied. I located the card and laid it on the bar and then proceeded to peel off the paper, exposing the most beautiful yellow roses with red tips. I'd have to ask Cain later what the color symbolized.

"Those are so pretty," Taylor said, admiring the bouquet. "My man never sends me flowers."

"Who said they're from my man?"

Bria shot me a look.

"Gurl, please," Taylor said, walking back to her station.

Bria smelled the roses. "Someone must really like you. Are you going to open the card?"

If I didn't open it, Bria would've wondered what the big deal was and why I was acting strange. I picked the card up and hoped Cain hadn't written anything revealing inside. I used the tip of my freshly manicured fingernail to open the envelop flap. I read the note.

I Reminisce…

A smile formed on my lips. Two words that said so much. I handed the card to Bria.

She read it and shrugged her shoulders. "Not a man of many words, is he? And what's with the Billy Dee Williams approach?"

I chuckled at her blatant sarcasm. "He said just enough. Sometimes less is more."

"Remember what I told you. Take things slow. I'll see you tomorrow, Diva."

Too late for that, I thought.

Bria vanished out the door, leaving me to admire my roses. I counted two dozen of the colorful flowers. He was definitely thoughtful—I just hoped it lasted. Most men barraged you with flowers in the beginning of a relationship but eventually it happened, they forget that flowers existed. I used to buy Bryce gifts from time to time to remind him of how nice it was to receive a small token from the one you loved. He had caught on after a while and I would get some sort of trinket from him every couple of months. It was the little things that count in a relationship and right now Cain was ahead.

I took my cell phone from my purse and dialed Cain's cell. He was talking to someone else in the background when he picked up.

"Thank you for my roses."

"You got them already?"

"I did and they're beautiful."

"Are they the yellow ones?"

"With red tips. What do they mean?"

"I'll have to tell you later. I'm golfing with my old man and he's minding my business right now."

I could hear his father talking but couldn't decipher what he was saying. I heard Cain remark to him "this is the one I was just telling you about" and I really started beaming.

"Cain, I'll let you finish your game. Call me when you're done."

"Can I come by tonight for seconds?"

I grinned. "Aren't you nasty."

"I was talking about the leftovers but I see where your mind is."

I laughed out loud. "I'll be home by eight so I'll see you then for *seconds*."

I put my phone away and turned around in my seat to face the band. They were playing a jazzy rendition of "Little Things" by India.Arie. When we were auditioning bands for Sunday brunch, Mello 4.5 outshined all the rest. They had an extensive repertoire, a classy sound, and four good-looking brothers behind the instruments. Sometimes there was a female singer with the group, but not every week. She wasn't with them today.

I looked around the dining room and got high from the energy. Everyone was enjoying themselves—eating, talking and listening to jazz. It was those moments at Rituals that I cherished most; this affirmation of our success. My heart filled with so much joy when I saw what Rituals had become for me and for those that came to dine with us. Those people could have been somewhere, anywhere else, but they chose to be in our establishment, for an afternoon of great food and entertainment. For all of that, I was truly thankful.

I saw Taylor embracing someone from the corner of my eye. I turned my head, only to see my parents over at the hostess station. My mother caught sight of me and traipsed over to the bar.

I kissed my mother on the cheek. "Hey, what are you doing here?"

"I thought I'd shut your father up and come for brunch today."

My father walked over and hugged me. "She means she was dragging me through the mall and she got hungry."

"Don't pay your father any mind. I already told you how we ended up here."

"Come on, I'll find you a table," I said.

"Are you going to eat with us?" my mother asked.

"I can sit with you for a bit. Let me grab a couple of menus."

I seated them at a corner booth and then scooted in next to my father.

My father looked around the packed dining room. "When are you starting the renovations?"

"Terrence scheduled it so that they start work in a couple of months."

"How long will you be closed?" he asked.

"According to your son, only a week. The job is going to take two weeks in total to finish, but we'll be open for business during the second week while they complete the job."

"I don't think you need to change the place at all." That was my mother.

"Mom, I realize you think it's perfect as is, but we really need to expand."

"You sure do because no one wants to wait too long to be seated at a table." That was my father.

My mother ignored us. "I know that song the band is playing. Bill, what song is that? It's an old one."

My father thought about it for a moment. "'Don't Go To Strangers' by Etta Jones."

"I thought I recognized it." My mother hummed along.

My father had not bothered to open his menu. "Jade, what's good?"

"You'd probably like the chicken prepared with artichokes and red peppers."

"I'll have that," he replied.

"Bill, you better look on the menu. There may be something else you want," my mother said.

"I don't need to look at the menu. I asked my daughter and she suggested something. You're worried about what I'm eating and I bet you don't know what you want yet."

"Now that's where you're wrong. I'm having the sweet potato waffles."

I snickered at their tit-for-tat conversation. My parents were like a comedy duo.

"I don't know about you two," I said.

"It's not me; it's your mother."

My mother glared at my father with feigned annoyance and resumed humming to the song. I told my parents that I would send the waiter over since they were ready and then left them to enjoy the music.

I checked on the kitchen staff, the wait staff, and then headed to the front to step outside for some fresh air. Taylor stopped me; I had missed a call from Milan. The message stated that she'd be back late tonight and she'd call me from work tomorrow.

Hopefully the time at home with her mother had done her some good. I'd been watching the news for any developments in the case but hadn't seen anything. If Eriq's wife had taken a turn for the worse, that would've been newsworthy but, then again, these days you never could tell what would get airtime.

I drifted outside to sit on one of the benches in front of the restaurant. The sun was high in the sky, causing me to squint and shield my eyes from the bright rays. I relaxed on the bench, closed my eyes, and inhaled. Light winds carried the smell of soul food and spring. The scent of spring could be so lush and romantic, with the perfume of flowers in bloom heavily suspended in the air. My mind wandered to the night before with Cain. I felt a rush go through my body, a surge in the pit of my stomach. He was so intense, so passionate; every touch had left me yearning for more. Cain had put his cards on the table from the beginning;

he wasn't afraid to express the depth of his emotion. A man that didn't try to hide his feelings was refreshing. It had been years since I'd been intimate with a man other than Bryce and Cain was making it so easy to get over him.

I SPOKE WITH A FEW OF THE PATRONS AT THE BAR and then began jotting down a few supplies that needed to be ordered. My parents had finished eating and had come over to say their farewells.

"How was everything?" I asked.

"Just fine," my father said. "The chicken was very tender. I'm positive your mother enjoyed everything because after she finished hers, she started eating mine."

My mother cut her eyes at my father and told me herself that the food was excellent. Then my roses caught her attention. She looked at them and then me, expecting me to say something.

"Yellow roses with red tips?" she commented. "Humph…means someone's falling in love."

I offered a nonchalant shrug and ushered them to the door. I expressed that it was a pleasant surprise to see them and let them know that I would call during the week. We hugged and parted ways. I went back to work, letting the spring in my step get me through the remainder of the day.

16

The next night, after work, I sat in Milan's living room listening to an update on Eriq's wife.

She was conscious, but couldn't recall anything about the accident. She suffered from a broken leg and collarbone. It was no surprise that Eriq thought there was no need to alert the police about their involvement since his wife was out of the woods. Milan was going along with the program.

"Today was the first day that both Eriq and I were in the office. We had lunch at the park and talked things over. We agreed not to say anything about the accident and from now on our relationship will be strictly professional."

I watched her through incredulous eyes. "That's it?"

"Don't look at me like that. I made my decision and I'm standing by it."

"And you feel comfortable sweeping things under the rug?"

"You and I both know accidents happen. This was an accident. If the details come out they will certainly be misconstrued. I don't want to deal with that."

"Milan, whether you want to deal with it or not isn't the issue."

"I don't need you to tell me the issue. I'm fully aware of what's going on. Jade, I need your support on this. I don't pretend to have all the answers, but I'm doing what I think is best."

"Are you sure you aren't doing what Eriq is telling you to do?"

"I'll admit I'm following his lead, but like I said, it was my decision. His wife is doing better and Eriq says he's going to be devoted to her every need. No one else has to be hurt as a result of this."

I sighed. "You're my girl so I have your back, but I want you to know that you're not handling this properly."

"I understand that and I respect your opinion. All I'm asking is that you respect my decision."

She had apparently made up her mind. I had no intention of debating with Milan over her life choices. I said my peace and she let me know that she was putting this ordeal behind her.

"I miss anything good while I was gone?" Milan asked.

"Terrence and Fitz took me to this hot club up in Harlem. Girl, I danced all night long with this fine brother named Omar."

"Did you get his number?"

"I did but I wasn't feeling him like that."

"Why? What was wrong with him? He still lives with his mama or something?"

"No. He seemed like he was on point."

"He was married?"

"Nope."

"You thought he may have been playing for the wrong team?"

"Will you stop with your lawyer tactics. I feel like I'm on the witness stand being cross examined."

"I don't get it. You said he was fine and you must've had a good time if you spent the entire night dancing with him."

I couldn't take anymore of her questions and blurted out the one thing that would put them to an end. "Girl, I slept with Cain."

Milan's jaw dropped. "I leave town for a minute and things start jumping off. When did this happen? "

"The other night. I made him dinner and we ended up in bed."

"I know you don't think you're getting away with that explanation. I'm going to need you to fill in the blanks between dinner and how you two ended up sleeping together. Start talking."

"Cain has really surprised me. He's nothing like what I thought he'd be. I went from thinking he didn't have a sincere bone in his body, to realizing he's a man of great depth, to wanting to spend all my free time with him."

"Skip the fluff; I want to hear the dirty stuff."

We giggled like two schoolgirls.

"Milan, when I tell you that this man has got it going on—it's an understatement. For the past two nights that man has rocked my body right."

"I can't believe this...you and Cain..."

"Believe it. He has explored and navigated every inch of my body. I get chills just thinking about it." My body shivered from the thought of him.

She chuckled. "If I knew my pep talk would lead to you two hooking up, I would've given it to you a long time ago."

"All I can say is...woo! Cain has got me open."

"Now this is what I like to hear. My girl is back in the game."

"I'm officially over the gloom and doom phase."

"I guess so...now that you're getting that ass tapped by Cain."

By now I was clutching my abs from laughing so hard. It was good to joke with Milan about men and relationships. It had been a rough year when it came to love; Milan and Nolan, me and Bryce, what a mess. This thing with Cain was a breath of fresh air, drama-free with a wealth of possibilities.

"The funny thing is, when I was dancing with Omar, I couldn't stop thinking about Cain. I would've never imagined dating Cain, definitely not sleeping with him, but when I'm around him, it feels right. I just go with the flow."

"Sometimes it's like that. You can't put a timeframe on romance. Some people wait months, even years, to have sex with someone. Others wait minutes. You, well, you waited seconds."

"Shut up, Lan." I snickered at her silliness. "I don't have a single regret. In fact, I want to do it again and again. He came over last night to eat leftovers from the dinner I made for him. Well, dinner wasn't the only thing he ate."

"Alright, I get the picture. I can see you're about to get perverted with this conversation."

"I'll spare you the intimate details. The clean version is basically that Cain and I have a chemistry we can't ignore. We enjoy each other's company. It's just that simple. When we're together we talk, we laugh...we click."

"I'm glad you gave him a chance, Jade."

"You know what, Lan? I am, too."

17

The third time my cell phone rang and the person on the other end refused to respond, I shut it off. This had been going on every hour on the hour since one in the morning. I had mistakenly thought it was Cain calling at first since, over the past few weeks, we had been engaging in late-night chats. Now my house phone was ringing every twenty minutes. I turned off the ringer in my room, but I could still hear the other phones in the house ringing off the hook.

It was almost four in the morning and I couldn't sleep; my crank caller was making sure of that. I grabbed the phone from my nightstand and dialed Bryce's number. His machine picked up. I called his cell and it went straight to voicemail. I hung up and got out of bed. There was no sense in lying there, wide awake.

I slipped on my robe and went down to the kitchen. The motion detector flood light was on in the backyard. An eerie feeling washed over me. I walked over to the back door and moved the blinds to the side to peer out into the yard. I didn't see anything. The neighbor's cat may have caused the motion detector to activate.

I turned to go to the fridge and saw a shadow run past the door in my peripheral vision. My piercing scream was enough to shatter the glasses in the cupboard. I ran to check that all of the doors were locked while I dialed 9-1-1 from my cordless phone. Five minutes later there were two police officers searching the perimeter of my house while I sat in the living room trembling. The officers told me whoever was out there had taken off. I recounted the calls that I had been receiving throughout the night and when they asked me if I had any idea who may be responsible, I said no. Although I had my suspicions that Bryce may have been to blame, I wasn't absolutely certain.

The officers said they would patrol the area for a while but convinced me that if anyone had been lurking that they wouldn't be back. I locked the door behind the officers and turned on every light in the house before heading to the living room and sitting in the corner of the couch with my knees pulled up to my chest. Strange phone calls, someone in the shadows in the wee hours of the morning; I'd never experienced anything like that. I wanted to call Cain but I couldn't drag him into such nonsense. I would keep this to myself and handle it my way.

The sun was finally rising and I had spent the night in the same position on the couch, listening for every little noise…and thinking about Bryce. Could he have possibly taken to harassing me? Bryce was intense but these tactics seemed to be out of his league. He was the man that used to make me feel so safe. Now I was sitting in fear in my own home. Whenever we were home together and I would try to put the alarm on before going to bed, he insisted it wasn't necessary, that he was there to protect me. At first I'd ignore him and set the alarm anyway, but eventually I felt that way, too. I was completely safe with him and realized that he wouldn't let any harm come to me. So it was strange when I came home early from Rituals one evening and the alarm sounded when I opened the front door. I punched in the code and disarmed it. Why Bryce had the alarm set as if we were turning in for the night baffled me. I went to the kitchen to answer the call from the monitoring station and found Bryce closing the back door. He had on jeans, his shirt was completely unbuttoned, his sleeves were rolled up, and there were soap bubbles on his forearms. I looked at the sink. It was empty; not a dish in sight. The phone continued to ring as he and I stared at each other.

"Answer it, Bryce."

He went to the phone and I bolted upstairs. I marched to my bedroom and into the bathroom. The tub was draining and I could smell my scented bubble bath all in the bathroom.

Bryce came up behind me. "I was about to take a bath. Get undressed. You can take one with me."

I looked at the nervous twitch in Bryce's smile. "Why is the water draining if you were preparing to take a bath?"

"I put too much water in the tub and I was letting some of it out. Then the alarm went off and I ran downstairs to see what was going on."

"Since when do you set the alarm?"

"It's silly, but, I was watching *Psycho* last night and that shower scene was a bitch." Bryce laughed nervously. "I was tired and knew I would probably drift off in the tub...so I set the alarm. You know...just in case Norman Bates is in the neighborhood."

My arms were folded across my chest. I wasn't buying it. I turned around, went into the bedroom, and over to inspect the bed. It was exactly how I had left it in the morning. Nothing out of place. I opened the closet door and looked inside. Then I went back to the bed and looked under it.

Bryce watched me. "What are you doing?"

I glared at him, before going down the hall to the guest room and performing the same inspection. Bryce followed me and stood watching from the doorway. I pushed past him, went to the TV room, and flipped through the *TV Guide*. Nine p.m. last night on AMC...*Psycho*, starring Anthony Perkins. I tossed the *TV Guide* back on the table.

Bryce smirked. "Are you done?"

"Bryce, if I ever find out that you had a woman in my house…"

"Jade, you're losing it. I told you, I was taking a bath."

"I know what you told me, but I also know what it looks like."

"Looks can be deceiving. Now I indulged your suspicions, but don't get carried away. I'm not going to deal with much more of this." He turned and went upstairs.

I wondered what kind of fool he must've thought I was to tell me that he was scared of *Psycho*; a movie he had watched a thousand times. I went back to our bedroom where he was changing his clothes.

"What happened to your bath?"

"I'm not in the mood anymore. You ruined it with your attitude. I'm out. I'll be back later."

I was furious. Leave it to Bryce to turn the tables as if he was wronged in some sort of way. I stormed to the basement and collected every cleaning product I had—Clorox, Ajax, Pine Sol, Soft Scrub, Ammonia *and* a Brillo Pad for good measure. I mixed a deadly concoction and then scrubbed the tub, tiles, sink, and floor until my hands were raw, breathing in toxic fumes until my head ached.

I ripped the comforter, blanket, and sheets from the bed and threw them in the trash. I thought about putting the mattress out on the curb, but decided I wouldn't be the one to drag that mammoth outside. I left the mattress stripped bare. I wasn't putting any of my linens on that bed. Bryce could continue to sleep on that one while I slept in the guest room.

I fell into bed, completely exhausted. It was after midnight when I heard Bryce coming into the house. His footsteps passed by the guest room heading to my bedroom. Seconds later, he groaned. He was swearing under his breath as he approached my new sleeping quarters.

I pretended to be asleep on my side when he called out my name from the door. He shuffled over to the bed and lay down beside me, reeking of a perfume that I didn't own. I rolled over with the speed of lightning and mushed him in the face.

"Get the fuck out!" I yelled.

He scrambled from the bed. "What the hell?"

"Get the fuck out and go back where you just came from." I was on my feet, pushing him out of the door. He opened his mouth and I slammed the door in his face.

He mumbled my name, repeatedly, before slinking off down the hallway. I cried through the night and swore to myself that this time, the relationship was over. When I emerged from the room the next afternoon, weak from crying, there was a Tiffany box on the floor outside the door. I picked it up and went downstairs and found three more Tiffany boxes, one in the living room, one in the TV room, and another in the kitchen. I sat at the kitchen table and opened the card that was propped against the box. The outside of the card had a picture of a teddy bear holding a compass and it read *I'm Lost Without You.* I opened the card and read what Bryce wrote inside.

Jade,

I can't stand it when we fight, especially when it's over a misunderstanding. There was no other woman with me yesterday. I would never disrespect you or your house in that manner and I would give my right arm to prove it to you. I'm sorry for the way I left and for coming home so late. Hopefully we can talk about this later. Please be open to hearing what I have to say to you.

Bryce

I opened the boxes one by one, shaking my head. As usual,

Bryce was trying to buy my forgiveness and this time he had paid a hell of a lot to be granted a reprieve. I laid the jewelry on the table—a platinum necklace with five diamonds, a diamond heart pendant, matching diamond heart earrings, and a diamond tennis bracelet. Would an innocent man go to these lengths? I knew the answer, but my anger was slowly melting away.

Bryce came home later that evening with flowers and more apologies. He made it clear he was apologizing for running out of the house and nothing more. According to him, he hadn't done anything to raise my suspicions. He even had an explanation for the perfume he was bathed in. Claiming that he felt bad for storming out, he went to the department store to find me a gift and walked in the path of an overzealous, perfume spraying saleswoman. After I threw him out, he knew nothing in any department store could rectify the damage; especially not the sweater he bought me. He was in Manhasset at Tiffany & Co. first thing in the morning.

I forgave him, not because I believed him, but because I didn't know what else to do. I loved him and couldn't see myself without him. I wasn't ready to let go. Imagine my feelings two weeks later when I almost broke my neck on a tube of lipstick—that didn't belong to me—lying on my back stairs. So much for ignoring the truth.

I stretched my stiff limbs and turned on the morning news. With the sun shining, I felt like I could get a little rest before going to the restaurant. I lay down on the couch and closed my eyes. What seemed like a few minutes of sleep ended up being five hours. It was almost noon and I was late.

Bria was more than annoyed when I strolled into the meeting

ten minutes late. She was in our office, laughing and smiling with Cyrus from the radio station, but her eyes told me that she was pissed.

It was one of our rituals to wine and dine prospective partners at least once a month in an effort to grow our business. Constant attention to growth—with a special focus on relationship building—was how we landed on top and plan to stay there.

I extended my hand to Cyrus. "I'm Jade. Nice to finally meet you."

Cyrus stood and shook my hand. "I've heard a lot about you and a lot of good things about your place."

Bria grabbed her portfolio. "Cyrus, lunch awaits."

Once we were settled in a corner booth with our drinks, Bria and I pitched our ideas to Cyrus. He was very excited we had chosen to partner with his station for our after-work networking functions and we were pleased that Rituals would be mentioned on the radio every week.

"If you're interested, we can broadcast live from time to time," Cyrus said.

Bria beamed. "That'll work."

"Cyrus, we're trying to do great things with Rituals. A live broadcast could help us reach out to people that wouldn't usually come out to Long Island," I said.

Cyrus nodded his head. "Well, let's make it happen."

We ironed out the details over a light lunch of Caesar salads and wrapped it up over refreshing lemon sorbet. Our first on-air, after-work event will be held two weeks after we reopened.

Bria walked Cyrus to the door and then came back to the table. "What is wrong with you, Diva? You look like something the cat dragged in."

I patted the puffy skin around my eyes. "Do I look that bad?"

"Worse."

"I had a rough night." I told Bria about the phone calls and the prowler in my backyard.

"People are crazy. Did the police find anyone?"

"No, but they asked if I had any idea who it may have been."

"Do you?"

My blank expression answered her question.

"Jade, my brother has better things to do than to ring your phone off the hook. And he wouldn't be sneaking around your yard in the middle of the night."

"I'd like to think so, but it isn't common for a random crank caller to have your home and cell phone numbers."

"Bryce ain't your culprit."

If Bryce had a gigantic sign that stated he was the one making the calls and creeping in the dark, Bria wouldn't have believed it. At that point, it really didn't matter what she said, because I knew who was to blame.

18

C ain met me out in the driveway. He opened my car door for me and then reached into my backseat and grabbed my overnight bag. Earlier in the day Cain had told me that he didn't want me leaving in the middle of the night and suggested I bring my clothes with me. His timing couldn't have been better because after last night, I was leery about staying at my house alone.

"I don't think it's a good idea for you to be riding around with the top down on your car late at night," he said.

"I do it all the time and it's not that late."

"I'd feel better if you wouldn't do it at this time of night."

What's the point of a convertible if you can't enjoy it? To keep the peace, I agreed that if I was alone, I wouldn't ride with the top down once the sun set. What I really meant was I wouldn't do it if I was going to see Cain.

I followed Cain to the den. He had the television on mute and paperwork spread across the table. I plopped down on the couch and grabbed the remote. My cell phone rang in my purse. I retrieved it and looked at the display but it was a blocked number. I switched the phone to vibrate and slipped it back into my bag. Cain looked at me but didn't say anything. I reached into my bag again and turned the phone off. A repeat of last night's crank-call-a-thon wouldn't be cool, especially at Cain's house.

Cain flipped through his papers and then turned to me. "It seems my weekend business at Eden has fallen for the third month in a row. Sunday business to be specific."

There was an awkward silence hanging in the air. Rituals has seen a drastic increase in our Sunday brunch crowd. It had to be affecting Cain's seatings, but that's the nature of the beast.

"I've always managed to keep my business and personal life separate," he said. "This is the first time that I feel I can't employ my crush-the-competition strategy."

He seemed frustrated. The reality of the situation was that regardless of what went on between us, we both had businesses to run. Our decisions were bound to affect each other.

"Are you saying that you're idly watching your numbers drop because of me?"

Cain looked down at his papers. "I haven't responded as quickly as I would have in the past."

"Cain, we're in the same industry; we're going to step on each other's toes."

I never thought I would be encouraging the competition to implement strategies that could chip away at my success. If Bria could've heard me, she would've killed me. But why shouldn't Cain and I have supported one another's efforts? We had two of the most successful eateries on the island and we shouldn't have been trying to harm each other's business.

"Saturdays are strong at Eden. Probably comparable to what Sundays are like at Rituals. I'm not concerned with growing my Sunday crowd, just holding it steady," Cain said.

I did not like the way that sounded. Cain was letting our situation cloud his judgment. Lovers or not, as long as we owned those restaurants, we had to compete against one another, but we *could* compete without trying to destroy each other. "What if you focused on Sunday evening? Our brunch ends at two...maybe you can feature a Sunday gospel dinner. It would definitely appeal to those getting out of church after three. Every week you can spotlight a different gospel choir."

Cain smiled. "That's a great idea. Are you sure you don't want to do that at Rituals?"

"I'm positive. Our jazz brunch is more than enough." I could almost hear Bria screaming bloody murder.

Cain leaned over and kissed me. "Absolutely amazing."

"The idea?"

"That, too...but I was talking about you."

I sat there, blushing like a teenage girl. At that moment, it didn't matter what Bria would say—this was between Cain and me, not Eden and Rituals. We were relating to each other as a man and a woman who only wanted the best for each other. We could help each other be more competitive, not just against one other, but against other establishments. And Bria thought no good would come from dating the competition. I was constantly benefiting from Cain's business savvy. We didn't always talk about work, but we'd had many lengthy discussions about what it took to survive the restaurant industry. I loved our conversations because Cain brought a diverse perspective on how to run a restaurant—he drew from his experience as a real estate investor, owner of a technology company, and franchisee.

Cain told me about his ownership of fast-food restaurants when we pulled up to a drive-thru and the cashier at the window knew him by name. At first I was thinking "boy does he get around" but he quickly told me that he owned the burger joint along with four others. He was also considering a couple of ice cream shops in the South, where warm weather didn't go on hiatus. I wasn't going to worry about a potential conflict of interest—I'd leave that to Bria.

Cain and I talked about which churches in the area were known to have the hottest choirs. I wasn't a member of a specific church but I did visit quite a few. Cain had been a member of Antioch Baptist Church in Brooklyn since he was a kid. Between the two of us we came up with fifteen choirs that would be perfect for Sunday evening gospel at Eden.

Cain went to the kitchen to get us a couple of glasses of iced tea. I watched him leave the room and smiled to myself. This is nice…me…Cain. Never once had I thought that Cain had an ounce of substance. He was definitely something to look at but his slick talk and roving eyes had rubbed me the wrong way. Who knew his *say anything* approach stemmed from a sincere interest?

Milan had been pushing me to date for years, even though I was with Bryce. On one occasion she gave me a reality check and commented that Bryce was dating so why shouldn't I do the same. She didn't think Bryce could change and I didn't think dating was in my cards—I was getting married. I had a man that loved me and we were headed to the altar, at least one of us was.

CAIN HANDED ME MY DRINK, rousing me from my thoughts. I patted the sofa cushion. Cain sat next to me and I snuggled up next to him.

"So what should we watch?" I asked.

We agreed on a movie on Starz in Black that managed to put us to sleep before it was over. I woke up in the middle of the night, still on the couch, covered by a blanket. Cain pulled me closer to him. I adjusted my body against his and went back to sleep.

The next morning I awoke to the scent of bacon frying. I released a loud yawn and launched into a full body stretch. Having spent the entire night on the couch, I felt surprisingly well-rested. I reached for my purse on the table and turned on my cell phone. Twenty-two messages. All from Bryce. The first message set the tone for the rest.

Beep. Hey, where are you? I just left a message for you at your house.

Beep. Your phone went straight to voicemail. A few minutes ago it was ringing. Alright, hit me back when you get this.

Beep. This is my third message.

The next few calls were hang-ups and the next round consisted of Bryce pressing the touchtone buttons and holding them. The last calls were more disturbing.

Beep. I'm on my way to your house right now and if you're there, you better answer the damn door.

Beep. Do you know what time it is? Where the hell are you?

Beep. You're lucky I don't have a key any more or I'd be in your crib right now—waiting for your ass.

The final message was difficult to decipher but, after playing it a few times, I was able to make out what Bryce was saying. It was short and not so sweet.

Bitch.

I pounded the keypad on my cell phone. Bryce answered his phone on the first ring. "Your behavior is out of control," I said tersely.

"I'm at work. What do you want?"

"What do *I* want? You left me twenty-two damn messages."

"And? Where the hell were you?"

"Home."

"No, you weren't, Jade. I was there."

"I was asleep."

"Yeah, okay."

I heard a click; Bryce had hung up on me. I was still chanting "hello" into the phone when I noticed Cain standing in the doorway, watching me. I closed my phone and tossed it into my bag.

"Good morning, sexy," I sang out in the cheeriest voice I could manage.

"Who's stressing you out so early in the morning?"

I cleared my throat. "Oh that? That was nothing. Just Milan complaining about work."

Cain opened his mouth to say something else but nodded instead. I steered our conversation in a different direction. "Something is making my stomach growl."

"Breakfast is ready," Cain said before leaving the room.

I slapped my palm against my forehead. I didn't know how long Cain had been standing there, listening. Why did I say that I was speaking to Milan? I tried to replay my conversation with Bryce to determine if I had called his name. I couldn't remember and I was getting nervous. I stood and attempted to smooth my wrinkled clothes.

Cain was spooning eggs onto my plate when I entered the kitchen. I sat at the table and sipped my orange juice.

"Can you take the day off from work?" he asked.

Relief washed over me. "Sure. What do you have in mind?"

"Don't worry; you'll enjoy it. Hurry up and eat so we can get dressed. Or, in your case, I should say undressed."

"I wish you would've woken me up last night."

"I tried but you got real evil when I told you to put on your PJs. I was scared. I've never seen that side of you before."

I laughed at Cain's exaggeration. "I'm sure I wasn't that bad."

"Yes, you were. My family jewels were in jeopardy when I tried to remove your pants."

"I kicked you?"

"Almost. Thank goodness I'm light on my feet."

I went around to Cain's side of the table and kissed his forehead. "I'm sorry, baby. Next time make sure you undress me *before* I go to sleep."

Cain tapped me on the ass. "Finish your breakfast so we can get going."

MY LEGS WERE OPEN, hips thrust slightly forward, feet firmly planted. I took my first swing…and missed.

"Try again," Cain said. "Remember what I told you; don't take your eye off the ball."

Cain and I were at his favorite course playing a round of golf. He stepped up to the tee and turned to me. "See how I'm standing? Now watch a master at work."

The little white ball went flying. He did have a nice stroke. "Watch out, Tiger," I said.

Cain refused to divulge where he was taking me when we left his house. Golf never crossed my mind. We stopped in the pro shop and Cain bought me the cutest outfit in pink, along with matching pink and white golf shoes. He rented my clubs and offered to buy me a set if, after today, I wanted to continue golfing. He owned an expensive-looking set of clubs that had surely cost a pretty penny, but judging by his skill, he was getting his money's worth.

We hopped in the golf cart and drove to the next tee. Though I wasn't doing too well on the course, Cain tried to make it fun. He approached the game with passionate discipline. I quit by the ninth hole, choosing instead to watch Cain play. When he finally wrapped up his game at the eighteenth hole, I said a silent prayer of thanks. It was one thing to watch Tiger Woods from the comfort of my sofa but this wasn't quite the same. I won't say I was completely giving up on golf, however, I needed to experience it in small doses.

Cain took me to a late lunch at Eden. We sat out on the deck eating crab cake salads, which consisted of two giant lump meat crab cakes atop tangy mixed salad greens. Cain poured me a third glass of wine.

I spoke with a mouthful of food. "Whoa… It's the middle of the day. Are you trying to get me drunk?"

"No. Nothing's better than good food and wine."

"Then why have you only had one glass to my three?"

"Because I'm driving."

"I have to drive home from your house. Remember?"

"I guess you'll just have to stay another night with me."

Cain didn't need to ask me twice.

19

O ver the next few weeks, Cain and I spent almost every night together. I was helping him with the plans for his pool party and couldn't wait to meet his friends and family. We were in my den, watching television and putting a menu together for the party. Actually, Cain was watching basketball while I worked on his party plans.

I was going to make a fantastic barbeque sauce that my aunt created and was never absent from our family barbecues. It had the right blend of spicy and sweet. I wasn't sure of all the ingredients so I asked Cain to get me the recipe from the file cabinet in my office.

"You don't want me fumbling through your stuff. Can't you get it?" It was clear that he didn't want to tear himself away from the game.

"First of all, I'm in the middle of writing the shopping list for *your* pool party and I need to know the ingredients for the sauce so I can add it to the list. The least you can do is go get the recipe for me. The Knicks will still be playing when you get back. Now stop giving me a hard time."

"Okay, baby. Tell me where it is again."

"In the file cabinet in my office. The recipes are in alphabetical order so you won't have a problem finding it." I was talking slow and exaggerating my words. "It's under the letter B."

"Okay, so now you're being funny."

"I'm sorry, baby. If you weren't being so difficult, you could've been back by now. Now be a good boy and hurry up and get it."

He smirked. "I'll show you a good boy later on tonight."

"Whatever you say."

Cain went to retrieve the recipe. When he returned, I asked, "Now was that so bad?"

"That's a good system you have in there. There are a lot of recipes in that file cabinet."

"Everything I've ever created is in there. I also have family recipes, recipes from cookbooks, cooking shows; you name it. It's organized by course, then subcategories within the course. That's my little gold mine in there."

"Can I sit down and watch the rest of the game now, or are you going to make me return to the mines to re-file this?"

I snatched the sheet of paper from his hand. "I can see you're in rare form tonight."

"You got me playing errand boy while I'm trying to watch the game."

"What are you complaining about? You didn't even miss anything. There was a commercial on the entire time."

"My bad." Cain slid over to me and kissed me on the neck. "Thank you for helping me, baby. I really appreciate it."

A smile crept across my face. "You're lucky I like you."

"Will you help me with the food prep later this week?"

"Now you're pushing it."

"Come on, Jade. I could use an extra set of hands. You know how many people I'm expecting."

"What's in it for me?"

"Whatever you want."

I ran my fingers through my hair while I pondered what it would take. "If I agree to help you prepare all of this food, you have to agree to take me somewhere for a day of relaxation. It doesn't have to be anything expensive but it has to be somewhere I can kick back and be pampered for the day."

"So let me make sure I understand the terms. If you help me with the party, all I have to do in return is take you on a day trip?"

"Yup."

"And does this help include food prep, cooking, and clean-up duty after the party?"

"Hmm, why not. I'm feeling generous."

"In that case I'm feeling generous, too. Forget your day trip. How would you like to go to Antigua for a week?"

I looked up from my list. "Are you serious? You want to take me to Antigua?"

"I haven't taken a vacation in a while and I'd love to have you lying next to me on a hot sandy beach wearing a skimpy bikini."

I squealed. "For real?"

"Yes I'm *for real.*"

"All because I'm helping you with your party?"

"No. *Just* because."

"I'm serious, Cain. You don't have to take me on a trip because I'm helping you."

"Are you trying to tell me that you don't want to go with me?"

"Hell no! I would love to go with you."

"Then we have a deal. Let me know when you want to go and we're there."

I put my papers down and captured Cain's face between my hands. I kissed his forehead, the tip of his nose, and then planted one on his lips. "You never cease to amaze me."

The crowd at the game started cheering. Cain's eyes darted toward the television. I let go of his face.

"Swish! That was all net, baby! Let's keep it up! Don't slack now!" He was on the edge of the couch, yelling at the television.

"I'm glad to see I have your attention."

I left Cain to his game and went to the kitchen for a drink of water. I couldn't believe he wanted to go to Antigua. My excitement was brewing. I hadn't been on a real vacation in over a year. I was already thinking about when would be the best time to go on our trip. Lazy, hot days on the beach, quiet nights and gentle breezes—what more could a girl ask for? I leaned against the counter and sipped my bottle of water.

Cain came into kitchen. "What are you doing in here?"

I lifted my bottle for him to see.

"Do you have any chips?"

I pointed to the snack cabinet. "I have pretzels."

"We need to get you some real junk food in here."

"Not if you want to see me in a bikini on the beach."

"I want to see you in one before we get to Antigua. You can wear your bikini this weekend at my pool party so I can get a taste of what's to come."

"I don't know about that. I don't want all your friends trying to holla at me," I joked.

"They're going to do that whether you have on a bathing suit or a turtleneck."

"I do have a cute new bikini. It's a red thong." I tried to hold in my laughter.

Cain stopped chewing his pretzels. "I'd love nothing more than to see you prancing around in your new suit, but please don't put on a thong at my party. I can't spend the entire time beating my friends off of you with a stick. Do me a favor and save that one especially for Antigua."

"I was thinking that maybe we can go during the week I close Rituals for renovations."

"Let me know when you have the dates and I'll call my travel agent."

"Are you always this easygoing?"

"When it comes to you...yes."

He came over to me and lifted me up on the counter. I wrapped my legs around his waist and my arms around his neck. His thick fingers gripped my hips. We were eye to eye. I watched him watch me. Cain sighed loudly and then looked away. He kissed me on the forehead and let go of me.

"I'm missing the game," he said.

I uncrossed my legs and lifted my arms from his neck. He grabbed his pretzels and left the kitchen.

His abrupt exit baffled me. I marched back to the den to find out what had happened. He was stretched out on the couch with his eyes closed. I plopped down near his feet and waited for him to acknowledge my presence. He didn't.

I cleared my throat. "What was that about?"

"What? I didn't want to miss the end of the game."

"The game is playing and you're lying here with your eyes closed."

"I'm listening to it."

I didn't want to push so I dropped it. "Okay, well, I'll be in my office doing some paperwork if you need me."

"Alright, baby."

In my office I thought about Cain's behavior. I had never seen him act so strange. It wasn't like him to not say what was on his mind. All I could do was to give him his space and, hopefully, he would feel comfortable enough to let me in.

20

People were everywhere. The music was pumping. There was a volleyball game being played on the lawn, eating at the tables on the patio, people lying on chaises poolside, and even quite a few in the pool enjoying the water. Cain's dad was at the grill making barbecue ribs.

I'd met him earlier in the morning and had instantly fallen in love with him. He'd given me a big bear hug and a kiss on the cheek when he came through the door. Cain was out back, setting up the yard, so it allowed his father and me to get to know one another. He offered to help me out in the kitchen and we ended up chatting the morning away.

Now I knew where Cain got his easygoing nature. He was tall like Cain but was light brown with grey hair. He was in great shape for his age. He told me that running five miles every day kept him healthy. I asked if he had a girlfriend and he smiled and said he had a few. He told me it had taken him many years to start dating after Cain's mother died and now he was making up for the time spent alone. I laughed when he said he had no intention of ever marrying again but he wouldn't mind shackin'. Those were his exact words…*shackin'*.

Cain's father believed for men and women my age it was best to avoid living together before marriage. According to him, that was the reason so many young people never married. They moved in, hit a rough patch, and then they were ready to jump ship. Yes, the same thing could happen once you're married, but those vows were supposed to mean something. Those vows served as a reminder to try a little harder to make it work—that a commitment had been made to another person—til death do you part.

He spoke of the joys of marriage and how much he'd loved his wife. He reflected on the early days, before the kids, when they'd lived in a studio apartment, barely making enough money to pay the bills, but having so much love that they didn't care. He said moving to Long Island was the best thing that he could've done for his family. Cain and his brothers had adjusted to life in the suburbs easily enough, riding bikes with their friends and getting in trouble like boys do. His wife having a kitchen big enough to cook elaborate holiday dinners and a dining room to eat them in—that's what made him happy. Those are the things he chose to reflect upon when thinking of the past, not the fateful day his wife had received the test results confirming that she had cancer. He said it had taken what felt like a lifetime to be able to think about his wife and feel joy and not sadness.

I not only got to know Cain's father in that kitchen, but through him, I also met Cain's mother.

He brushed the ribs with the sauce I made. "Cain told me you're a great cook. I see he wasn't lying," he said.

"I can do a little sumthin-sumthin."

"And you're modest."

Just then, Cain came up behind me and wrapped his arms around my waist. "Don't let her fool you, Pop. She's far from modest. This is Ms. Cocky."

"Now don't you go lying on this girl," his father replied. "She's nothing but sweetness."

"Thank you, Pop," I said.

"So now he's Pop?" Cain asked, grinning wide.

"I told Jade to skip the formalities and call me Pop. I prefer Pop over *Mister* and *Sir* any day; especially from someone so pretty."

"So this is where I get my weakness for a pretty face." Cain leaned over and kissed my cheek. "Well, *Pop,* I need to borrow Jade for a moment."

"Go ahead, Son. I'm not trying to steal your lady friend from you."

"Don't worry, Pop. I'll be back to get me some of those ribs," I said.

Cain gave his father a playful punch in the arm, grabbed me by the hand, and led me into the house. There were a couple of people loitering in the den so he pulled me upstairs away from the noise.

Cain took me to his bedroom, closed the door behind us, and immediately covered my lips with his. He pressed my back against the door as he bombarded me with urgent kisses. He gripped my ass while sucking on my neck.

"Don't leave any marks," I whispered.

Cain didn't answer; he scooped me up in his arms and carried me to the bed. He started to lie on top of me.

"Cain, what are you doing? You have a house full of people down there."

"I don't care about that. You've been driving me crazy all day with that outfit you have on. I can see straight through your dress."

I was wearing a pale gold, off-the-shoulder, bell-sleeved cover-up that stopped a few inches below my ass. Underneath I wore a slinky white bikini that showed through the sheer fabric.

I scooted away from Cain and stood up. "You're going to have to control yourself. We have company. We cannot be up here doing the nasty with a party going on downstairs."

He stretched out on his back and groaned. "Come on, Jade. We could have a quickie. Nobody would know."

"I don't do quickies," I said, enjoying his torment.

He lay there, trying to convince me of the positive aspects of a quick rendezvous but to no avail.

"I can't believe you dragged me up here to get your freak on. Pull yourself together."

He sighed and then sat up. "I really came up here to put on my swimming trunks. I wanted you to come with me since we haven't had a moment together all day. But once I got you in here all alone, I couldn't resist touching you."

"We'll have plenty of time for this later, *after* the party. So behave yourself and put on your trunks so we can get back downstairs."

Cain reluctantly got off the bed to change his clothes. I giggled at the way he was frowning and taking his time to get over to the dresser. While he searched for his trunks, I lay across the bed like I was doing a *Playboy* photo shoot. I started on my side, then slowly rolled over to my stomach and winked at him. I ran my fingers through my hair and blew him a kiss.

"If you don't want any trouble, you better stop lying there like that trying to tease me," he said.

I licked my lips. "I'm not teasing you."

"See now you're playing with me." He approached the bed.

I sprang up and sat on the edge. "Okay. Okay. I'll stop," I laughed. "Get changed."

He didn't budge. He was deliberating whether to seduce me now or wait until later.

"I promise, I'll stop," I repeated.

Cain flashed me a smile while shaking his head from side to side. "You and me…right here…later."

I watched him strip and wished I hadn't stopped him a few moments ago. He stepped into his trunks and then extended his hand to me. I slipped my hand in his and we went back down to the party.

His father gave us a knowing look as we came out the door into the yard. Cain still held my hand as he walked to the edge of the pool and dipped his foot in. I kicked off my sandals and was about to put my toe in the water when Cain's dad called my name and said that the ribs were done. My head was turned toward Pop when I suddenly felt Cain's arms grab me around my waist and pull my body with his as he jumped into the pool.

I managed to take a deep breath before we made contact with the cool water. As we sank to the bottom of the pool, I wriggled free of his grip. I swam to the surface and caught my breath, treading in the middle of the pool. I was ready to strangle Cain but he hadn't resurfaced yet. I looked around but didn't see him. I thought maybe I had kicked him when breaking free of his arms. Just as I began to panic, something brushed against my leg. I looked down and Cain popped up from under water. He was laughing. I swung my hand against the surface of the water and splashed him in the face.

Through clenched teeth, I asked, "Why did you do that?"

Cain swam up next to me and squeezed my ass under the water. "That was payback for upstairs."

"I'll show you payback." I pushed him under by his shoulders and held him there.

He grabbed my thighs and pulled me under with him. We frolicked underwater; stealing secret touches no one could see. We came up for air, continuing to tussle with one another.

"No roughhousing in the pool!" Pop shouted.

We stopped pushing and pulling on one another and laughed that we were being reprimanded like two children. Everyone was getting a good laugh at our expense. A couple of people jumped in the pool during our skirmish and a couple more were thrown in, so Pop wasn't only talking to us.

Cain pulled me to him and gave me a peck on the lips. "You mad at me?"

"I might be…but you can make it up to me later."

We shared another kiss in the middle of the pool. When we separated, I looked toward the patio and saw Milan watching us, smiling.

I swam over to the edge of the pool where she was standing. "Hey, girl, when did you get here?"

"Just as you took your flying leap into the water," she said.

"Can you believe he did that?"

"Stop frontin'. You know you loved it."

"Don't let me have to pull you in." I reached out as if I was going to grab her ankle and she jumped back. "Give me a second. I'm getting out."

I swam to the shallow end and came out of the pool. My cover-up was plastered to my body. Cain had a stack of towels sitting on a cart if, anyone needed one. I peeled off my cover-up and toweled off. I slipped on my sandals and went to spread my towel across a lounge chair. Milan sat on the lounge next to mine.

"I was starting to think you weren't coming," I said.

"You know how long it takes me to get ready for anything. I couldn't find the right outfit."

"You look great. Did you bring your suit?"

"I look too cute to be getting in a pool."

She did look nice in her pink ensemble, a wrap top and mini-skirt.

Cain emerged from the pool. He wrapped a towel around his waist and then came over to us.

"Long time, no see." He bent over and kissed Milan on the cheek. "I've owed you that for quite some time now."

Milan looked at me and I shrugged. "What for?" she asked.

"For telling your friend to take a chance on me." He nudged my legs so he could sit at the end of my lounge chair. "She wouldn't have given me the time of day if it weren't for you."

Milan laughed. "I'm glad I could help."

"You ladies want something to eat?" Cain asked.

"I was about to get down on those ribs before you tossed me in the pool."

"To make amends I'm gonna hook it up for you. Milan, you want something?"

"Not yet, thanks."

Cain squeezed my thigh and then went over to the grill for my food.

"Y'all are cute together," Milan said.

I looked over at him, fixing my plate. "I'm really digging him, Lan. His friends are cool, his family is nice, and he's so open with his feelings. I've really stepped outside of the box with him and I just hope it works."

"You deserve to be happy and it seems that Cain makes you happy."

"He does. Bryce never would've shown a public display of affection in the middle of a party. Actually, I couldn't even trust Bryce to show up to a party. I couldn't trust him at all."

"Why are you even bringing him up? Let it go. You're on to bigger and apparently better things."

"You're right. No more comparisons between Cain and Bryce."

"Good. Now I'm going to go mingle."

"Do you want Cain to introduce you to one of his friends?"

Milan poked her breasts out. "I got this."

Milan strutted across the yard where people were playing spades. Cain took her seat and handed me my plate. It was piled high with ribs, macaroni salad, BBQ shrimp, and corn on the cob.

"You're not eating anything?" I asked.

"I brought enough for both of us. You thought you were going to eat all of that by yourself?"

"I was sure as hell going to try. But you can help me."

Cain took a rib from my plate and bit into it. "Jade, you threw down on this sauce."

I tasted it. "I did, didn't I?"

"Pop needed to hear that one. Modest, my ass."

"I like your dad. We had a good time this morning."

"Yeah, well, he told me that you're a keeper."

I smiled as I took another bite of my rib. "Am I a keeper?"

"Look at you cheesing. I may keep you around for a bit."

I moved my plate out of his reach. "Don't make me have to ask you again."

"You know damn well I have no intention of letting you go. Now, unless you want to take another unexpected swim, you better pass that food this way."

I picked up a shrimp and fed it to him. He got up from his chair and joined me on my lounge. Cain was facing me so he didn't see Pop walk up.

"Look at you two. Sitting in one chair. Eating off one plate. Boy, you could've fixed two plates of food. And there are about fifty empty chairs back here and you squeezing your big ass on her seat. Excuse my language, Jade."

I laughed at what Pop was saying.

"Did it occur to you that I want to be this close to Jade? I'm trying to get my mack on and here you come messing things up. How do you know I didn't tell Jade there were no more plates?" Cain answered.

"If you did tell her that nonsense, she wouldn't have believed a word of it. Ain't that right, Jade?"

"Not a word. But it's okay, Pop. I don't mind sharing with your son. He's a caring and giving man."

Pop nodded. "Uh-huh. I smell love in the air."

Cain glanced at me, then looked back at his father. "Come on,

Pop. Why are you over here messing with me? Don't you need to check on the food?"

"My work is done here. I'll be at the grill, if you need me." Pop walked off.

Cain and I avoided one another's eyes. "Your dad is funny," I said.

He put another shrimp in his mouth, chewing while he spoke. "Yeah, he's a trip. Always trying to embarrass me."

"That's what parents are for. I'm sure mine will do the same thing when you meet them."

"You plan on making that happen any time soon?"

"Whenever you're ready. I'd love for my parents to meet you."

"So this is getting serious?" he asked.

"You tell me. Is it?"

"That's what I asked you." Cain stood up and straightened his trunks. "My romantic scheme backfired. You're hogging the food. I'm going to get my own plate." He winked at me before he walked away.

I don't know why I didn't answer his question. I had sat there and told Milan I was falling for him; I should've been able to share that information with him. I could've kicked myself. He fixed his food and sat across the yard talking to some of his friends.

Meanwhile, Milan was having a good time. She made some new friends rather quickly. She was playing cards with three guys, all of whom weren't bad-looking. Milan knew how to turn on the charm. I didn't have to worry about keeping her entertained while I helped Cain with the party.

I walked over to the bar for a glass of wine, leaving my cover-up with my towel on the chair. I was all bikini. Out of the corner of my eye, I saw Cain watching my every move. I was searching the bar for a bottle of Chardonnay when a brother that looked like he spent every day in the gym stepped up next to me, muscles bulging out of his tank top. He asked what I was drinking, his lips almost touching my ear as he spoke. Cain leaned forward in his chair. The guy was all up in my space. I played it cool, acted like I didn't see Cain.

I had polite conversation with Muscles while we sipped our drinks. Cain sat as still as a statue, plate in hand, eyes glued on me. When the brother finally got around to asking if I was seeing anyone, I pointed to Cain, looking rather tense in his chair. Cain nodded at the brother and Muscles nodded back before taking off with his rum and Coke. I raised my glass to Cain and did a catwalk stroll back to my seat. I reclined on the lounge and sipped my wine. Cain eased back into his seat and resumed eating his food. Every so often I would find Cain staring in my direction. When I'd catch him, he would shake his head and continue his conversation with his friends.

I lay soaking up the sun with my eyes closed. A shadow fell over me. I knew who it was but I didn't open my eyes.

"Your bikini is going to get me in trouble."

I looked at him and smiled. "I think this is getting serious."

He sat on my chair and held my hand. "I was getting jealous when I saw that guy trying to rap to you."

I sat up so we were face to face. "You had no reason to be. I wasn't paying him any attention."

"Let's get rid of all these people. They're keeping me from what I really want to do."

"Enjoy the day with your friends and family. I'm not going anywhere. We have the entire night to be together."

Chaka Khan's "Ain't Nobody" came blaring out of the speakers. The deejay had turned the music up.

"Come on. Dance with me."

"You want me to put on my cover-up? I don't want to get you into any trouble."

"Naah, these cats realize you're my girl. That one clown must've been a friend of a friend but he knows now."

We went over to the patio where the deejay was set up. The party was in full swing. We joined the crowd that was already out there shaking their booties. I gave Cain my laid back sexy dance, hips swaying from side to side. We flirted while we danced, trying to see who could put it on the other one. Cain was no match for me. I whirled, twirled, bumped, and bopped to the music; left him in need of a drink to cool down. After our dance, we swam some more, ate even more, and drank the most. We partied the rest of the day into the late night.

At around one a.m., Cain escorted the last guests out the door. Pop had done most of the clean-up while we partied so Cain and I had little to do after he left. I tinkered around in the kitchen while Cain handled the backyard. As tired as I was, I was still buzzing. Now I understood why Cain needed help to pull the barbecue off. The crowd swelled to at least two hundred by the late evening. Poor Pop couldn't leave his station at the grill for more than a few minutes at a time. He loved it, though. Cain tried to shoo him away from the grill so he could relax but he refused. He said he liked being around young folks' energy—it kept him young.

Cain had to be exhausted. He'd been working nonstop since four in the morning. I came over to pitch in at eight and the house was spotless. The yard furniture was set-up and the sterno racks were already on the table. There wasn't much left for me to do, other than help prepare the food.

The day was wonderful, full of fun, but I was sure Cain must've been glad it was over. When he finished out back he came into the kitchen and motioned with his head for me to come. I sauntered over to him. He patted me on my ass and then nudged me toward the staircase. He followed close behind me as we ascended the stairs. He began to untie my bikini top as we reached the top of the landing. I slipped it off and tossed it over my shoulder at him as I sashayed down the hallway, where we retired to his bedroom.

I COLLAPSED ON TOP OF CAIN after riding him like a jockey in the Belmont Stakes. Cain held me to him, the rise and fall of his chest lulling me to sleep. He traced patterns on my back, still damp with perspiration. Every time I tried to move, he protested and tightened his arms around me.

"You uncomfortable?" he asked.

"No, I thought you were."

"This is where I wanted to be all day. Let me have my moment."

It had been a long day and my fatigue was getting the best of me. I was trying hard to stay awake and talk with Cain. One minute, I was mumbling into Cain's chest, the next I was dreaming.

I dreamt that I was driving my car but wasn't getting very far. I pulled over on the side of the road and realized that I was trying to drive on four flat tires. The highway was deserted except for me. Strong winds were blowing sand into my face. I waited for a passing car for help but there were none. I was stranded.

21

I uncorked a bottle of Riesling and poured two glasses for the women at the end of the bar. My bartender called in sick and I was filling in for him. It was midweek and slow enough that I could muddle my way through making drinks. If someone requested something I was unfamiliar with, I discreetly referred to the Bartenders Guide and did the best I could.

I was placing the wine in front of the ladies when a voice called out from behind me.

"Excuse me, Bartender, can I have A Screaming Orgasm?"

I smiled. "One moment, Sir." I placed a couple of menus in front of my customers and then returned to the opposite end of the bar.

"Courvoisier?"

"No, I said A Screaming Orgasm. I haven't had one of those in a while."

"And you won't be having one now." I filled a brandy glass halfway with the amber liquid and placed it on the bar. "One Courvoisier."

"Thanks." Cain smiled his sexy smile at me. "Maybe later?"

I leaned over the bar and kissed him on the cheek. "What's up, Black Man? What are you doing in my establishment?"

"Checking on my lady. I haven't laid eyes on you since the party."

You would've thought we hadn't spoken every day, two or three times a day. I was having a busy week, conducting interviews for additional wait staff and meeting with marketing reps from the different spirit makers.

"Do you want something to eat?" I asked.

"I'll have something light. What's good?"

"We have a roasted potato soup today that's absolutely delicious."
I signaled Jeff, who was covering the front section of the restaurant,
placed Cain's order and then went to work filling drink orders.

"You actually look like you know what you're doing."

I looked up from the apple martini I was mixing. "Looks can
be deceiving. One of my bartenders is sick, another had a death
in the family, and the other's on vacation. Talk about bad timing.
How was your day?"

"I reviewed proposals all day from contractors in Atlanta. I
narrowed it down to four. I'm going to fly down there tomorrow
morning for a couple of meetings and come back tomorrow night.
You wanna come with me?"

"I'd love to, but I can't. I have a slew of meetings myself all day
tomorrow."

Cain and I complained about trying to run businesses and feeling that there was never enough time to get everything done. But
he had it worse than I did. He was running multiple businesses
in multiple states and was responsible for the success of each and
every one. Cain admitted that since we'd been dating he'd been
taking more one-day business trips when possible. It wasn't
uncommon for him to be on the road for weeks at a time—not
because he had to—but because there was nothing for him to
rush home to. I could only imagine the women scattered across
the country anxiously awaiting Cain's next visit.

"So what do all of your lady friends think about your quick
business trips? They must be upset that you aren't spending more
time with them," I said.

"My lady friends? Oh…I get it. Well, that's easy. They just
come to see me. In fact, there are three women waiting for me at
my house right now."

Typical. Make a joke when a serious response would be most

appropriate. "Cain, there were women in your life before you and me...a young, fine brotha traveling the country for weeks at a time must have friends to make him feel welcome."

Cain chuckled. "Jade, of course I have friends."

"I thought so."

"But they're just that; friends."

"Nothing more?" I asked with doubt in my voice. "You don't have someone in Atlanta who's jumping for joy that you're thinking about opening a restaurant down there?"

"There may have been one person that was excited when she found out, but that was before I told her about you."

"Okay. So that explains one state. What about your honeys in D.C., Connecticut, North Carolina, and Kansas?"

"First of all, I don't have any businesses in Kansas. Secondly, I do not have honeys around the world. I thought we covered this before...and I told you I wasn't seeing anyone."

"Humor me."

"Listen, Jade. There were a couple of women I was dating. One was in Atlanta, the other was right here in New York. Neither situation was serious and all parties knew that."

I believed Cain but insecurity rapidly crept up on me. He had admitted to having a relationship with a woman in Atlanta and now he was opening a business down there, where she lived. By any woman's standards, Cain was a great catch. This woman might've been plotting at that very moment how to dig her claws into my man. She probably couldn't wait until she could lure him with her big country booty.

A smile spread across my lips as I listened to my own crazy thoughts.

"What's funny about what I said?" Cain asked.

I wiped the smile from my face. "It's nothing you said, just something I was thinking."

Cain's soup arrived and I resumed making drinks. It would've been silly of me to harp on his past relationships when I had Bryce—my own unresolved drama. No. I would let this ride. If he wanted a woman in Atlanta, then that's where he would be spending his time, not with me. But there he was, in my restaurant, sitting at my bar, eating his dinner. I really had nothing to worry about and wouldn't create something, either.

CAIN WAITED OUT FRONT WHILE I LOCKED UP Rituals for the night. We were going to swing by the supermarket for a pint of Häagen-Dazs French vanilla to satisfy my craving and head back to my place. We rode in separate cars, chatting with each other on our cell phones. As I made a right turn onto my street, a red motorcycle was coming out of my block, passing slowly by my car before speeding off down the road. My instinct told me it was Bryce. I had never seen him on that particular bike before, but motorcycles were his toy of choice. He had a blue Katana and a black Harley; the red one must've been a new purchase.

Thankfully, Cain and I were not in the same car, or surely Bryce would've made a U-turn. I pulled into my driveway and Cain parked behind me. I wanted to have him pull into my garage but didn't think I could make such a request without raising a red flag. I hurried Cain into the house and sent him to put the ice cream in the freezer. I ran up to my bedroom and watched from the window to see whether or not the red motorcycle would return. Maybe I was being paranoid. It could've been anyone on the motorcycle. I didn't see a face through the helmet and as far as I knew, Bryce didn't even own a red motorcycle.

It took a long time before Bryce could get me to ride on the back of his bikes. He had been riding for years but I didn't think it was safe. It took a lot of convincing—and promising that he would go slowly—for me to put my safety in his hands and climb on that first time. I tightened my arms around Bryce's waist like a vise grip and buried my face in his back. I refused to open my eyes. He cruised on the Meadowbrook Parkway to Jones Beach. He had to pry my arms from his nearly crushed ribs and help me off the motorcycle. My legs wouldn't stop shaking and I didn't want to take the ride back. We went down to the beach and sat by the water as the sun set. After an hour or so of calming my nerves, Bryce got me back on the bike. The moonlit ride home was romantic. He took it nice and slow and as I became more comfortable, I began to enjoy the experience. After that night, I would ride with Bryce all the time. I even had my own helmet— something cute that didn't cover my face. In the summertime I would put on my cut-off shorts and a wife beater and hop on the back. I would get such a rush when we'd speed down the highway at top speed. Bryce was a bad boy to the bone and when I rode with him, I was his rebel sidekick.

Headlights brightened the street and a Volkswagen Beetle passed the house. I couldn't stay on my knees, peeking through the blinds all night. Bryce wasn't coming back. I took a quick shower, threw on my sweats, and joined Cain in the TV room with two bowls of ice cream. The lights were dim and he lay back on the couch, listening to smooth jazz.

We ate while the music played softly in the background. I reached over to place my empty bowl on the coffee table and experienced a sharp pinch at the base of my neck. I did a few neck rolls and rubbed the source of my affliction. It was most likely Bryce-related tension.

Cain put his bowl down. "Come sit over here."

I sat on the floor between his legs and he started massaging my neck and shoulders with a firm circular motion. "Is that better?"

I nodded my head. "I should leave bartending to the professionals."

"Are you sure that's what it is?"

"What do you mean?"

"While you were upstairs I was thinking about our conversation at the restaurant. You don't trust me, do you?"

I leaned my head against Cain's knee. "I trust you."

"Jade, talk to me."

I got up and sat next to Cain on the couch. "My imagination was getting the best of me. That's all."

"That explains earlier. How about the way you've been acting since we came home?"

"I didn't realize I was acting any different than usual."

"So everything's alright?"

"Everything is fine."

"And you're not upset I'm going to Atlanta tomorrow?"

"Why would I be?"

"Okay, Jade. Keep thinking that I don't know you."

Cain collected our bowls from the table and stood. I followed him to the kitchen and watched him rinse out the dishes. "Leave them in the sink. I'll wash them later."

Cain dried his hands and then came over and kissed me on the cheek. "I'm going to get going. I have an early flight tomorrow. I'll call you when I get back."

I walked Cain to the door and let him out. He didn't bother to give me a real goodnight kiss before leaving.

I went upstairs to prepare for bed. I decided I wouldn't fall asleep with the television on; a bad habit that needed to be broken. I turned off my lamp and crawled under my covers. I lay in the dark, not used to the late-night quiet of my house. As I dozed off, the unmistakable sound of a speeding motorcycle pierced the silence. I leapt from the bed and looked out of the window. I waited for a few minutes but didn't see anything. I lay back down and rubbed the dull ache that once again seized my neck.

22

My girls and I were on our way to see a black stage play at the Beacon Theater in Manhattan. Bria had gotten the tickets for us and was basically forcing us to attend. I didn't even know what this one was called. It might've been *Mama, Don't Throw the Baby Out with the Bathwater* or maybe it was *Baby, Don't Throw My Mama in the Bathwater*. Either way, I couldn't remember. Bria dragged us to one of these plays about six months ago and I nodded off in the middle of it. She was pissed at me but had to admit later that the play was awful. I could only pray that whatever we were seeing this time wouldn't be so bad.

Neither one of us wanted to drive so we decided to take the Long Island Rail Road into the city. We waited on the platform for the two o'clock out of Mineola. It was already ten minutes after two and Bria had launched into her *we're going to be late* mantra.

Originally we were supposed to take the one o'clock train, but Milan had arrived at the station five minutes after the train departed. I had been listening to Bria repeat the same thing for the last hour and a half.

I couldn't stand it anymore. "Bria, please. We're going to get there in plenty of time," I said. "The train is a little behind schedule and the play probably won't start on time anyway."

"That's not the point. We were supposed to leave at one. That gave us enough time to get to the Beacon," Bria replied.

Milan threw her hands up. "I already apologized for the mix-up. Am I going to hear about it all day?"

"Will you two cut it out? Here comes the train now," I said.

We boarded the relatively empty train and sat in seats facing one another. There were a few loud-talking sisters sitting together in the middle of the car, probably going to the same place that we were.

It had been a while since the three of us spent an afternoon together. I'd been spending most of my time with Cain, Milan had been devoting herself to her job and Bria was teaching an evening culinary class at the community college. I had planned to work that day but Bria wasn't trying to hear that.

Milan stared out the window as the train started moving. "Today is a good day to be on the beach," she said.

Bria disagreed. "It's too hot for that. I prefer to have my ass in an air-conditioned theater with a drink in hand. Jade, you don't need to chime in 'cause we know where you want to be."

"Oh really? And where is that?"

"Where were you last weekend?" she asked.

"At Cain's pool party, which you declined to attend."

"And the weekend before that?" she needled.

"Probably with Cain. I don't remember."

"Probably my ass. You know you were up underneath that man."

"I wasn't *under* anything. I was *with* Cain. Is there a problem?"

"Why would I have a problem with what you do? I was just saying."

"Just saying what? You made an unnecessary comment regarding my whereabouts as if you had a problem with it."

Milan's head moved back and forth, like she was watching a tennis match.

Bria screwed up her face. "What are you getting all sensitive for? It was a joke. If your ass can't take a joke, then let me know."

"Where's the joke, Bria? I like Cain...we spend time together... so I repeat, what's the problem?"

"If you want to jump from one man to the next, then knock yourself out."

"I am not 'jumping from one man to the next.' Your brother left me."

"You leave him, he leaves you; that's what y'all do. This isn't the first time you two broke up."

"But it's the last."

Milan laughed at my wisecrack and became the recipient of the icy glare I had been getting.

Bria turned back to me. "Bryce is trying—"

"Trying to harass me."

"Jade, my brother doesn't get down like that."

"Your brother isn't a saint." I raised my voice and the sisters in the middle of the car turned around. "In fact, your brother—"

Milan interrupted. "Now, ladies, we're supposed to be out for a nice day. Not to argue over silly things. Let's leave the drama for the play."

"Who's arguing?" I said. "Are we arguing, Bria?"

"You might be, but I'm not."

We started to laugh.

"I did get a little riled up," I admitted.

Milan chimed in. "Yeah, you did. Bria was only kidding but it's not like she was lying. The past couple of months you have spent every free minute with Cain."

"Who asked you anyway?" I said.

"Don't worry, Bria; we can all spend some time with Cain when his gospel Sundays start at Eden," Milan joked. "Jade, did you tell Cain to contact Pastor Abbott from my cousin's church?"

I nodded and then gave Milan a look that told her to put a sock in it.

Bria shook her head. "Helping the competition; real smart, Jade."

There was no point in discussing the particulars with Bria. She was in attack mode and even if I explained that his plans would have a minimal impact on our business, she wouldn't want to hear it.

Since the purpose of our outing wasn't to talk about Cain and me, I opted to change the subject. "Bria, what's the name of this play?"

"*Mama, I'm Having a Baby.*"

Milan snickered. "We've seen one too many mama plays. I can't figure out why you love these things."

"It ain't serious drama, but in case you haven't noticed, Broadway isn't running over with black theater. If this is all we have, then I'm going to support my brothers and sisters," Bria said.

I spoke up. "Milan, you can't say the music isn't good. Remember the one we saw with Shirley Murdock, Cherrelle, and Christopher Williams? They tore it up."

"It's entertainment," Bria quipped. "Act like you're not too bourgeois to enjoy it."

"These stage plays may be all we have, but I still think we can stand to raise the bar a bit. That's just my opinion; however, regardless of what I may think about the quality, I still plan to have fun today," Milan replied.

"...With your snooty self," I teased.

It wasn't uncommon for the Diva Squad to get together and have a few disagreements. Our spats were rarely serious and we didn't dwell on our differences of opinion. We didn't hold grudges and if something was bothering us we let one another know. That was the sign of true friendship; you could tell each other off and carry on as if nothing ever happened.

I SAT IN THE DARKENED THEATER watching the main character clinging to a doll wrapped in a blanket, crying that she would never give up her baby. Her mama was trying to convince her that the baby had a better chance at a fulfilling life with the rich husband and wife looking to adopt her child.

The girl and her mama sang a heart-wrenching duet, which ended with the mother trying to take the baby from her daughter. As the mother pried the baby from her daughter, neither actress noticed that a piece of the blanket was still in the daughter's folded arms. The daughter did a quick spin to turn her back on her mama leaving the room with the baby, which yanked the blanket, causing the doll to fly out across the stage. The two actresses scrambled to recover the doll. The audience was silent.

Milan let out a loud cackle. People turned around in their seats to see where the laughter was coming from. I clamped my hand over her mouth and pushed her head down toward her knees. Every time she would calm herself down, she would erupt again. She couldn't control herself. I started to laugh at Milan laughing. Bria was shushing us and giving us the evil eye at the same time. When other people in the audience started to shush as well, I grabbed Milan by her arm, pulled her out of her seat and up the aisle toward the exit.

We burst into the lobby and howled. Milan had tears running down her cheeks.

Through her laughter, she asked, "Did you see that shit?" She was holding her stomach, trying to catch her breath.

"How could I miss it?" I chuckled.

"Were we the only ones laughing at that spectacle?"

"A few other people laughed a little, but you took the cake."

She struggled to compose herself. "Was I really that loud?"

"I'm sure the bartender heard you out here in the lobby."

The guy behind the bar nodded his head, confirming that I was right.

Still giggling, Milan said, "I may need to stay out here until intermission."

The bartender offered her a napkin to wipe her eyes. We ordered a couple of drinks and waited for the break. Milan replayed the scenario for the bartender and he said he wished he could've seen it for himself.

"Bria is really going to have a fit now," I said.

"She better not. That was hilarious. I don't want to hear her mouth."

"Just get all of your laughter out now because you'll set her off if you start up again."

"I'll try..." Again she was cracking up.

The audience began clapping, signaling the end of the first half of the show. Bria filed out along with the other theatergoers. Her scowl reached us before the rest of her did.

She wedged herself between us. "We might as well not even bother to go back in there after the intermission."

Milan kept a straight face. "Why not? I'm enjoying the show."

I lifted my glass to my lips to conceal my smirk.

"After the ruckus you made in there, I'm too embarrassed," Bria said.

"You act like I was laughing for no reason. You mean to tell me that little bald-headed doll flying across the stage didn't make you laugh?"

I almost spat out my drink. Bria refused to answer.

Milan continued, "That stiff, black, bald doll flipping out of the blanket didn't amuse you even a little bit?"

Bria conceded. "I guess it was funny...but not that funny."

"Then stop trippin' because I'm going to watch the second act. I don't want to miss it if they mess up again."

Bria smiled. "Let's get back to our seats before everyone one else. Lan, try to keep your trap shut for the rest of the show."

Milan crossed her heart. "I promise...I'll try."

AFTER THE SHOW WE STOOD OUTSIDE THE THEATER, deciding what to do next. I suggested we go around the corner to a new Italian restaurant on Amsterdam for dinner.

The wait was at least an hour for a table. We parked ourselves at the bar and ordered a round of drinks. I sipped my white wine and surveyed the room. It was obvious that people had come straight over from the play. We should have left the show a few minutes early to beat the crowd.

The conclusion of the play was a little better than the first act. The young mother had managed to get herself together. She cut the deadbeat dad loose but let him know that he would always be able to have a relationship with his child. She found a job and was even working toward getting her own apartment. She was determined to make a life for herself and her baby.

Honestly, I was glad when it was over. If I had to sit through one more tearful number, I would've screamed. Milan did her best not to make a peep through the rest of the show, though I did see her cover her mouth to stifle a laugh more than once.

"Bria, what did you think of the play?" I asked.

"It would benefit a lot of teenage girls to come and see it."

I hadn't thought about it that way. "You know, Bria, you're right. They could learn from the hardships faced by the young mother."

Milan offered her opinion. "Teens these days are having sex earlier and earlier and aren't ready to deal with the repercussions. So many young girls aren't protecting themselves, either. They think these guys love them and will do anything for them. Then, at the first sign of trouble, these girls find out it isn't true."

"There's always a lesson to be learned from these plays. Like I said earlier, they ain't winning any Tonys but they're delivering a message to our communities. That's worth more than any award," Bria preached.

Bria made a good point. One person's entertainment is another person's inspiration. We have enough cynics knocking what we do as a people; I wouldn't be one of them. I was going to make an effort not to knock these productions and to see as many as possible. Well, at least one a year...I don't want to overdo it.

We had dinner and then hopped a cab uptown to Blaze, the club Terrence had taken me to. When we got to the door, Bonecrusher remembered me and let us in without our paying the cover charge. He jabbered something about three beautiful women and going broke while he escorted us to the V.I.P. section. He told the bartender our drinks were on the house and said for us to call him if we needed anything. He winked at Bria before he walked away. Bria smiled and commented that he was cute in a big bear-ish kind of way. She stood twirling one of her locks, watching Bonecrusher disappear into the crowd. I never did understand her taste in men.

Both Milan and Bria were on the dance floor getting their groove on. I was up in the V.I.P. nursing my drink. I wondered what Cain was up to while I was out there thinking about him. I took out my cell and dialed his house but got his answering machine. I called his cell and didn't get an answer. I tried again, figuring that he didn't hear it ring the first time, but he still didn't pick up. I really wasn't in a party mood. I wanted to curl up beside Cain in his bed and sleep off the five glasses of wine I'd drunk. I peered over the balcony and located Milan on the dance floor.

I had to yell over the music to tell her that I was leaving. I told her to stay and enjoy herself and to let Bria know I had left. She shrugged her shoulders, gave me a quick hug, then resumed dancing with the cutie she had for a partner.

I caught a cab to Penn Station and managed to make it to the train with only a minute to spare. If I'd missed that train I would've had to wait a whole hour for the next one.

I looked out the window, anticipating the moment I would cuddle up next to Cain. I tried him at home again. It wasn't like him not to answer his home or cell phone. Then I remembered him mentioning that he had a private party booked at Eden that night. I believed he'd said there were over two hundred people expected. It was after midnight so I was certain that the party was over, but my poor baby was probably still wrapping things up from the event.

By the time the train had pulled into the station I had already made up my mind to go over to Eden and drag Cain out of there. I wanted to go home and get in the bed and I wasn't going to be alone.

I pulled into the lot at Eden. It was empty, with the exception of Cain's truck and another car. I wanted to surprise him so I quietly opened the door and slipped inside. There was music playing but I didn't see anyone; the lights were dim. I stepped past the hostess station and looked toward the back of the restaurant. Two figures were sitting at one of the tables.

Staying out of sight, I walked slowly toward the back. Cain was at the table with a woman. I inched a little closer. He held her hand in his and they appeared to be having an intimate conversation. He stood, still holding her hand. She got up from her chair and stood in front of him. They were saying something but I couldn't hear them over the music.

I watched them from the shadows. They embraced. Not a short hug but a long passionate embrace. She turned her face and laid it against his chest. I couldn't believe my eyes. It was Cutie Pie. Just as I was about to speak up and say something, Cutie Pie looked up at Cain and they kissed on the lips. I had seen all I needed to see. I stealthily backed up to the door. Even though I wanted to spit fire I left as quietly as I had come.

I slammed my car door and gunned the gas pedal. As I drove

past the other car in the lot, the license plate caught my eye. It was customized. I screeched to a stop behind the car to read the plate. Vonnie.

I pulled off, my mind racing as fast as my car. Vonnie. I knew that name. I felt the tears beginning to well up. My cell phone rang. I choked back my tears and answered. It was Bria, making sure that I made it home in one piece. She asked me was I okay, said that I didn't sound right. I did my best to reassure her that I was fine, told her that I was feeling nauseous, that I had too much to drink. She reluctantly let me off the phone. No sooner than I pressed the end button did I start crying. I wiped my eyes with the back of my hand so I could see the road. How could I have been so foolish? I'd jumped in headfirst when I should've known better.

23

I entered the house, leaving all the lights off. I slumped down on the couch in my living room and replayed what I had seen. Cain and that woman had kissed on the lips. Hot tears seared my face. They had hugged, her clinging to him, and then kissed. It was an endearing kiss...a full lip kiss...full of emotion. Who knew what happened after I left. Who knew what was happening at that very moment.

What was he doing with Cutie Pie anyway? I mean Vonnie. No wonder she'd been ready for a catfight the night I'd seen her at the club. We were screwing the same man. She was privy to that information but I wasn't. I'd assumed that there was more than that between Cain and me, but obviously I'd been wrong.

Damn. Why was her name nagging at me? Vonnie? Vonnie? Then it hit me. Vonnie...Chivon. Cutie Pie was Chivon. Cain's ex-girlfriend.

But why hadn't Cain mentioned that she was his ex-girlfriend the day I'd seen him chatting with her and Blondie at his restaurant? Apparently Cain was still with Chivon. Now it was making sense. Chivon's behavior toward me wasn't because we were screwing the same man—it was because I was screwing *her* man.

I got off the chair and flicked on the lights. I needed a drink. I fixed myself a Hennessy—straight up. I drained the contents of my glass in two swallows and poured myself another. As I raised my glass to my lips, the doorbell rang. It was probably Cain. He must've seen my number on his caller ID. I put down my drink and stumbled to the door.

I flung the door open. "What, dammit?"

It was Bryce. He opened the storm door and pushed past me.

"Close the door, Jade," he calmly replied.

Every time my mouth opened, the louder I got. "Why are you here?"

"Stop yelling and close the door."

I stared at Bryce through bloodshot eyes. I left the door hanging wide open, barreled past him to the living room, and returned to the couch.

He closed the door, and then stood in the archway, watching me. "I don't know what's wrong with you, but my sister was worried about you. She asked me to come and check on you."

"How noble of you," I hissed.

"Bria said when she spoke to you, she realized that something was wrong. She thought maybe someone had carjacked you at the train station, or was holding you against your will. I can see you haven't been harmed in that way, but something's wrong. What is it?"

I took a few deep breaths and tried to get a handle on my anger. "Bryce, I appreciate you coming over here but I'm fine. Call your sister and let her know that I'm okay and you can go back to whatever you were doing."

Bryce sat down next to me. He put his hand on top of mine. "You mean more to me than that. If you have a problem, I want to help."

I started to laugh. It wasn't a sweet melodic laugh; it sounded almost sinister. "*You* want to help me with my problems? *You* are the cause of my problems." I was angry at Cain. I was angry at him. I wanted to be left alone. My laugh turned into a broken sob.

Bryce sat silently, perplexed by my behavior. He put his arm around my shoulder. I tried to shrug it off but he wouldn't let go. His persistence was frustrating me. I began to cry harder. He pulled me into his arms. I stopped struggling. I leaned my head against his shoulder and let go of my emotions.

Bryce wiped the tears from my cheeks. He smoothed my hair away from my face, tucking it behind my ears. He kissed my forehead, kept saying that everything would be okay. Told me he was here for me and always would be. He rocked me in his arms. The next thing I knew, his lips were all over my face. He was kissing my tears. He lifted my chin and kissed my lips. I didn't look at him. I kept my eyes shut tight.

He kissed me again, soft and tentative. I thought of Cain and immediately felt guilty but then my mind flashed to him hugged up with Chivon. I kissed Bryce back. I opened my eyes in time to see the surprise register on his face. This time, when he kissed me, it was filled with desire. His breathing sped up and his hands were up and down my back.

Bryce gently pushed me back on the couch. His lips made contact with my neck, my chest. He touched my breasts, told me how much he missed this. I lay still, listening to him, trying not to think. He unbuttoned my shirt and I didn't stop him. Bryce deftly freed my breasts from the front-clasp bra I was wearing. He laid his head on my stomach, rubbing his face against it. He slid his hands underneath my skirt and pulled down my panties.

He looked down and at my body and took a deep breath. "I've missed you."

He quickly shed his clothes and laid his body next to mine. He began to caress my breasts. Bryce maneuvered his body to climb on top of me.

I bolted up. "I can't do this. I'm sorry." I pushed him so I could get off the couch, causing him to fall to the carpet. I clutched my shirt together, then bent over to pick up my panties. "Bryce, I'm sorry."

"What the fuck, Jade?"

Now that was the Bryce I knew. I hadn't recognized the considerate, compassionate man a few moments ago.

"Please don't make this a big deal. I'm sorry I let things get this far but I can't do this with you. We can't go backwards."

"Are you fucking kidding me? I'm laying here butt-ass naked, about to make love to you, and you pull this shit?"

"Bryce, get dressed. We were about to make a mistake."

"Fuck no! I ain't getting dressed and I wasn't making no mistake by making love to my woman."

"See, that's the problem right there. I'm not your woman and what we were about to do wasn't making love."

"Then what the fuck was it, Jade?" he asked, his anger escalating.

I buttoned my top and stepped into my panties. My night was catapulting from bad to worse.

I kept my voice at an even tone, no sarcasm. "We were caught up in the moment. If we would have continued, we both would have regretted it tomorrow."

"Why don't you be honest and say what this is really about?" He walked over to me and grabbed between my legs. "You've been giving my pussy to someone else?"

I slapped his hand off of me and backed away from him. "Don't be raunchy, Bryce."

"Then answer me. Somebody else is getting my pussy?"

"I don't want to complicate things with us. I don't want to confuse you about where we stand."

"Answer me!" he roared.

I jumped, then hurried to the other side of the room, putting some distance between us. He followed me and grabbed between my legs again. "Who's getting this?"

This definitely wasn't the right moment to tell him that I was involved with someone. I tried to reason with him. "Stop grabbing on me, Bryce. It's unnecessary. You don't see me putting my hands on you. Now get dressed."

He didn't move. He stood glaring at me, his chest puffing up with anger. What the hell was I thinking? I wasn't thinking. Now I had Bryce's naked ass standing in front of me, acting like a raving lunatic. My eyes started to water. He blinked a couple of times, seemingly snapping out of his rage.

Bryce always had a temper but lately it seemed as if he couldn't control his anger. He turned away from me to retrieve his boxers. He sat down on the couch and put his head in his hands.

"I'm sorry, Bryce."

"It's my fault. I came over here and took advantage of you while you were going through some shit. That was low."

"I should've stopped you." I sat on the chair across the room. "I didn't mean to give you the wrong impression."

"When I kissed you, I was praying that you wouldn't slap me. But when you kissed me back, I thought you had a change of heart about us. For a moment, I thought you'd come back to me."

"I'm sorry about that."

"Pardon me for putting my hands on you. I'd never hurt you."

"You need to seek professional help for anger management. You made me extremely uncomfortable." I wasn't going to tell him but he was scaring me with his aggressive behavior. I thought I was going to have to make a run for the door.

"If I get counseling, will you consider giving us another chance?"

"Bryce, you have to get help for yourself, not for me. Our problems run deeper than your anger. I don't want to rehash. It's late, I've had too much to drink, and I need some sleep. You can let yourself out."

"I don't mean to hurt you. I've been through some shit that messed with my head and sometimes I can't control—"

"Now's not the time."

"I'm not letting you go…I'll do anything to keep you in my life," he muttered, more to himself than me.

I left him sitting on the couch, looking pitiful. I was truly sorry for getting him worked up but I wasn't feeling him, or the situation. I had just lain there. I hadn't even touched him. He didn't seem to notice, or maybe he didn't care. I guess he was happy to take whatever he could've gotten.

I lay across the bed in my clothes and thought about Cain. Was I so naïve that I thought he was different than Bryce? No, he was just that good of an actor. I drifted off, mid-thought, into a fitful sleep.

24

I woke up with a splitting headache. The phone was ringing but I couldn't move to answer it. The machine picked up.

Good morning, beautiful. Sorry I missed your call last night. I want to see you today. Oh, by the way, I got our tickets for Antigua. In a few weeks, we'll be lying on the beach. Call me when you get this.

I rolled over and sucked my teeth. *We won't be lying anywhere,* I thought.

I stumbled from the bed and went downstairs to make coffee. I walked by the living room and stopped. Bryce was lying on the sofa, still in his boxers, knocked out sleeping. I called out to him and he stirred.

He stretched and then opened his eyes. "I fell asleep. I was sitting here thinking about us and must've nodded off."

I shook my head and went to the kitchen. A few minutes, later he came into the kitchen, fully dressed, and helped himself to a cup of coffee. The phone rang.

I looked at the caller ID. "Hey, Bria…No, I have a headache… Yup, he came by… He's right here." I handed Bryce the phone. "After your coffee, you can let yourself out."

I left him in the kitchen, talking to his sister, and went upstairs to get myself together. I wasn't going to spend the day sulking in the house.

I WAS HAVING A ROUGH DAY. I locked myself in my office a few times when I sensed my emotions bubbling to the surface. The mind was good for reminding me of things I wanted to forget. Snapshot images of last night kept reappearing to blur my vision with fresh tears. Sunday brunch was rocking and there I was in my office fighting the impulse to go home. I had work to do and the jazz pouring through the restaurant was trying to lift my spirits.

Before leaving the confines of my office, I checked my face in the mirror. Sad eyes stared at me, asking *old* questions about a *new* man. Why, why, why echoed in my head. I slammed the compact shut and left the office—questions unanswered. Unfortunately there would be no schmoozing with customers today. I told Taylor if there were any problems to let Winston, the manager, handle it. I was not to be disturbed.

I stayed in the kitchen all day, keeping myself busy alongside my chefs. The kitchen staff shared lighthearted conversation while preparing meals. There was a different energy back in the kitchen; exactly what I needed. I didn't have to wear my dining room smile; I could keep it real. I wasn't in the mood for chit-chat. I worked silently, giving instructions only when necessary. I noticed a few prolonged glances from questioning eyes but I kept working. I sliced through the facts. Chopped into the image of Cain kissing another woman. Diced up the nasty exchange between Bryce and me. Minced the dull ache of repeated betrayal into tiny pieces. Grilled the decisions I'd made. Seared my seething anger. Roasted it all until Bryce, Cain, and I were done.

An evening calm settled over the restaurant. Hours after jazz brunch ended, I had emerged from my self-imposed isolation. I was at the bar drinking a glass of wine when Terrence came in with someone I had not laid my eyes upon in quite some time.

"What's up, guys?" I said, producing my first real smile of the day.

Terrence sat on the stool to the left of me and Malik took the one to my right. "Malik, it's good to see you."

Malik was a friend of Terrence's from NYU. He's what I call a "goody"—a good-looking brother with a good job who loves to have a good time. Malik had it going on and there were a lot of women that could testify to that. If Terrence and I didn't have that damn rule not to date each other's friends, I would've been all over Malik like syrup on a waffle. Instead, we'd settled for shameless flirtation over the years. We both knew it was harmless fun, nothing would come of it, but we did it anyway.

Malik kissed me on the cheek. "You're looking good, girl. Life must be treating you right."

Terrence butted in. "She looks tired to me. What, no sleep last night?"

Leave it to Terrence to put me on the spot and call it like he saw it.

"I've been here all day...working. Not gallivanting like some people."

"Gallivanting?" Malik laughed. "We just came from the auto show at the Coliseum and stopped in for a bite to eat."

"I wanted to go to Dave & Buster's to watch the game and throw back a couple of beers but this brother insisted on coming in here," Terrence said.

"I had to check my girl; it's been a while."

"If you ventured out of Brooklyn more often ..."

"Don't bust my chops." Malik hugged me. "Work has a brother busy as hell. You know I love you."

"Man, come on with all that nonsense." Terrence stood. "Jade, hook us up with a table, please, before I lose my appetite."

I led them to a table and told them their waiter would be over momentarily.

"Sit down for a few minutes, girl." Malik slid over, making room next to him in the booth.

"Only for a minute, then I have to get back to work."

"Since when is sitting at the bar, drinking, considered work?" Terrence cracked.

"I was taking a break," I said defensively.

Malik stifled a laugh. "Yo, Terrence, that must be the equivalent of a coffee break. It's called a cocktail break."

"You clowns need to take this act on the road," I said, amused by their wisecracks.

Between the two of them, the laughs kept coming. I was enjoying their company so much, I ended up joining them for dinner. Terrence and Malik were a welcome distraction and badly needed cure for the blues.

I HAD MANAGED TO AVOID CAIN FOR FIVE DAYS. He'd been blowing up my cell, home, and work phones, trying to track me down. His last message had been a mixture of anger and concern. He called me rude and inconsiderate for not returning his calls and then said he hoped everything was okay. I didn't have any words for him and had no intention of calling him back. Besides, he didn't need me. He had another woman to keep him warm at night. I'd let him figure out on his own why I had stepped off.

Milan was coming down to Rituals for lunch. As soon as she came through the door, I could tell she was upset about something. We sat at a table away from the lunchtime diners. I waited for her to start talking to find out what was bothering her. Yet another ritual I'd adopted—sitting face to face at a quiet table ready to resolve problems. I had an open door policy. Though usually the person across from me was an employee with a work-related gripe, my friends and I had spent many hours at the restaurant with the same mission—resolution.

She tapped her fingers on the table. "I may have to resign from my job."

"Now what?"

"That bastard, Eriq. I found out he's been trying to sabotage my chance at making partner."

"Why would he do that?"

"How about the little issue with his wife. Since she came home from the hospital, her memory started to return in bits and pieces. Eriq decided to fill in the blanks before she remembered everything. So his wife has given him an ultimatum, get rid of me or she'll alert the police about our involvement."

"I tried to tell you that this would come back to haunt you."

"That asshole has launched a smear campaign at the office that will more or less result in me never making partner."

"Can't you fight back?"

"Not without airing my dirty laundry. Jade, at this point, I'm ready to walk away."

"But you've worked so hard to get where you are."

"I'll have to start over somewhere else."

I didn't want to see that happen. "Let's try to figure something out before you do that," I said.

"I'm open to any ideas you can come up with."

"Why don't you come by tonight and we'll brainstorm. Bring your PJ's so you don't have to drive home late at night."

"Sounds like a plan." Milan got up to leave. "I can't stay for lunch; I'm working on a big case, but you can cook something tonight."

"Girl, get out of here. I'm not cooking. We can order Chinese."

"That'll work, too. Catch ya later."

STOMACHS BULGING FROM TOO MUCH CHICKEN LO MEIN, we were stretched out in the TV room weighing Milan's options for dealing with her situation at work. I was never one for quitting and didn't want Milan to throw in the towel just yet.

Milan, on the other hand, didn't appreciate that her fate was in the hands of a former lover. She wanted to leave before her reputation as an attorney was damaged.

"I have no one to blame for this situation but myself," she said.

"That's water under the bridge."

"I had a good man and I messed it up. Do you know, on that first night with Eriq, there was a moment when I could've stopped everything? We were in his office, partially disrobed, when his phone rang. It was his wife. I sat there telling myself to get up and get dressed. His wife calling at that moment was a sign. While he was talking to her, I actually said to myself that this wasn't right and that I shouldn't get intimate with this man. Then I turned right around and ignored my inner voice."

"We all do that sometimes."

"The sad thing is I didn't have any real feelings for Eriq. It was pure lust or maybe it was the excitement of doing something forbidden. Fucking a partner at the firm. A married man. No one knowing about it. That was the turn-on. I've always played things safe. For once I ventured outside of the box."

This was the most Milan had ever shared about her affair with Eriq. In the past, she would say "it just happened" and offer nothing more as an explanation. Surely, she didn't think things would come to this.

"We were spending too much damn time together. He knew

what he was doing. He ignored me enough for me to wonder why, then charmed me enough until I wanted more and more. He sucked me into his game and my stupid ass fell for it," Milan said.

"Stop being so hard on yourself. You can't change what already happened."

Milan's eyes were full of desperation. "What have I done?"

"Made a few mistakes…"

Milan wasn't listening to me. She was finally letting out what she'd been holding in for so long. I let her speak uninterrupted. She told me how awful it was to go to work every day fearful that Eriq's lies were circulating throughout the entire firm, scared that her well-deserved reputation as a hot-shot lawyer was deteriorating. She tried to avoid Wallace Black whenever she could. She didn't know what he may have heard. Milan was spending sleepless nights stressing over what was said and who heard what. She put up a good front in the office but she was full of fear…and regret. To lay with another woman's husband, never in a million years did she think she was capable of such an act. What bothered her most was how much she'd enjoyed doing it. Her affair with Eriq had ignited a fire inside of her. It was a foreign feeling—being the bad girl. They carried on their indiscretions for five whole months. According to Milan, it was a confusing five months. Where she felt guilt and regret, she also felt alive. Her secret fueled her, energized her, excited her. Her lovemaking with Nolan was different as a result. She was less inhibited, more giving, totally adventurous. And it didn't go without notice. Nolan was curious to know what had caused Milan's transformation. She explained that it was natural for women to peak sexually at her age. She said that she was simply responding to her body's demands.

The hardest part for her was lying to Nolan. She couldn't ignore her wrongdoing when she looked into his eyes and spoke untruths. Milan said she repeatedly told herself that she would end it with

Eriq, but she didn't. She'd kept going back for more. She had become what she despised—a cheater and a hypocrite.

"How many times did I reprimand you for staying with Bryce after he disrespected you?" Milan asked.

It was a rhetorical question; she wasn't really looking for an answer. Confessions continued to pour out of her. She said she had preached one thing and lived another. She had treated Nolan the same way Bryce had treated me. Disrespected the man she loved. She said it became hard to look at herself in the mirror. That was the reason why she'd refused to share the sordid details with me. She was a hypocrite.

"The day I got busted was the worst day of my life. Nolan called me a whore. I didn't even want to know what you thought of me."

I remembered that day all too well. Nolan had left Milan's house and had driven straight to mine. He was physically shaking when he came in. Picture this big, football player type falling to pieces. Twice he had to run to my bathroom because he was on the verge of throwing up. Nolan was repulsed by what he had seen in the pictures. He told me what was in them and I didn't believe it. I asked over and over if he was certain it was Milan. He yelled at me as if I were the one cheating on him. Screamed at the top of his lungs that she was a tramp; accused me of knowing the entire time. I assured Nolan that I was just as horrified as he was at Milan being photographed performing oral sex on some man. I knew nothing about it. At first, I thought Nolan had to be mistaken but when Milan called, crying, I realized it was the truth. Nolan snatched the phone from my hand and called Milan every kind of loose woman imaginable. I had to pry the phone from his clenched fingers; no easy feat. I told Milan I'd call her back as soon as I calmed Nolan down. That never happened. His verbal rampage turned to bewildered tears. Nolan experienced an emotional meltdown. At that moment, I was angry with Milan, too. She had one of the good guys and she crushed him. I knew the feeling all too well. Betrayal was an unforgettable bitch. Though I didn't believe it, I'd tried to convince Nolan that there had to be a reasonable explanation and I promised I'd find out what I could. He knew his eyes hadn't deceived him, yet there was still a glimmer of hope in them. I'd seen that glimmer in my own eyes many times before.

I consoled Nolan as best as I could. When he heard Bryce coming in, he collected himself and prepared to leave. I hugged him and told him to call if he needed me. He and Bryce exchanged a brief greeting and then he left.

Bryce wanted to know what was going on and I unleashed my own pent-up anger on him. I cursed him out, called him a cheating mofo who didn't deserve to be with me. He thought I was crazy. It was funny how your own feelings of hurt resurfaced when you heard someone else's similar experience.

When I finally called Milan back that night—after Bryce and I finished the fight I started—she refused to elaborate on anything. She admitted she had cheated with Eriq and told me about the confrontation with his wife, but that was it, never a discussion on what led to the cheating.

I brought my mind back to the present.

"Have you spoken to Nolan?" I asked.

"No. He could barely look at me the day we met for lunch at Rituals. When he did, he looked at me like he wanted it to be the last time. I could see the pain I inflicted on him in his eyes. Nolan asked for space so I haven't tried to contact him. Have you spoken to him?"

"We've had a couple of conversations. I didn't want to mention it because I didn't want to upset you."

"I can't feel any worse than I already do. Did he ask about me?"

I lied. "The last time we spoke, he asked how you were doing."

Milan cocked her head to the side. "You are the worst liar. I don't know why you even try."

I fidgeted in the chair. "What are you talking about?"

"I appreciate the effort, Jade, but I know Nolan didn't mention me."

"Okay. He might not have asked but he wanted to."

Milan smiled. "If it's meant to be…"

"Yeah," I said, feeling a bit melancholy.

"Why are you sounding depressed? Your love life is all good."

"That's what you think. I haven't spoken to Cain in days and please don't ask me why."

"Why?"

"You don't know how to follow instructions, do you?"

"Nope. What happened?"

"I saw him with his ex-girlfriend and they didn't seem to be broken up to me."

"Well, what did he say about it?"

"He didn't. I've been avoiding him. He doesn't even know I saw them together."

"Jade, I would at least give him a chance to explain himself."

"What for? My eyes don't lie."

"Contrary to what you may think, you don't always know everything."

That was why I wasn't going to mention this to Milan. Now I had to defend my decision as to why I was no longer involved with a man who had a girlfriend.

"I may not know everything but I know what I saw. So can we drop it?"

"And I know what I see every time I see the two of you together.

A man who cares deeply for you. You owe him an opportunity to explain."

"Let's get back to fixing your problems. I'm not interested in repairing mine."

We stopped talking about men and got back to business. We weighed the pros and cons of Milan leaving the firm or staying to fight. By the end of the night, I was convinced Milan would not only have her partnership, but Eriq would be doing everything in his power to make it happen.

25

Bria came into the kitchen cracking her whip at two waiters that were neglecting their tables. I was busy plating a slice of banana cheesecake for the dessert tray and hadn't noticed them goofing off in the corner. I thought she came in the back looking for them but she came over and stood in front of me.

"There's someone out front waiting to see you."

"I don't have any appointments today." I wiped my hands on a dishtowel. "Can you finish this? I was about to drizzle the rum sauce over it."

I pushed through the swinging doors and Cain was standing at the hostess station. As I approached the station, Cain turned to walk out the restaurant; I followed. He was seated on the bench, leaning forward, forearms resting on his thighs, hands tightly clasped. I took my time reaching him.

"Can you sit down, please?"

I sat at the opposite end of the bench, blankly staring at him.

He spoke in a low, gruff voice. "I'm not sure what's going on but I deserve an explanation."

I was unfazed.

He continued. "I've called, left numerous messages and still, not a word from you." He stopped talking and mirrored my expression.

I broke my silence. "First of all, I don't owe you anything, but since you came down here, I'll satisfy your curiosity. I haven't returned your calls because I figured you had your hands full with Chivon."

"Chivon?"

"Yes, you do know who I'm talking about right? Chivon…your ex-girlfriend. My bad, I mean your girlfriend."

"Where did you get that? I told you Chivon and I broke up years ago."

"I know what you told me but I also know that you can't believe everything you hear."

"What would make you think Chivon and I are still together?"

"You did, actually. I was lucky enough to be at the right place at the right time."

Cain's eyes widened. At that moment, I could almost see the light bulb switch on. "So that was you speeding out of the parking lot the other night?"

"Right after I saw you hugging and kissing your girlfriend."

"Jade, it's not what you think."

"Then why don't you enlighten me."

Cain went on to explain that I was right; it was indeed Chivon that he was with that night. However, she was there for the private party that was held earlier in the evening. It was a thirtieth birthday party for her friend, Tioni, the girl with the blond hair. After the party, Chivon had stayed behind, saying that she had a few things she wanted to discuss with Cain. They chatted over drinks, having a conversation that was long overdue. She admitted it was unfair for her to blame him for the loss of their baby and apologized for putting that burden on him.

They finally had a chance to discuss their feelings and mourn their loss together, something they had never done since she'd had shut him out so many years ago. Chivon told him she'd been in a relationship with a wonderful man for the past year and they were engaged to be married. She also let Cain know she had seen me partying at the club in Harlem and confessed that she acted like a bitch toward me. When he asked her why, she explained that seeing me with him at Eden had made her jealous. Even though she had moved on with her life, she couldn't help feeling jealous because Cain never looked at her the way she had seen him looking at me that day.

When I had seen them the other night, Chivon was about to leave. The hug and kiss that I had seen was their moment of closure. There was nothing romantic to the kiss and if it looked like it, it was because they were both emotional from discussing their loss as parents.

I was so ashamed. "I'm sorry, Cain." For a person who's never wrong, again I was apologizing to someone. "I misinterpreted the situation and I jumped to the wrong conclusion. When I saw you, I couldn't believe you were with someone else. I started to question everything that had transpired between us."

"All I want to know is can we move forward?"

"I would like that...but I still have one question."

"What is that?"

"Why didn't you tell me it was Chivon when I saw her in Eden the first time?"

"I hadn't seen Chivon since we had broken up. I was shocked when I saw her walk through the door with Tioni. They came in to book Tioni's party. I didn't want you to feel uncomfortable or think there was something between us. As far as I was concerned, she was my past and I was looking at my future. I didn't discuss her because I didn't want to put any doubt in your mind about us. In retrospect, I definitely should've mentioned she was my ex-girlfriend, but at the time I thought it served no purpose. You and I had just shared an intimate evening at my house, in the Jacuzzi, and I didn't want anything to overshadow that. That's why I had no problem ending the conversation I was having with them or even holding your hand in front of her."

So many things ran through my head. First off, I should've told

Cain what I had seen; we could've straightened things out days ago. In a short amount of time, my feelings for Cain had grown in ways I could've never expected. I kept telling myself that things seemed too perfect and I was waiting for something to go wrong. I used the incident with Chivon as a way to prove that I was right for thinking things weren't always as they seemed; however, my proof wasn't what I thought it was.

Now I was sitting next to this man who I thought couldn't be trusted and I was the one at fault. What happened the other night between Bryce and me shouldn't have happened, but it had. I needed to clear my conscience and hoped that Cain would understand.

I was nervous and didn't know where to begin. "I apologize for not returning your calls. When I saw you with your ex-girlfriend, I thought the worst about you. I know firsthand how difficult it is to get an ex out of your life. I've been trying to—"

"It's not difficult when you've found someone that makes you happy. There's no room for an ex in my life and I think you feel the same."

I couldn't continue. What would be the purpose of telling him that Bryce and I had shared a kiss? I certainly couldn't bring myself to say that we were both naked but didn't have sex. My imagination had run wild after I had seen Cain and Chivon. What type of thoughts would he have if I mentioned that I had come close to sleeping with Bryce but had changed my mind at the last minute? I decided it was best not to say anything. If I tried hard enough, I could actually convince myself that what happened between me and Bryce was just a kiss. Right?

Cain distracted me from my thoughts. "What was that look for? You do believe me about Chivon, don't you?"

"Of course I do."

"Once I realized you obviously weren't speaking to me, I thought you must've had second thoughts about us. I tried to figure out what I had done wrong. The only conclusion I could come up with was that when we first started seeing each other, you'd just ended a relationship. I thought maybe we were moving too fast for you or maybe you got back with him."

I shook my head and swallowed the lump in my throat. "I'm relieved that we were able to resolve this."

"Is there something else bothering you?"

"No."

Cain moved closer to me on the bench. "I missed you all week."

"That makes two of us," I said, wishing I could shake my feelings of guilt.

"Promise me one thing. The next time something is wrong, talk to me about it."

"I will."

"Can I come over tonight?" he asked.

"Why don't I come over to your place? I have a meeting not far from you and I can shoot over there afterward."

I didn't want to risk Bryce dropping by while Cain was at my house. I needed to make sure Bryce and I were on the same page after the other night. That was definitely a setback in terms of the boundaries I had already established between us.

"Alright, I'll see you at my house later on." Cain stood up to leave. "You sure you aren't going to disappear on me again?" he said jokingly.

I got up and hugged him. "I wouldn't do that. I'll be over later."

After we shared a brief kiss, I watched him walk to his car and drive off. I was relieved things were okay between us, but at the same time, I was unsettled about the other night with Bryce. I turned to go back inside the restaurant and was startled by Bria standing on the steps looking at me. I walked past her.

She pursed her lips. "It must be hard juggling two men."

I ignored her and went inside. I hadn't mentioned what had occurred with Bryce and me, but I was sure that he didn't spare any details. He never did. I refused to stay under her judgmental eye for the rest of the day, so I collected my things and took off. I called Bryce from my cell phone and asked him to meet me at the park. I was going to run a couple of miles and figured he could run with me, sort of like the old days.

I WAS ON THE GRASS STRETCHING WHEN HE ARRIVED. He peacocked over to me like he owned the world. He was in great shape and he realized it. He sat down on the grass in front of me and extended his hands so we could help each other stretch. He leaned back, pulling me forward, stretching my hamstrings, then I leaned back pulling him into a stretch. When we were warmed up and limber, we started our run.

We ran through the park at a comfortable pace. On the phone, Bryce had asked why I wanted to meet but I told him that I needed to speak to him in person.

"It's beautiful out today," I said, trying to set the tone with small talk. "Not much humidity, which is rare for this time of year."

"You didn't ask me to meet you to talk about the weather."

Obviously he wasn't in the mood for small talk.

I abandoned the chitchat and got to the point. "I want us to be friends, Bryce. There are too many years between us for us to be at each other's throats."

"I want more than that."

"Can't be any other way."

"You seeing someone?"

"Not important."

He stopped running. I slowed down and then came to a halt a few yards ahead of him. I waited for him to walk up to me.

"We should be civil. Friends. Nothing more," I reinforced.

"What about the other night?"

"It shouldn't have happened."

"Is that all you wanted to tell me?" he asked.

"Yes."

"Okay, *friend*."

Bryce shot off, leaving me standing there watching his back. He was hoping for a different outcome, but it wasn't possible. I turned and sprinted in the opposite direction.

I zipped along the path, feeling as if a weight had been lifted. Bryce finally understood that we were through. I could move forward with Cain guilt-free. I ran fast. I had lost time to make up and Cain was waiting.

26

Cain and I sat in my parents' backyard snacking on chips while my father grilled his famous blue cheese burgers. We were leaving for Antigua in a week and I thought it was a good idea to bring Cain by to meet them before we left.

My father could get along with just about anyone. He liked to talk and appreciated a good conversationalist. My mother wasn't so easily won over. She was more of a listener, always ready to pounce if someone said something out of line. But I wasn't worried; Cain can hold his own. All he had to do was be himself and I knew my parents would find that he was good enough to be with their daughter. Already he and my father had discussed everything from sports to politics and shared many of the same views. My mother was impressed with his business endeavors and had probably determined that he would be able to support me if it ever came down to it.

I went in the house to help my mother with the salad. She gave me one of her looks. "Now I know why we barely see you these days."

"You see me all the time."

"He's a good-looking man."

I smiled. It amused me when my mother tried to have girl talk with me. She went back and forth between mother and friend.

"Mom, he is not only fine, but smart, sensitive, caring, generous...you name it."

"So he makes you happy?"

"Extremely."

"What about you-know-what?"

"What?"

"How is he in bed?"

"Maaaa! I can't believe you asked me that." I covered my face.

"You didn't think I thought you were a virgin?"

"Do we have to have this conversation? You're embarrassing me."

"Jade, please. You're a grown woman. I understand that you have sex. If you didn't, I would think something was wrong with you...so?"

"It's fine, Mom." I couldn't help wanting to run out of the kitchen.

"Looking at that strapping man, I'm sure it's better than fine."

I started backing out the room. "I'm going outside. I can see you don't need my help in here."

My mother's laughter followed me into the backyard. Cain and my father wore puzzled expressions at my mother's outburst. I told them don't even ask.

"Dad, did Cain tell you that he plays golf?"

"Yes, he did. We already agreed to get together some time soon for a round."

"I'm going to take your father to the course in Douglaston where I play with my Pop."

"My dad is a beginner so you go easy on him," I said.

Cain winked at me across the table. I looked to see if my father caught it and he winked at me, too. That was my father's way of telling me that he had seen the exchange and also giving Cain the thumbs-up.

My mother came out the back door with the salad and my brother in tow. I didn't know he was coming over. I introduced him to Cain and he joined us at the table. He gave me a slick look after shaking Cain's hand. I expected a smart comment about my rapid rebound the next time we were alone. If there was one thing I knew, it was how my brother's brain worked.

Terrence and my dad immediately started talking business. Even though my father had retired, he liked to know what was going on with the company at all times.

I asked Terrence, "Is everything set for next week?"

"No, Jade," he replied. "I meant to tell you…nothing is ready."

"Stop playing with me."

"Then stop asking questions you already know the answers to."

"Well, I won't be here so I'm asking you now."

"Sis, I got this. If I need anything or a decision needs to made on something, then I'll ask Bria."

"You can always leave a message on my cell or my machine at home. I can check it from Antigua."

"Chill out."

I dropped it. Between my brother and my father, things would go smoothly.

Cain took advantage of the opportunity to pick the brains of two architects at one time. He had made the decision to build Eden2 in Atlanta and was asking my father and brother a few things that he had concerns about. Little did he know, those two would never stop talking about their craft. We had long finished eating and I'd left the table and come back a few times and they were still going at it.

A few hours later, I literally had to drag Cain away from their discussion on cars, boats, and whatever else they were rambling about. It was time for us to leave and he was acting like he wanted to stay all night.

I said my goodbyes to everyone and when I hugged my brother, he whispered that Cain was cool; not like that loser, Bryce. I pushed him and told him that I was glad I had his approval and suggested that the next time, he bring his harem with him. He pushed me back. I was about to shove him when my mother stepped between us and reminded us to act like the adults we were supposed to be.

On the drive home, Cain and I talked about all the things we wanted to do in Antigua. I wanted to do the shopping and sight-seeing; he wanted to go jet skiing, scuba diving, and hiking. We compromised somewhere in the middle with eating and relaxing. I could barely contain my excitement and couldn't wait to get there.

27

E riq arrived at the office at six in the morning, greeted by a cigar box on the center of his desk. It was a box of Cuban cigars that the founding partner, Wallace Black, gave to the attorneys to reward a job well done.

Walking around the desk, Eriq patted himself on the back. It was the first time Wallace had graced him with the expensive smokes. He thought it must've been for the big medical malpractice case that he had won.

Eriq put his feet up on the desk and opened the lid on the box. He froze. Inside the box was a tape recorder, not cigars. He jumped up from the desk and ran to his office door. There were no other attorneys in yet but he closed it to be safe.

His hands shook as he pressed the play button. Female voices spoke one after the other. Each voice saying something different, yet the same.

*I slept with Eriq on numerous occasions…Eriq told me he was going to leave his wife… Can you believe that bastard said if his wife didn't pull through, he would need me to get him through the hard times? … We fucked in the office after everyone left for the night… He told me he wasn't married…. Eriq forced me to do it …Eriq made me uncomfortable with his constant groping… He loved to fuck in the supply closet… He threatened to fire me if I didn't give him a little taste… Eriq said that he was divorced…*the comments went on and on.

Eriq recognized each and every voice from Ashley to Zena. They were all paralegals who worked for the firm at one time or another. Many of them still did. A tape like that could ruin him. He pounded the desk with his fists.

Over the years, he had had a hard time trying to resist all those cute asses in those tight little skirts. But they knew better than to kiss and tell. Eriq loosened his tie and rested his head in his hands. His nerves were shot. He counted to ten to calm himself.

He rationalized—the women were all consenting. He distorted—they were disgruntled employees with an ax to grind. He denied—they were lying.

The voices stopped. Eriq welcomed the silence until another woman started to speak. This time it was only her voice, no one else.

I loved fucking Eriq. We shared a lot of good times. When his wife was out of town, we would even make love, if you could call it that, in their bed. I didn't care he had a wife; what Eriq and I shared was special. I couldn't have him all the time, but I was happy to take what I could get…

Eriq broke into a cold sweat. That was Chanel Black, Wallace's daughter, speaking on the tape. The forbidden fruit. The most enticing of them all. He couldn't turn away from her long legs and lowcut blouses. Her body called out to him and he had to answer. He didn't care that Chanel was the boss's daughter.

Eriq removed the bottle of Johnny Walker Blue from his bottom drawer and took a swig.

…He made promises, lots of them. He said he was going to leave his wife, but he didn't have to. I was fine with the situation. I knew what I was getting. Eriq and I would take weekend trips upstate and stay in cozy bed and breakfasts. He told me that he loved me and I believed him. So I dealt with his situation. I accepted that he had a wife at home. Like I said, I could deal with just about anything…anything…except for the fact that Eriq was also sleeping with my mother…

Eriq shut off the tape. He couldn't listen to anymore. His shirt was sticking to his back, drenched with perspiration. He shoved the recorder back into the cigar box and buried it in his desk. He scrambled to the door, sticking his head out into the hallway to make sure no one was loitering, then dashed to the bathroom. He splashed water on his face over and over, trying to wake up from his nightmare.

The bathroom door opened and Wallace walked in. "Good morning, Eriq. I thought I was the only one who came in this early."

Eriq snatched a few hand towels to dry his face. He did his best to sound normal but only managed a falsetto, "*Good morning.*"

"You don't look so good. Are you feeling alright?"

"I may be coming down with the flu or something."

Wallace patted Eriq on the back. "You'd better take care of that. I want to see you this afternoon. I need to make a final decision on the new partners and I want to get your opinion on a few things."

"Yes, Sir," Eriq muttered.

Wallace left the bathroom.

Eriq checked himself in the mirror. His face was drawn and ashy. He was nauseous. His shirt was no longer crisp but damp and crumpled. With slumped shoulders, he ambled back to his office and slammed the door behind him.

28

Milan had sounded so excited on the phone that I had taken the liberty of setting up a bottle of champagne at a table in the back. She was almost running when she came through the doors. I stepped out from behind the hostess station and she grabbed me in a tight hug. She was jumping up and down so I joined in. I held her hand and pulled her to the champagne that was waiting for her. I poured her a glass and then filled mine.

Milan cleared her throat. "You're looking at the newest partner at Stowe, Black, and Helms."

I beamed with pride. "Congratulations. I knew you could do it, Girl."

We tapped glasses and took a sip before sitting down.

"I wouldn't be here, if it weren't for you," Milan said. "I wanted to quit."

"You're a partner because you deserve to be. I simply helped you get past the road block. Now tell me what happened."

In true lawyerly fashion, Milan told me every single detail of her encounter with Eriq. When she arrived at work, she wasn't in her office for five minutes before he busted down the door, making accusations. She was calm and didn't let him rattle her. He'd gone on and on about her not knowing who he was and that she wouldn't get away with what she was trying to do. Milan didn't respond. She let Eriq tire himself out with his tantrum and once he crumbled in the chair like the broken man he was, she launched her attack.

Milan lashed out at him for trying to ruin her reputation and career. He sat, listening like a little child, as she chewed him out for the way he had handled the situation. She told him that he had two options. He could either do damage control and recommend to Wallace that he make her a partner, or he could hand in his resignation. Eriq went crazy when she told him to submit his resignation. He ranted that he could fight it and told Milan that the tape was nothing, that he could talk his way out of it, that she didn't have any real proof. That was when Milan slid a manila envelop across the desk. His hands were shaking when he picked it up and opened it. She wasn't sure if he was trembling because of fear or anger, but she was enjoying it just the same. Eriq stared at Milan's proof, pictures of him cheating with Wallace's wife. His mouth fell open. He asked Milan how she had gotten a hold of the pictures. She informed him that it was amazing what you could get when you talk to the right people.

The paralegals had been easy. Milan provided me with a list of twelve paralegals she wanted to "interview" and told me that we had to act quickly. I called the girls, one by one, at the law firm, informing them that they had been entered in a drawing by a coworker and had won a free lunch at Rituals. I set three lunch appointments a day—starting at eleven and ending at two—over the course of four days. Milan took over from there. She met the scheduled girl in front of Rituals and led her to a quiet table we had designated for the occasion. I instructed my staff not to interrupt the meetings. I served as their waitress. After I took the orders Milan, worked her magic.

She had a great relationship with the paralegals and always treated them with respect, unlike the other predominantly male attorneys. She simply asked about Eriq and they sang like birds— told every nasty detail. She had also promised them the tape wouldn't go any further than Eriq's ears. She told the girls to look forward to a change around the office. Milan knew once she had Chanel on board, she would only have to play the tape to one person, Eriq.

Milan asked Chanel to meet her for lunch, launching phase two of the plan. Since Chanel had been doing her externship at the firm, she viewed Milan as a mentor and they had become pretty close. Milan had always heard the rumors about Eriq and the paralegals, but she wasn't sure about Chanel's involvement with him. She decided she was going to come out and ask her if they were true. Chanel told her everything. Milan realized that after Chanel was so honest with her, she would have to give a little to get a little. She didn't mention the accident, but she confided in Chanel about her own affair with Eriq and how he was jeopardizing her promotion. She asked Chanel for her help. Chanel heard our plan and agreed to let Milan record the intimate details of her liaison as long as Milan promised that her father would never hear the tape. Chanel had been played by Eriq and wanted Milan to take him down.

Chanel told Milan that her feelings about Eriq had begun to change when she had seen him being extremely attentive to her mother at a dinner party at her parents' house. After that night, her mother would be missing for hours on end and it always coincided with Eriq's unaccounted-for time. Chanel had hired an investigator to follow her mother and he had delivered to her the pictures that would ultimately seal Eriq's fate. Chanel had not yet decided what to do with the photos. Milan's trouble made it easy for her to get Eriq away from her mother without hurting either of her parents.

ERIQ BECAME QUITE COMPLIANT, BEGGING MILAN not to go to
Wallace with the information. Milan ran down her list of
demands. She had told him not only did she want his recommen-
dation, but he was to retract every negative comment he made
about her to the partners. She had also insisted that he get a
handle on the situation with his wife. She would be damned if
that woman would be the demise of her career. Milan knew
Eriq's wife would not risk losing her husband. She had so many
opportunities to leave him and never had. She was all bark and
no bite. Milan made Eriq call his wife on the speakerphone and
tell her that he had done his best to get Milan fired but Wallace
wouldn't hear of it; he thought she was too valuable to the firm.
Eriq swore to his wife that she had nothing to worry about—
nothing would ever happen between him and Milan again—that
he wanted to go for marriage counseling. He called Milan a
tramp with no class who could never compare to what he had in
his beautiful wife. Milan had made him add that line. She figured
his wife would eat up the flattery and be more prone to believe
that he had no interest in a tramp. By the end of the call, Eriq
had his wife eating out of the palm of his hand and she wasn't
thinking about Milan.

Milan told Eriq that she expected the utmost professionalism
from him and as far as she was concerned the situation was
behind them. With a wave of her hand, she dismissed him from
her office. Later that afternoon, Wallace had met with her and
delivered the good news. She had made partner.

"You made partner...I'm so proud of you," I said.

"Even though I had to get a little grimy?"

"Especially because you got down and dirty. You fought back
and that's what I'm proud of."

"I feel like I'm finally back on track. I've learned so much from this."

"What, to keep your legs closed in the workplace?"

"Definitely that!" Milan laughed. "But seriously, life is a game and you have to know how to play it. I sat back and played by Eriq's rules and he tried to screw me. I have to be on top of my game at all times. I'll never play by someone else's rules again."

"I hear that, my sister." I called a waiter over and asked him to get Bria from the kitchen.

Bria emerged from the kitchen and came over to the table, all smiles. "What are we celebrating?"

"The newest partner at Stowe, Black and Helms," I said.

"Congrats, Diva! Pour me a glass."

"Thank you, Bria. It feels so good to be me." Milan finished her drink. "I hate to leave you guys but a few of the lawyers at the firm are taking me out for drinks. I had to come over here first, though, to tell you the news."

"Don't drink too much, Partner," I instructed.

"Partner...I like the sound of that. Bye, Divas." Milan kissed us both on the cheek and then floated out the door.

"We should throw her a party when you get back from your trip," Bria said.

"A party is a good idea. We can have a small get together, celebrating our reopening and Lan's promotion."

Celebration. The ultimate ritual.

"I can't believe you're going to Antigua alone. Aren't you going to be bored?"

"I plan on getting spa treatments, doing some reading and plenty of relaxing."

"Where are you staying?"

There was no avoiding the topic. "I'll be at the Antiguan Palm Resort."

"I'm jealous. While you're off getting pampered, I'll be here teaching my night class."

"I'll do my best not to rub it in."

"I appreciate that."

"I'll refrain from mentioning that I'll be lying on the beach in a few days, or that I'll be poolside sipping daiquiris. I won't even bring up that I'll be swimming in warm tropical waters so clear you see the sand between your toes."

Bria rolled her eyes at me and then pinched me in the arm as she got up to return to the kitchen. "Have a good time, Diva."

29

I was squeezing a few small items into my overstuffed luggage when the doorbell rang. I wasn't expecting anyone so when I looked through the peephole, I was surprised to see Cain standing on my steps.

"Hey, Baby. Shouldn't you be at home packing?" I asked.

"I'm all packed but I need to talk to you."

"Come on in then."

He followed me into the living room. "Jade, I have to fly to Atlanta tomorrow. The engineer called and said he needs me down there. They ran into some construction problems on the restaurant site."

"We're supposed to be leaving tomorrow," I complained.

"I know, Baby, but I have to be in Atlanta as soon as possible. I want you to go on without me tomorrow and I'll come down the day after."

"I don't want to go without you. We can both leave the day after tomorrow."

"No, I want you to go ahead. You can start getting pampered, and by the time I arrive, you'll be ready for me."

I wasn't particularly happy with this last-minute development, but it couldn't be helped. I didn't want him to feel bad for having to take care of business. "Alright, Baby," I said. "I'll see you the day after tomorrow."

Cain sensed my disappointment. "I'll be there before you know it. You won't have a chance to miss me."

We kissed goodnight and Cain left. I finished my packing and then went to bed. My flight was leaving early in the morning and I wanted to get a good night's sleep.

THE AIRPLANE CABIN WAS SILENT, most people sleeping through the six-hour trip. I didn't sleep on planes. I liked to take the time to absorb the glory and wonder of the Almighty's creations, like the never-ending blue sky that wasn't always visible through the clouds when my feet were firmly planted on the ground, or the rays of the sun, unfiltered, shining in my eyes without being reflected through pollution-induced haze. I stared out my window at the billowy white clouds below, imagining they were a soft, feathery mattress to lie down upon. There was no way I could sleep through this.

The captain announced that we were beginning our descent. We came through the clouds and I marveled at the ocean in shades of blue and green, gently rippling, the sun glistening off the surface. No matter how many times I traveled to the Caribbean, I fell in love all over again with the crystal clear water. I wouldn't set foot in the water in New York; its murky gray color and odor to match was beyond frightening.

I looked down on the small uninhabited islands scattered in the ocean. I wouldn't have minded being stranded on one of them with Cain. We could catch fresh fish and cook it over an open flame. Okay, maybe I was getting a little carried away. There was no way in hell I could've lived without my kitchen and a roof over my head.

The plane touched down and I was brimming with excitement. I stepped off the plane into a gorgeously hot, sunny day with low humidity and a light island breeze. I bustled through the crowded airport and waited in the long line to get through customs.

A couple with three busy children were behind me in the line.

The youngest child hollered at the top of his lungs the entire time while his older sister kept running in circles around me. The parents, of course, were oblivious to the havoc their children were wreaking. I kept my cool because in a moment, I'd be on the beach, drink in hand.

Outside the airport, cab drivers saw that I was traveling alone and bombarded me. I respectfully declined and located the shuttle to my resort. There were two couples already seated in the van. The driver got in, verified we were all going to the right hotel and then pulled into traffic.

I engaged in polite conversation with the couples during our drive to the hotel. Some people were so free with their information. Within a few minutes time, I knew where the people lived, what they did for a living, about their families, and if I had asked, I probably could've gotten their social security numbers.

The van drove through the resort gates, entering a luxurious estate with acres of lush, sprawling lawns surrounded by tropical gardens. We pulled in front of the hotel and the driver unloaded the van. A bellman immediately retrieved my bags and brought them inside the hotel.

Fabulous columns and sparkling marble floors graced the elegant lobby. I went to the front desk to check-in and the young lady already knew who I was. I read her name tag and was certain I didn't know anyone named Colette. She explained that she had received a call from my travel companion and he'd informed her that he wouldn't be arriving until tomorrow, but he wanted to make sure my name was on the reservation. Colette commented that my companion described his beautiful lady friend perfectly. Cain was so thoughtful. She handed me the key to my villa and told me someone would be over in a little while to familiarize me with the spa services offered at the hotel. She signaled for a bellman to take me over to the residence, as she called it.

We took a short jeep ride to the other side of the resort. The property was enormous. The bellman parked the jeep in front of a villa the size of a single family home on Long Island. I stepped from the truck in disbelief that Cain had gone to this extreme. I was expecting a hotel suite, nothing this extravagant.

I went up the cobblestone path to the residence and walked through the door into an airy villa. I waited in the foyer, checking out the décor, while the bellman went upstairs to take my bags to the bedroom. He quickly returned, thanked me for the tip I handed him, and left me to explore the place.

Linen-colored walls and terracotta tile extended from the foyer down the hallway. I meandered into the living room and was greeted by three dozen red roses. I read the card.

Missing You...Love Cain

I took a rose from the vase and sniffed it. I carried it with me as I walked through the rest of the villa. The living room led outside to a patio that you could step off and be right on the beach. In the kitchen there was a Viking range and refrigerator filled with water, fruit juice, and soda. The breakfast nook sat in front of a large picture window that made you feel like you were looking at a painting of the ocean.

I went to check out the upstairs. Two bedrooms, two baths, and a sitting room, more room than Cain and I possibly needed. The master suite was inviting with its queen canopy bed draped with gossamer fabric. French doors opened to a terrace and a light breeze swept through the room.

I began to unpack my bags. I had packed too many things for one week. I hung my outfits, ranging from cut-off shorts to linen dresses, in the closet. There wasn't much closet space left for Cain's clothing. I put my lingerie into the drawers and arranged my toiletries on the counter in the bathroom.

By the time I finished unpacking, I could hear the shower calling my name. I gathered my bathing essentials and turned the water on in the steam shower big enough to fit ten.

I stayed in there for at least a half-hour, letting the steam invigorate me. Clean and refreshed, wearing my plush new robe, I traipsed downstairs for a bottle of cranberry juice. I sat in the living room and looked out onto the beach. I was considering whether I wanted to call in for room service or get dressed to go out and eat at one of the many restaurants at the resort when there was a knock at the door. I tightened the sash on my robe and went to answer. Colette told me to expect someone to come conduct a profile for my specialized spa treatments. I was prepared to tell them to leave the literature, that I'd read and fill it out later.

I opened the door and my mouth dropped open. There stood Bryce, smiling like the Cheshire Cat.

"Surprised?" he asked.

That was an understatement. It took a second for my brain to register what my eyes were looking at. I blinked a few times, not sure I was seeing what I thought I saw.

I closed my mouth, then emphatically started shaking my head. "Oh, hell no," I said.

"I was in the neighborhood and thought I'd drop by." Bryce laughed at his own joke. "Not funny? Okay, how about I had business in Antigua and heard you would be here at the same time as me?"

My mind couldn't formulate the words to express the emotions I was feeling. I closed my eyes, praying that when I opened them, he wouldn't be standing there. Unfortunately, he was.

My mouth finally started working. "How about this one? Your sister told you that I was here and somehow you got it twisted that you were invited to join me. What the hell do you think you are doing? I can't believe you're stalking me. Why would you just show up here?" My voice was pleading with him, begging him to disappear.

"Can I come in?"

"No, you can't come in. I came to Antigua to get away, to relax, to regroup. *You* don't fit into those plans."

"Are you here to think about us?"

"Bryce, what fucking planet are you on? There is no us! How many times can I say it? There...is...no...us! Don't pop up at my house, don't call my phone with your hang ups, and stop speeding up and down my street on your motorcycle. Yeah, that's right, I knew that was you."

The smile slid from his face. He gritted his teeth, speaking through tight lips. "You think my feelings aren't worth shit, don't you?" He leaned in close to my face. "Don't you?" he yelled.

I jumped. "Bryce, that isn't— "

"I get it now," he said, talking over me. "You told me that you didn't want anything to do with me and I didn't listen. I had to give it one more try. I came here to show you that I was serious and made a fool of myself, following behind you, hoping that you would take me back."

Just that fast, he calmed down, was acting like he hadn't been upset a few seconds ago.

I measured my words carefully. "We're through, Bryce. Following me here wasn't right and you can't stay."

"The next plane leaves in a couple of hours. I'll be on it."

I opened my mouth to respond but he hurried down the walkway toward the direction of the hotel.

The first thing that crossed my mind was thank goodness Cain wasn't arriving until tomorrow. I didn't like this feeling. I was going to have to tell Cain what had been going on with Bryce lately. Bryce's behavior was becoming unpredictable and irrational to the point where I hardly recognized him.

I called the front desk to see if Bryce was registered at the hotel as a guest. He wasn't. I breathed a sigh of relief. I played it safe and ordered dinner to the villa. I didn't want to take the chance of bumping into him if he was still on the resort premises.

A nice breeze blew through the villa. I wandered out onto the patio. There was a beige rope hammock hanging from two coconut trees. I climbed in it and let the light winds swing my body from side to side.

I must've dozed off because I woke up to the setting sun and the doorbell ringing. I almost broke my neck, trying to leap from the hammock.

I opened the door and the server pushed in a cart full of covered dishes. I had only ordered a caesar salad. He arranged the dishes on the table, then removed the lids revealing my salad, assorted breads, a bowl of fresh cut fruit, and a slice of rum cake. He placed a bottle of red wine on the table, filled a glass with sparkling water, then pulled my chair out for me. After inquiring if I needed anything else, he politely excused himself.

I carried my salad and water from the table to the sofa and turned on the television. I stumbled across one of my favorite movies from back in the day; *New Jack City* with Wesley Snipes. I had seen that movie too many times to count but I was always drawn to Wesley playing the hell out of his Nino Brown character. I got comfortable on the sofa and ate my dinner.

It wasn't long before the movie was watching me. I had managed to eat the salad, but the fruit and cake was in the refrigerator. I did have a glass of wine, which most likely was the true catalyst for me falling asleep on the couch, coupled with getting up at five in the morning. I slept soundly, curled up on the soft sofa.

A noise jarred me from my sleep. I lay still and listened for a moment. The front door was opening. I wondered if it was someone from the hotel coming to retrieve my dishes. Perhaps they rang the bell and I didn't hear it.

I sat up, straightened my robe, and quietly crept around the corner to the foyer where I was met by Cain coming through the door with his bag. I screamed.

"I hope that means you're happy to see me," he said.

Cain dropped his bag in the doorway and I ran over to hug him. I held him by the face and kissed him hard. "You're early."

He hugged me again, lifting me off my feet. "If you could've seen your face last night...I knew I had to get here tonight. I wrapped up my business by early afternoon and then caught the four o'clock flight to Antigua."

"I'm so glad you're here. I hated that I wasn't going to see you until late tomorrow."

He kissed me again. "How do you like the place?"

"Are you kidding me? I love it. Come see." I grabbed him by the hand and pulled him from room to room, highlighting what I loved about each one.

He stopped me before I could drag him upstairs. "Why don't you show me where the shower is? I could use one of those."

We went upstairs and I directed Cain toward the bathroom. When he walked into the bedroom, he commented that the villa was tight and he might never want to leave. I told him that I had thought the same thing when I had first arrived. The encounter with Bryce tried to edge its way into my thoughts but I pushed it aside. There would be time to discuss that.

I asked Cain how everything had gone in Atlanta. He said construction had hit a snag because of a discrepancy in the blueprints. He had called my brother to get his opinion on the problem. I hadn't realized that he had Terrence's number, but he told me that he tracked him down at Rituals. They had managed to resolve the problem without too much of a delay and he had hightailed it out of there.

"I have to head back to Atlanta right after our trip to check on their progress."

I couldn't stop smiling. I had planned to see the historical sites on the island by myself in the morning but now Cain could come with me. He settled in while I went on and on about all the brochures, detailing things we could see and do while we were there on the island. I was bombarding Cain with more information than he needed at the moment; all he wanted to do was to take a hot shower. I left him to unwind and went to flip through some more tour materials.

I was downstairs reading about scuba diving lessons for Cain when he called my name. I put the books down and went upstairs. He was standing in the middle of the bedroom with a towel wrapped around his waist.

He turned out the lights. "I wanted you to see this full moon."

We went out onto the terrace and looked up at the heavens. The moon, large with a yellow glow, illuminated the night sky. The stars looked close enough to reach out and touch. Cain stood behind me, wrapping his arms around me.

He slid his hands over my hips. "What are you wearing under there?"

"Nothing."

Cain moaned and turned me by my waist to face him. He untied my sash; my robe fell open. He reached inside my robe and drew my body to his. He kissed my forehead, the tip of my nose, my lips.

He lured me back inside the bedroom, leaving the french doors open.

I let my robe fall to the floor and tugged Cain's towel from his waist and let it drop. The moonlight cast our naked shadows across the room. I stepped closer and watched the space between the shadows disappear.

Cain pulled me down on the bed. A slow and seductive exploration of my body began, his lips touching every inch, no part being neglected. I lay on my stomach as he kissed down my spine. The sensation of his mouth, tasting and nibbling, sent pulses through me. I turned over and pulled Cain on top of me.

His mouth covered mine and my moans combined with his as our tongues connected. I sucked his bottom lip, gently biting and licking before sucking it again. I caressed the back of his head as we fell deeper and deeper into the kiss. We were feeding off of each other's intensity, reacting to the urgency, communicating without words. I wrapped my legs around his waist, invited him inside of me. Cain stared into my eyes as he rubbed his hardness in my wetness. He watched me as he eased inside. I closed my eyes and moaned.

"Open your eyes," he whispered. "I want you to see me feel you and I want to see you feeling me."

I reconnected with him, observed the effect that my good lovin' was having on him. With each thrust, I watched a subtle change in his face. I saw his pleasure escalating, which turned me on even more. His stroke was long and deep. My moans sounded more erotic with each meeting of our hips. I took in everything that made him a man, his mind, his body, his soul, his spirit. I wanted to close my eyes and lose myself in the moment, but couldn't. I didn't want to take my eyes off Cain. I loved seeing what I was doing to him.

Our rhythm transitioned from soft and smooth to hard and fast. I was drifting toward that special place. I matched Cain's pace in pursuit of my orgasm. The more my hips rolled, the more his brows wrinkled. His mouth alternated between hanging open and clenched teeth.

"I'm about to come!" I cried out, surrendering to the feeling.

Cain's eyes were glazing over and he struggled to keep them open. My wetness was all over him. He lost it. Cain shut his eyes and buried his face next to mine. He gripped my hips and slid in and out of me, repeating over and over how much he loved being inside of me. I raised my legs, opening them into a wide V, granting him full access. He worked the middle until he could go no deeper. I whispered in his ear that my nani belonged to him. He uttered a loud guttural moan as he let go and released his fluid. Cain held me tight while he slowed his stroke to a halt, mumbling incoherently. He lifted himself off my body and lay next to me.

Our cries of passion now silent, I could hear the sound of the ocean as it faintly drifted through the open doors. I closed my eyes and listened to the ebb and flow of the tide.

Cain shifted. "Jade, are you asleep?"

"No."

"I love you."

I wasn't expecting that. I opened my eyes. He was lying on his side, looking down at me. I was falling in love with him, too, but I didn't realize that we were at the stage where we would start saying it. I didn't know if I was ready to put myself out there yet.

"Are you sure you aren't caught up in the moment?" I said. "I mean, we're on a beautiful island…on a romantic night…"

"I'm in love with you, Jade, and it has nothing to do with where we are."

I stroked Cain's face. "You're right. It has nothing to do with the island…you're always in touch with your feelings and not afraid of them."

"That's not exactly true."

"What do you mean?" I asked.

"Do you remember the night I was at your house watching the game?"

I chuckled. "That could be just about any night you were over. Could you be a little more specific?"

"The night you were helping me plan the pool party."

I nodded. "I remember."

"We were in the kitchen and you asked was I always so easy-going."

I finished his sentence. "And you said when it comes to me."

"That was the moment I realized that I loved you."

I was a bit confused. "But you left me sitting on the counter and then refused to even look at me when I asked you what was wrong."

"At that moment in the kitchen, it hit me like a brick, and I wasn't prepared for it. The last time I loved someone...well, you know what happened. Then here you come and finally decide to take me seriously. You made me feel things I hadn't let myself feel in years. I was caught off guard by how fast my feelings for you had grown."

I sat up. "Thank you for always making me feel special. Thank you for being you. Thank you for this trip. Thank you for the beautiful roses downstairs. Thank you for everything." Now that I thought about it, he did sign the card *Love* Cain.

"You're welcome."

I kissed him, hoping he would feel the words that my mouth couldn't say.

"Thirsty?" I asked.

"Parched."

"I'll be right back." I tipped downstairs to the kitchen and grabbed two bottles of water. I ate a small chunk of honeydew melon from the bowl of fruit. It was sweet like sugar. I took another piece and then closed the refrigerator.

I handed Cain a bottle and climbed over him onto the bed. I was about to bite into the melon when he asked, "What are you eating?"

"The sweetest melon that came with my salad."

"You didn't bring me any?"

"Here, you can have this piece. I had one downstairs."

I leaned over and fed him the melon I had in between my fingers. Some of the juice dripped on his chest. I didn't bring any napkins so I used my tongue to clean it off.

Cain leaned his head back. "Mmm."

I flicked my tongue over his nipples until they hardened. My mouth wandered from his chest to his stomach, savoring the taste of his skin along the way. I wandered further down, licking the tip of his penis. Cain moaned again. I tasted and teased him until his toes curled. Just when he couldn't stand anymore, I took him into my mouth and sucked until he was close enough to touch the stars in the sky.

30

We had been in the shower so long, soaping each other's bodies, the entire bathroom was filled with steam. I was washing Cain's back, chattering away about the sites I wanted to visit. I suggested that we start with a tour to Devil's Bridge.

"What kind of name is that?" Cain asked.

I told him what I had read in the brochures about slaves committing mass suicides there and also the legend that the devil lives below the surf.

"Sounds morbid," he said.

"The name is a bit eerie but it's actually a beautiful natural bridge carved by the sea."

"Alright, we'll go to Devil's Bridge and then come back here for lunch. After lunch, I want to get a massage. My muscles are a little stiff from flying yesterday."

I slapped his butt. "You sure that's what it was?"

He turned around and squeezed my ass. "Making love to you all night definitely played a part in it, too."

"Then, by all means, get your massage because I plan to keep you busy again tonight."

We finished our shower, got dressed, and then went downstairs to have a light breakfast out on the patio. The table had been set with fresh fruit, cereal, and breads. A pitcher of orange juice was on the table. Cain sat down as I filled the glasses. I placed his glass in front of him and he pulled me down on his lap.

He kissed my shoulder. "When I start looking for a house in Atlanta, I want you to come with me."

"Do you really think you're going to need a house in Atlanta? Maybe an apartment would be more practical."

"I'll be spending a lot of time there getting Eden2 off the ground. Atlanta is going to be my new home. I want to be comfortable and I want you to feel at home when you come down. We can't be cooped up in an apartment."

"What are you going to do with your house on Long Island?" I asked.

"Nothing. I'll still be living in New York. Atlanta will be my home away from home. Besides, my baby is in New York. I'll have to divide my time between both places."

This was where things got complicated. They always do. Right after you begin to catch feelings you get thrown a curveball. I didn't want Cain to move to Atlanta. Call me selfish, all I knew was that I liked having Cain in my life—on a daily basis. I'd become accustomed to waking up next to him in the morning. If he was in Atlanta that wouldn't be an option, except maybe on a quick weekend rendezvous.

No one understood more than me that starting a business took sacrifice and commitment. I was trying to grow my own, but I wondered if Cain would be committed to growing what we had once he was in Atlanta. He'd be around all of that Hot-lanta booty, charming the ladies that came to his restaurant. Certainly there would be women pursuing him—attractive, progressive women—and I'd be nowhere near to remind him of what we shared. My relationship with Cain was so new, how would we know what we could have together if we were going to be apart most of the time?

I found myself in a position where I had to put my faith in a situation that I wasn't comfortable with. Distance spelled disaster. Then again, Bryce and I were basically under the same roof and he had run the streets like a wild dog. In that case, proximity had meant nothing.

I should've been sharing Cain's excitement, but the mention of Eden2 elicited the opposite reaction. Sadness and doubt hid behind my smile. Old feelings of insecurity churned in my stomach. I didn't want to spend my days, or nights, wondering if Cain was with someone else.

I sighed and looked out at the ocean. The water was calm. I almost wanted to run upstairs to put on my suit and lose myself in the warmth, wade away the anxiety.

Cain saw me gazing at the beach. "We could always stay here today and do the tourist stuff tomorrow."

"No, let's get out and experience the island. We'll only be gone a few hours, then I'll lay out on the beach while you go for your massage."

"Will you be wearing your thong?"

"You'll have to wait and see."

WE OPTED TO TAKE A PRIVATE JEEP TOUR instead of the group tour to Devil's Bridge. Our driver told us that he was taking us on a special scenic route. We drove along paved roads framed by lavish mansions and extravagant resorts to bumpy dirt roads running through small towns. Our driver wanted to give us a taste of the varied local flavor on the way to Devil's Bridge.

It was surreal, being on a bridge where our ancestors had chosen death over slavery. Truly a site to behold. We took pictures, standing on top of the bridge with the rough water crashing against the rock. Cain stood near the edge and kept pretending that he was going to jump into the raging waters. I threatened to push him if he didn't cut it out. We left there, clothes a little wet, and headed back to the resort.

I wanted to go back to the villa and change out of my damp shorts. Cain claimed he was ravenous so I told him to go ahead without me; I would meet him at the restaurant.

I went through my closet and couldn't decide if I wanted to wear an entirely different outfit or if I should put on my bathing suit with a pair of shorts and a tee since I was going to the beach after lunch. Cain should've known better than to let me come back to the villa alone. He would've rushed me along and there would've been no deciding between three outfits. I would've thrown on a pair of shorts and been right out the door. Now I was sitting on the bed acting as if I had to decide whether or not to push the red button to launch a nuclear weapon.

Twenty minutes later, I was walking down the cobblestone path in a summer dress with my suit underneath. I laughed to myself at how long my wardrobe change had taken. Cain had probably finished his lunch and was on his way back to the villa.

I approached the outdoor restaurant and didn't see Cain. I immediately knew I had taken too much time. Then I spotted him sitting with someone. They were engrossed in conversation. Cain had a stern look on his face. I could only see the back of the other person's head. Cain didn't see me coming.

I neared the table and my stomach churned. I focused on the man that Cain was talking to and my steps quickened. I rushed to the table and almost knocked it over, I bumped into it so hard.

"You alright, Baby?" Bryce asked.

I looked at Cain.

"Are you, *Baby*?" Cain asked.

"Cain…" I started off slow. "I don't know what you must think right now, but I can explain."

Cain leaned back in his chair and put his hands behind his head. "Bryce here has already clued me in about a lot of things."

I sneered at Bryce. "You have sunk to an all-time low. It wasn't enough for you to destroy our relationship; now you want to ruin my life?"

Bryce snickered. "Why would I want to ruin your life? You know how much I love you. You are my life. I told you that when we were holding each other and kissing that night."

"That was a mistake!" I spat without thinking.

Bryce smiled. Cain pushed back from the table and stood up.

Bryce stood and extended his hand. "Hey listen, Man, Dane, it was nice to meet you."

Cain looked at Bryce, then at me, and walked away.

Bryce sat back down and picked up a French fry from Cain's plate. "He's a nice guy. I'm glad I had a chance to meet him."

I stared at Bryce, my hands gripping the side of the table, trying not to rip his head off.

Bryce stopped chewing. "Sit down, Babe. Let's order some lunch. I was thinking maybe we could go sightseeing later. I wanted to check out that natural bridge but Dane told me you two went there this morning. He was a real chatty fellow until I told him that I was your man. After that, I thought he was a mute or something."

"Are you crazy!" I shrieked.

"But I think what really got him..." Bryce reached into his shirt pocket and placed a velvet box on the table. "...was this right here."

"What is that?" I said, afraid to ask.

"Your engagement ring." Bryce opened the box and the diamond glistened in the sunlight. "Since I didn't get a chance to show you yesterday, I showed your boy Dane to get *his* opinion. Phat, isn't it? Look at that bling. Had your boy speechless."

That did it. I slapped the shit out of him. I heard gasps coming from the surrounding tables but didn't even turn around. Right then, it was just Bryce and me.

Bryce chuckled, grabbed another fry, and kept talking. "There's a dinner cruise tonight so I hope you brought a sexy dress with you so we can celebrate."

I leaned down and put my face all up in his. "Hear me and understand me. If you even attempt to contact me, I promise you…you will regret it. From this point on, you're dead to me." I stormed off, listening to Bryce's laughter echo in my ears.

Once I was clear of the restaurant, I started to run toward the villa. I needed to explain to Cain the situation between Bryce and me. I could only imagine what Bryce had told him. Unfortunately, some of it was probably true.

The front door was open but Cain wasn't anywhere in sight. I took the stairs, two at a time, up to the bedroom. There he was— tossing his clothes into his suitcase. He briefly looked at me and then continued what he was doing.

I asked a dumb question. "You're leaving?"

"I'm catching the next flight. But feel free to stay and enjoy the rest of your trip. I did promise you a week in Antigua."

He was so dismissive. I would've felt better if he would've shown me that he was upset. His detached tone was killing me.

"Cain, we need to talk."

He stopped packing. "What's there to talk about? You neglected to tell me things I needed to know prior to this moment."

"I…but…there isn't anything to tell," I stammered. "I mean, not how you're thinking."

"You don't know what I'm thinking, Jade." He resumed throwing items in his bag.

"Bryce and I aren't together, if that's what he told you. He's been trying to reconcile with me but I kept telling him it wasn't going to happen."

"Then what's he doing here, Jade?"

"I don't know."

"You saw him yesterday?"

"Yes, but—"

"Did you tell him you were in a relationship?"

"Well, no, but—"

"That says it all right there."

He closed his suitcase and headed to the door. I blocked his way.

My voice broke. "Give me a chance to explain."

"One question, Jade. Were you with him a few weeks ago?"

"Yes, but—"

"No wonder I was the only one saying 'I love you' last night. Don't think I didn't notice. I thought maybe you needed a little more time, but I was wrong. The man you love, your *fiancé*, just crashed my party."

He gently moved my arm and proceeded down the hallway with me on his heels.

I started talking, all of my sentences running together. "He came over the night I saw you with Chivon...we kissed...things got out of hand but nothing happened, I swear to you...I stopped it...I was angry at you but I didn't want to be with him...Cain, I love you."

He stopped and turned to me. "If you didn't love me last night, then you certainly don't love me today." He went down the steps, leaving me standing at the top.

I heard the door close, slumped down to the floor and cried. I had witnessed my future become my past.

31

I don't know how long I sat at the top of the stairs wailing, but eventually I dragged myself out to the patio. I was empty inside. Every time I managed to stop crying, I reflected back to Cain's face when he'd said that I didn't love him and the tears would start flowing again. I was making myself sick. My head ached furiously and the slightest movement intensified the pounding in my brain. I kept hoping Cain would come back to the villa after he'd had time to calm down. The door never opened.

I lay in the hammock, replaying what had gone wrong and came up with one thing. Me. I had gone wrong, one too many times. I was wrong for allowing Bryce to be a part of my life for so long. I refused to be truthful with myself about why I had stayed with Bryce, about why I wouldn't let him go. It had nothing to do with love. I had stayed with Bryce because I didn't want to be alone. I had made Bryce the center of my world. I had let him disrespect me and explain away his actions because I believed that, without him, I would've been miserable. Meanwhile, I had lived in misery almost the entire time we were together. We'd break up for a week or two but then I'd end up taking him back. I didn't care what anyone thought—not even me. I didn't want to deal with my reality. I'd ignored the obvious—that I was being a fool. I figured I was being a fool for love and that was okay. It wasn't. It never was. Eventually it had become too complicated to lie to myself, extremely difficult to convince myself that Bryce would change, and virtually impossible to tell myself that he loved me and would do right by me. Those lies I used to tell myself began to eat away at my insides and still, I had done nothing. I had stayed. Planned to marry him. I could no longer place the blame on Bryce; I was disrespecting myself. Bryce had never felt compelled to respect me as long as he realized that I would accept the shit that he was offering. Time and again I had shown him that he could do practically about anything to me and I'd still stick around. Bryce had done me a favor when he abandoned our relationship. He had forced me out of the vicious cycle I was never strong enough to leave. There were many times I thought about leaving him, but I didn't want to feel the pain of being by myself. The exact pain I was feeling now that Cain had left me.

I couldn't place the blame on Bryce for the nonsense in Antigua. It could've been prevented, but I had chosen to avoid the situation instead of dealing with it. Bryce should've been told that I was seeing someone else. I was even lying to Bria to avoid dealing with Bryce. My relationship with Bryce was unhealthy and my breakup with him was even more so. I should've halted his relentless pursuit of me and informed him that things had changed in my life. He was under the impression that his old tactics would still work on me. Like I said, I couldn't blame him. They had worked in the past, repeatedly. It was my responsibility to tell him that I had found someone new.

I was so wrong for not telling Cain how I truly felt about him. I couldn't even be honest with him about my feelings. I was holding back with him because of unresolved issues I had with myself. I kept thinking Cain was too good to be true because of the drama I had endured with Bryce. I waited for him to show me something negative because, after Bryce, I figured that was what I should expect from men. My views had become distorted. I tried to withhold my feelings long enough for Cain to mess up;

that way I could always say at least it didn't get too serious. Well, that was exactly what he thought. He thought that I didn't love him.

Cain deserved my love and devotion; he was the man with whom I could have shared a wonderful future. I had messed all of that up. Cain revealed that he loved me, wanted me in his life, asked me to help him find a house that we would enjoy together and I revealed nothing. Not how I felt, not what I had been through in the past, not even what I wanted for the future. Instead of embracing what I had in Cain, I focused on what I wouldn't have once he moved to Atlanta. Distance shouldn't matter if you're with someone you truly care about. You have to know what it takes to make it work—trust, honesty and commitment—the main ingredients in the recipe for love. But there was more to the recipe than that. I finally understood that you could have a pile of ingredients but knowing what to do with them was the key. You had to use those ingredients and develop rituals. Rituals for sharing—oneself and one's feelings. Rituals for growing together. Rituals for resolving conflicts and misunderstandings. And best of all—rituals for celebrating life and love. The recipe for love took the finest ingredients and turned them into the sweetest thing you'd ever tasted. That was what was missing with Bryce. Cain had added those ingredients to my life but I didn't recognize the taste nor did I fully appreciate the flavor.

Most importantly, I was wrong for thinking that I was never wrong. I swung back and forth in the hammock, thinking what a high price I had paid to learn something about myself.

32

I was on the first flight out the next morning. I didn't want to be in Antigua without Cain and it wouldn't have been right for me to remain at his expense. I had worked out a deal with the hotel for them to mail Cain a credit voucher for the unused time.

I didn't let anyone know I had returned home early. I wanted to be by myself. I spent my days holed up in the house, watching television and thinking about Cain. I wondered if he went to Atlanta, or if he came home. Wondered what he must be thinking about me. I wanted to call but I didn't know what to say to him. Every time my phone rang I prayed that it was him. I'd check the caller ID, see it wasn't him, then let it roll over to the machine.

The remote had become my best friend. I ran up and down the channels, stopping on TBS. *Love Jones* was on TV again. That was the last movie I needed to be watching, but I tortured myself anyway…and cried the whole two hours it was on. I was in bad shape. On the couch in the fetal position with a pile of crumpled tissues strewn across the cushions, I fell in and out of restless sleep. Disturbing dreams replayed in my subconscious mind. They revolved around me, trying to get close enough to Cain to apologize. Just as I would reach him, some obstacle would pop up, preventing me from speaking with him. I'd wake up frustrated—determined to have a resolution between us. Since there was no chance of Cain and I reconciling in reality, I forced myself back to sleep to try and talk to him one more time in my dreams.

After a couple of days of seclusion, I broke down and called Milan. She rushed over and I relayed the events of my disastrous trip.

Milan shook her head. "What would possess Bria to tell that fool where you were? Not to mention, where you were staying."

"I don't even want to think about that. Bria should've kept her mouth shut but this wouldn't have happened if I was straight up with Bryce about having a new man in my life."

"Have you spoken to Cain?"

"He hasn't called me."

"Have you called him?"

"I can't, Lan. I don't think he wants anything to do with me."

"You won't know unless you try."

"He left me in Antigua. I think that's an indication he's through with me."

"Jade, call the man. Trust me. Don't give up so easily. I'm saying that because Nolan and I have been speaking to each other. After I took care of Eriq, I decided to work on Nolan. We've been working through our problems. My point is, I wasn't going to let go without a fight and neither should you."

Milan tried her best to feel my pain, but she was basking in the joy of her reconciliation.

"My love life is jacked up but I'm happy for you," I said. "You can bring Nolan with you on Sunday night to our re-opening gathering at Rituals."

"Can you make those shrimp puffs that I love?"

"I haven't made those in ages. I'll have to look for the recipe."

"Well, hop to it because they must be on the menu. I hate to run off, but I'm having dinner with Nolan tonight."

"Behave yourself, Freak. I know it's been a while."

"I'm going with the flow. Whatever happens—happens."

After talking to Milan, I wasn't going to let Cain slip away without letting him know how I felt. I made up my mind to call him later, after I had showered and beautified myself. I was looking a little crunchy from lying around like a brokenhearted loser for a few days.

I WAS IN MY OFFICE LOOKING FOR THE SHRIMP PUFFS recipe. I checked my file cabinet, but it wasn't there. I searched in a couple of other places in and around my desk but it still didn't turn up.

My system was impeccable and I couldn't understand why I was unable to locate what I needed. Then I realized why. The entire "S" appetizer folder was missing, which was strange since I hadn't used these files in quite a while. Not since…Cain's pool party…that's right…Cain's party. I had sent him to my office to get a recipe for me. He couldn't have possibly taken my files—could he?

I paced the room. Why would he need to take my files? It dawned on me. Cain mentioned that he wanted to revamp the menu for Eden2 in Atlanta. But did that mean he would take my recipes? It had to be him. He was the only one that had been in my office other than me.

I snatched the phone from the base and dialed his home number. His voicemail picked up. I left him a terse message.

Cain, I suggest you call me immediately. I believe we have something to speak about.

I slammed the phone down. It wasn't the message I thought I would be leaving when I decided earlier to call, but I hadn't known then that he was a thief.

I waited for the rest of the night for Cain to call me back. When I woke up on the couch the next morning, it was obvious that he wasn't going to.

33

I walked through the doors at Rituals and my breath caught in my throat. Two of the walls had been knocked down, opening up the room immensely. The seating capacity had nearly doubled. There was now a second bar in the rear of the restaurant and a cozy lounge area next to it. The place looked absolutely marvelous.

I pulled out my cell and called Terrence. "My brother, you have outdone yourself. Rituals looks amazing."

"There a few final touches that still need to be done but we worked as fast as we could to get it completed in a week. I had two crews in there working around the clock."

"Who loves you more than me?"

"Probably your mother…and maybe a few of my honeys."

"Thank you, Terrence. I couldn't ask for a better brother, I mean it."

"You knew I was gonna take care of you."

"You'll be here Sunday night, right?" I asked.

"Of course. Bria told me some of the things on the menu and my mouth started watering. She was in the kitchen while we were working, practicing some puffed shrimp or something."

I hung up with Terrence and wondered if it was possible. I called Bria and asked her to meet me at the restaurant. She showed up an hour later in true diva fashion. Sunglasses, hat, short dress, and high-heels.

"Before you get started, I owe you an apology," she said. "I would've never told Bryce where you were if I knew you were going to be with Cain."

"You shouldn't have told him where I was, regardless of whether I was alone or with someone. But I owe you an apology also. I'm sorry for lying to you."

"I noticed you had turned into quite the Pinocchio."

"Bria, sit down." We sat at a table up front. "Bryce and I aren't getting back together. I'm going on with my life and I want to be able to share it with you. The way things are now, I can't tell you anything because it goes right back to your brother. You have to accept that I've moved on and respect our friendship by keeping my business private."

Bria reached across the table and grabbed my hand. "You're right, Diva. I'm sorry my actions helped to ruin your trip."

"Well, hopefully you can help me from making a bad situation worse. Do you somehow have one of my recipe files?"

"Yeah, didn't Bryce tell you?"

"He didn't tell me anything."

"The morning I spoke to him at your house, I told him to ask you for your shrimp puffs recipe."

"He didn't ask me for anything. Then again, I was so pissed off that he was still there from the night before, I told him to let himself out."

"I asked Bryce why you sent the entire file but he mumbled something about he wasn't looking for shit. I ignored him because I figured he had an attitude because he didn't get none."

I rolled my eyes. "Bria."

"Sorry, Girl, I thought you knew I had it. What did you think happened to it?"

"I thought you may have been right about me dating the competition."

"You thought Cain had taken it?"

"I almost accused him of it."

"Girl, you can't pay me any attention. That was me being a hater. I was still holding the torch for you and Bryce. I know better than anyone how much my brother loves you. I really thought you two would've worked out your problems."

"Not this time."

"Jade, Bryce probably never told you but my mother and father put him in the middle of things that no child should be involved in. My mother knew my father was cheating and she knew Bryce was with him most of the time. She started to conveniently have men leaving the house when Bryce would be coming in from school so that he would have something to report to my father. Of course this affected how he regarded both of my parents, but it really affected his perception of relationships. It affected me, too, but not like it did Bryce. He tried to be a good man for you and yes, he did fall short. I guess I'm asking that you have a little compassion for him and why he's the way he is. He'll probably never be happy in a relationship, but he saw hope with you."

I nodded. "I wasn't aware of the full impact your parents had on him."

"He asked me to tell you that he's sorry. Bryce never thought you would consider him a *stalker* or feel unsafe around him. He realizes that he was wrong, Jade. He got caught up, started obsessing over making things right with the two of you. He understands it's not going to happen. And *I've* accepted that it's over and I want you to know you can talk to me about anything. Even Cain."

"I can't believe it. No more ride or die shit? It's a miracle. Something good did come out of my horrible trip." I laughed.

"I'll admit I was a little out of control. Listening to my brother constantly crying the blues and then when Cain came on the scene, I felt like I was losing a sister and a partner all at once."

"This is *our* dream, Bria. *We* built Rituals together. Cain and I were getting close, but personally; not professionally. It doesn't matter any more...it's over now."

"Forgive me?"

"Of course. Hey, wait a minute. Why *did* you need that recipe? You hate shrimp puffs."

Bria hesitated. "You do remember the night your ass cut out on me and Lan at the club?"

"Do me a favor and try to work on the sarcasm next."

Bria laughed. "Do you want to hear the story or not?"

"Alright, go ahead and tell me."

"Girl, after you left the club, I sat in the V.I.P. lounge talking to Ernest until the place closed."

"Ernest? Who's Ernest?" I shrieked, "You mean Bonecrusher?!"

She turned her nose up. "I mean Ernest. That's his name."

"I know, I know. And?"

Bria said she was telling him about our restaurant, the type of food we made and so on. During the course of their conversation, he'd mentioned that when he was in the Marines with Terrence, the guys used to sit around and talk about things they missed from home. Ernest said Terrence used to go on and on about these shrimp puffs his sister would make. He said Terrence made them sound so good he'd wanted to try one ever since.

"I see where this is going," I said.

"He was cute and he wanted to take me out to dinner. Instead, I offered to make him those shrimp puffs he'd heard so much about. I called you the next day to get the recipe, Bryce took the file, and the rest is history."

"Wow. You're seeing Bonecrusher...you didn't even tell me."

"I know you're not talking."

"Okay, I won't go there. How did the puffs turn out?"

"They didn't taste like yours."

"Don't worry, Girl. I'll hook it up for you."

Bria and I walked around the newly renovated Rituals, discussing the future direction of our establishment.

I beamed with pride. "Diva, we've done good."

"No, Diva, we've done *great*."

Glasses were raised in a toast. Everyone had to add in their two cents before we could take a drink of the champagne. I was last. I kept it short and sweet. "Here's to…things to come." Responses of *cheers* and *hear-hear* rang throughout the room but I wasn't quite finished. "And…congratulations to my girl, Milan, for making partner at her firm." Glasses clinked.

My parents were present, as were Bria's parents. Terrence actually brought a date, a cute doctor who seemed to have reeled him in. Bonecrusher, I mean Ernest, had come and was ecstatic he would finally get to sample the shrimp puffs. Milan and Nolan came in together hugged up like the old days. Needless to say, Bryce had the good sense not to show up and I was thankful.

I went to the kitchen for more hors d'oeuvres. The music was pumping and I couldn't help dancing while I refilled the platters. The doors opened. I looked up, expecting to see Bria, but it was Cain standing in the doorway, sexy as hell, in a black Armani suit. I froze.

He came into the kitchen. "I got your message."

"Uh…oh. I didn't mean to leave that."

"You didn't? I thought you wanted to talk." He shrugged. "Maybe you changed your mind. I realize this may not be the best time, but I have something I want to say to you." Cain stepped closer to the prep table. "After I told you how important it is to discuss our problems I turned around and did to you what you had done to me, I shut you out."

"Cain, I want to explain to you what really did happen and if you don't think we can move forward, I'll understand."

"You don't have to explain. I was wrong."

"But I want to. You deserve to know the whole truth."

"I already do."

"No, you don't."

"Jade, I do. When I left Antigua, I ended up on the plane with that knucklehead, Bryce. He sat in the seat next to me and started rambling about how much he loves you, saying he would do anything for you. He was on the verge of tears. I stood up to switch my seat; I would've killed him if I didn't. He stopped me. He said he had to do what was right because he'd hurt you deeply." Cain leaned over the table. "I know that you've been telling him to leave you alone for months and he wouldn't listen. He confessed that he lied about the two of you being back together and sleeping together that night."

"He told you we slept together?"

"Among other things..."

"I'm sorry that night ever happened. It was wrong and I should've told you about it."

"Maybe, maybe not. That entire night was a big mix-up on both of our parts. I trust you, Jade. I shouldn't have let Bryce corrupt what I already knew; that I want you in my life. I needed a few days to get my mind right, but here I am."

Bria popped her head in and asked if she should take the hors d'oeuvres. I nodded and she whirled in and whirled back out.

Cain and I stayed in the kitchen and talked. Apparently Bryce said I didn't need to tell him that he was a dead man because he saw it in my eyes. At that moment, he realized that I would never take him back. That's what made him tell the truth. It finally clicked that there was no us.

"Bryce claims he only wants you to be happy and if it means that he has to step aside for me, then that's what he'll do."

I couldn't believe it, but I was relieved. "Can I say something now?"

"By all means."

"I'm not always right."

"Okay…"

"Lately, I've been wrong about so many things, especially you. I doubted your feelings because I was trying to suppress mine. I left that ridiculous message on your machine. I'm so glad you didn't answer; I was about to accuse you of something completely ridiculous."

"Don't tell me. It's not important. Jade, you don't have to tell me everything; only the things that matter."

I smiled. "So do you think we can move forward?"

"It depends."

"On?"

Cain smiled. "If you can promise not to be so damn cocky."

I giggled. "I promise."

"Jade, I don't want you to change a thing. Now come here and give me a kiss. I missed you."

I came around to the other side of the table and wrapped my arms around Cain. We stood in the middle of the kitchen, kissing through song after song. We were missing the entire party.

I pulled away and looked into his eyes. "In case you didn't know, I love you, Cain."

"Yeah, I know."

"Now look who's being cocky."

I grabbed his arm and pulled him out of the kitchen. "Let's go join the festivities."

I looked toward the bar and I stopped in my tracks. Standing at the bar talking and laughing with Terrence and Bonecrusher was Omar—tall, fine and dimples showing. Omar looked my way and winked at me.

I tugged Cain back toward the kitchen.

He looked confused. "What's wrong?"

I grinned as I pushed him back through the door. "I have just one more thing to tell you."

AUTHOR'S NOTE

Recipe for Love started as an inkling. I knew I had a story to tell and I knew the time had come to tell it. It was one of those things that you profoundly feel and instantly accept as fact. Actually, I desired to write this novel long before I committed those first words to paper. If anything, *Recipe for Love* was overdue.

At the inception of *Recipe for Love*, I wasn't certain what I was going to write. I did have a basic premise—I intended to map the journey of a young successful woman. What journey? No clue. I didn't quite know how the story was going to end. Though once I began to develop the main character, it became apparent that her professional life was in order yet her personal life was in disarray. Her disparate worlds landed her at a crossroad. I decided to spend some time and linger at that crossroad. The place where right and wrong, good and bad, the highest high and the lowest low all reside. To see what happens when someone who thinks she has all the answers discovers that she is grievously mistaken.

Jade's story takes place on the brink of both her past and her future—the promise of new joy and the ache of old pain. I aimed to explore the range of emotions familiar to so many of us who have loved before. However, this story is about more than romantic love. It deals with sisterly love, brotherly love, parental love, love of self and loving what you do.

My passion lies in cooking and I have spent countless hours creating and following recipes. If there's one thing I know, cooking is not an exact science. You can always add a little bit more, take something away or make substitutions to get the result you want. The cook in me thought, "Wouldn't love be easy if it could be followed like a recipe."

I approached this story the way I approach a recipe in my kitchen. Every day I'd sit at my computer and create. I'd look at what I had and visualize what I wanted it to be. The joy in cooking is the process of putting the ingredients together *just so*, watching the dish take shape, and finally, the scrumptious end result. In writing this book, I became engrossed in the process. I couldn't wait to come back the next day to see what would happen to the characters. To check the oven to see what I needed to add or tone down. Decide whether the content in the pot needed to simmer or boil. I wanted *Recipe for Love* to appeal to a variety of tastes; for that to happen, it had to be delectable. Plain and simple.

I needed to explore what made my characters tick and soon learned it was hardly an easy task. It's like trying to distinguish the faintest echo of a particular spice in a dish. Ingredients tend to meld together and take on a life of their own. You know it tastes familiar but it can be a multitude of things. So you roll the many flavors around your mouth and attempt to put your finger on the one specific flavor. We all have layers in our personalities, hidden experiences, wants and desires that contribute to who we are. I aspired for my characters to have the same level of complexity. That sense of *do you ever really know someone*. I sought to travel below the carefully constructed exterior, asking along the way, what makes this person behave the way they do? How did this person get in this predicament? Can they find their way out? In trying to discover who they were, I finally put my finger on the *Recipe for Love*. Sure, the *Recipe for Love* may vary from person to person but they all share one common theme. You want your recipe to turn out right.

As I was completing *Recipe for Love*, I decided I wanted to invite you to experience the same sweet indulgences as the characters. My original recipes for the dishes that were mentioned in the story follow the novel. I must thank all of my taste testers for allowing me to stuff them with food. Mom, Dad, Selena, Courtney, Shannon, Mia, Joanne, Denise, Xalya and Olu—you guys are real troopers. I couldn't have eaten all of that food! I have to shout out my brother, Chris, who throws down in the kitchen (and on the grill) and feeds us all on a regular. Now he's a brother who's figured out that ladies LOVE a man who can cook.

Thanks to my agent, Sara Camilli, for your commitment. It's been a journey and I appreciate all of your efforts.

Shinda, I love you! Kappa Lambda, Delta's love is the sweetest love! Nik and Shelly, thanks for making an exception to the "no book" rule. And to my family (from parents to siblings to nieces to aunts, uncles and cousins), thanks for being my world.

Stay tuned…

www.shamararay.com

www.facebook.com

ABOUT THE AUTHOR

Shamara Ray is a graduate of Syracuse University. She develops business training programs for Fortune 500 executives. She has a penchant for the culinary arts and enjoys entertaining friends and family in her Long Island home. She is currently working on her next novel. Visit the author at www.shamararay.com and on Facebook.

READER'S DISCUSSION GUIDE

1. Was Jade careless to begin a new relationship only weeks after a complicated break-up?

2. Why do you think it was so difficult for Jade to be honest with Cain? Bryce?

3. What same act did each character have to perform at one point or another and what was the impact on those around him/her?

4. Milan's betrayal of Nolan ultimately jeopardized her career. What are your thoughts on getting intimate with a colleague?

5. Bria's and Bryce's views on relationships, love and marriage were greatly influenced by their parents' destructive behaviors.

6. What's your best advice for overcoming the harmful effects of unhealthy relationships (romantic, business or friendship)?

7. What character did you identify with most and why?

8. Would you go into business with your best friend? Date your best friend's sibling?

9. Can a couple that has different or conflicting definitions for what love is have a successful relationship?

10. What's your idea of a deliciously sexy date, meal or vacation?

11. What's your own personal Recipe for Love?

RECIPES

GRAND MARNIER PANCAKES WITH CINNAMON CREAM

Pancakes
   1½ cups all purpose flour
   1 tablespoon baking powder
   3 tablespoons sugar
   ¼ teaspoon salt
   1¼ cup of milk
   2 eggs
   2 tablespoons melted butter
   5 tablespoons Grand Marnier

Cinnamon Cream
   1 cup cold whipping cream
   2 tablespoons confectioners sugar
   1 teaspoon cinnamon
   ½ teaspoon vanilla extract

For cinnamon cream:
   In a chilled metal bowl add the cream, sugar, cinnamon and vanilla. Whip cream with a hand mixer on medium speed until the cream begins to hold soft peaks. Transfer to a plastic container, cover and refrigerate.

For pancakes:
   Mix dry ingredients in a bowl. Add eggs, milk and melted butter and mix on low speed with a hand mixer until smooth, about 45 seconds. Fold in Grand Marnier into pancake batter.

   Preheat griddle over medium heat. Lightly grease. Pour ¼ cup batter onto griddle for each pancake. Cook until bubbly. Turn over and cook until browned.

   Top pancakes with a dollop of cinnamon whipped cream.

   Makes approximately 10-12 pancakes

PEACH PANCAKES WITH VANILLA SYRUP

Pancakes
 1½ cups all purpose flour
 1 tablespoon baking powder
 3 tablespoons sugar
 ¼ teaspoon salt
 1¼ cup of milk
 2 eggs
 2 tablespoons melted butter
 ½ teaspoon vanilla extract
 3 peaches
 ½ teaspoon cinnamon
 1 tablespoon light brown sugar

Vanilla Syrup
 2 cups water
 2 cups light brown sugar
 2 tablespoons vanilla extract

For vanilla syrup
Add water, brown sugar and vanilla to a saucepan and bring to a boil on medium high heat, stirring frequently. Cook until syrup begins to thicken, approximately 10-15 minutes. (Do not overcook or syrup will become too thick. If this happens, thin with a small amount of water, stirring frequently.) Cover and remove from heat. Makes 1 cup.

For peaches:
Peel and slice peaches. Add sliced peaches, cinnamon and 1 table-spoon of brown sugar to food processor. Pulse until coarsely chopped. Set aside.

For pancakes:
Mix dry ingredients in a bowl. Add eggs, milk, vanilla extract and melted butter and mix on low speed with a hand mixer until smooth, about 45 seconds. Fold one cup of chopped peaches into pancake batter.

Preheat griddle over medium heat. Lightly grease. Pour ¼ cup batter onto griddle for each pancake. Cook until bubbly. Turn over and cook until browned.

Serve pancakes with warm vanilla syrup.

Makes approximately 10-12 pancakes

WAFFLES

1 cup of all purpose flour
2 eggs
¾ cup milk
2 tablespoons vegetable oil
1½ teaspoon baking powder
1½ teaspoon sugar
½ teaspoon salt
½ teaspoon vanilla extract

Mix dry ingredients in a bowl. Add eggs, milk, vanilla extract and oil and mix on low speed with a hand mixer until smooth, about 45 seconds.

Pour ½ cup batter into heated waffle iron. Close lid and cook until golden brown.

Makes 4 waffles

BERRY PUREE

8 ounces strawberries, hulled
6 ounces blackberries
6 ounces raspberries
½ to 1 cup of sugar

Rinse berries. Add berries and ½ cup of sugar to food processor. Puree until smooth. Taste for sweetness. If necessary add more sugar for desired sweetness.

Place fine mesh sieve over a bowl. Strain berries through sieve to remove seeds. Serve over waffles

APPLE NUT COMPOTE

4 granny smith apples
½ cup chopped pecans
1 cup of water
2 tablespoons butter
1 tablespoon cinnamon
½ teaspoon lemon extract
1 cup brown sugar

Peel apples and cut into wedges. Remove core and seeds. Add all ingredients except the nuts, to a sauce pan. Bring to a boil over medium-high heat. Turn heat to low and simmer apples until tender. With a slotted spoon, remove apples from liquid and place in a bowl. Boil liquid until it thickens to a syrup. Return apples to pot and stir in nuts.

Serve over waffles.

SWEET POTATO WAFFLES

1 cup mashed sweet potato
1 cup of all purpose flour
2 eggs
¾ cup milk
2 tablespoons vegetable oil
1½ teaspoon baking powder
2 teaspoons sugar
½ teaspoon salt
1 teaspoon cinnamon
⅛ teaspoon nutmeg
1 teaspoon vanilla extract
½ teaspoon lemon extract

Bake one medium sized sweet potato in 400 degree oven until tender (about one hour). Let cool.

Mix dry ingredients in a bowl. Add eggs, milk, vanilla extract, lemon extract and oil and mix on low speed with a hand mixer until smooth, about 45 seconds.

Mash sweet potato and measure one cup. Mix one cup of sweet potato into waffle batter, stir until incorporated.

Spray waffle iron with nonstick spray. Pour ½ cup batter onto heated waffle iron. Close lid and cook until golden brown.

Serve with cinnamon cream or vanilla syrup

Makes 4 waffles

SCRAMBLED EGGS WITH CARAMELIZED SHALLOTS

6 eggs
1 cup thinly sliced shallots
1 ounce diced cream cheese
2 tablespoons salted butter
½ teaspoon salt
⅛ teaspoon black pepper

Melt butter in a nonstick skillet over medium-low heat. Add shallots and sauté until golden brown, about 15 minutes, stirring frequently. Be careful not to let shallots burn.

In a large bowl, whisk eggs with salt and pepper until incorporated. Whisk in diced cream cheese. Add eggs to skillet with shallots and cook over medium heat, stirring constantly with a spatula until eggs set, about 3-4 minutes. Eggs should be moist and creamy.

Serve immediately.

Makes 2 servings

CRAB OMELET

3 eggs
½ cup lump crabmeat (drained, picked for shells and rinsed)
½ cup shredded gouda cheese (not smoked)
⅓ cup heavy cream
1 minced garlic clove
1 tablespoon chopped fresh parsley
1 tablespoon chopped fresh dill
½ teaspoon salt, plus additional ⅛ teaspoon salt
¼ teaspoon cayenne pepper
1 tablespoon butter

In a bowl whisk eggs, ⅛ teaspoon salt and dill. Set aside.

Melt butter in a sauté pan over medium heat. Add garlic and sauté 1 minute, be careful not to let it burn. Add crabmeat, parsley, ½ teaspoon salt, cayenne pepper, and heavy cream and stir gently until heated, about 3 minutes. Add cheese and stir into crabmeat. Remove from heat.

In a 10-inch nonstick skillet, melt butter over medium heat. Add eggs to skillet and cook until eggs are just set. Lift edges of omelet with spatula to let uncooked eggs flow underneath cooked portion, about 3 minutes. Spoon crabmeat on one half of the omelet. Use spatula to fold uncovered half of omelet over crabmeat. Use spatula to slide omelet onto plate.

Makes 1 serving

TURKEY SAUSAGE

1 pound ground turkey (not white meat)
2 teaspoons salt
3 tablespoons ground sage
¼ teaspoon black pepper
½ teaspoon red pepper
1 teaspoon onion powder
1 teaspoon vegetable oil

In a bowl, mix all ingredients with your hands until well-blended. Mixture should be smooth. Form into small 4-inch patties; approximately 1-inch thick.

Cook in a lightly greased skillet over medium heat until browned on both sides and cooked through.

Makes 24 patties

CHICKEN SOUP

1½ pounds diced chicken cutlet
3 cups diced red potatoes
1 cup diced onion
1 cup diced celery
1 cup diced carrots
⅓ cup olive oil
2 dried bay leaves
1 tablespoon salt (an additional ½ teaspoon according to taste)
1 teaspoon black pepper
1 tablespoon onion powder
1 tablespoon garlic powder
1 teaspoon dried oregano
8 cups water
2 cups dry egg noodle pasta (no yolks dumplings)

In a large, 8-quart stockpot, heat olive oil over medium-high heat. Add onion, celery, carrots, salt, pepper, onion powder, garlic powder, oregano and sauté over medium-high heat for 3-5 minutes, stirring frequently.

Add chicken and sauté for 3-5 minutes. Stir in potatoes, add water and bay leaves. Bring soup to a boil. Stir, then reduce heat to medium-low. Simmer for 1 hour. Add egg noodle pasta and simmer for an additional 15 minutes until noodles are tender.

Makes 6-8 servings

ROASTED POTATO SOUP

3 pounds russet potatoes
1 quart light cream
3 chopped garlic cloves
1½ teaspoon salt
⅛ teaspoon black pepper
2 cups grated sharp white cheddar
¼ cup chopped green onion

Bake potatoes in a 400-degree oven until tender (about an hour), turning once halfway through baking process. Let potatoes cool. Cut potatoes in half and scoop flesh from the skins.

In a large bowl, roughly mash potatoes. Potatoes should be chunky. Stir in 1 cup shredded cheese.

Bring cream, chopped garlic, salt and pepper to a low simmer over low heat, stirring frequently. Do not bring to a boil. Once heated, simmer an additional 10 minutes; continue stirring.

Add ½ the potato mixture to cream. Be careful when adding potatoes to hot cream. Stir to incorporate potatoes and cream. Let simmer 3 minutes, stirring. Add remaining potatoes and stir 3 minutes until incorporated and heated. Soup should be thick and chunky. Add remaining cup of cheese and stir. Remove from heat and stir in green onion.

Ladle soup into bowl and garnish with additional cheddar cheese.

Makes 4-6 servings

GRILLED CHICKEN SANDWICH
WITH ROASTED RED PEPPER & MOZZARELLA

4 thinly sliced chicken cutlets
8 ounces mozzarella cheese thinly sliced
2 roasted red peppers (in jar)
½ teaspoon salt
¼ teaspoon black pepper
½ teaspoon onion powder
½ teaspoon garlic powder
¼ teaspoon paprika
½ teaspoon dried oregano
2 tablespoons olive oil
4 ciabatta rolls

Basil Mayo
¾ cup mayonnaise
3 fresh basil leaves
1 garlic clove
¼ teaspoon black pepper

For basil mayonnaise:
Combine ingredients in a blender or food processor. Blend until smooth.

For chicken:
Thinly slice mozzarella cheese and cut each roasted red pepper in half.

Season chicken with salt, pepper, onion, garlic, paprika and oregano.

In a saute pan, heat olive oil over medium-high heat. Add cutlets to pan and sear until golden brown, about 4 minutes each side. Top each cutlet with a roasted red pepper and the sliced mozzarella cheese. Melt cheese, then remove from heat.

Cut rolls in half and lightly toast cut sides. Place chicken atop bottom half of roll. Spread basil mayonnaise on top half and serve.

Makes 4 servings

BUFFALO BLUE CHEESE BURGERS

1 pound lean ground beef (ground turkey or chicken can be
substituted)
¼ cup diced onion
¼ cup diced celery
3 tablespoons hot sauce
1 teaspoon salt
¼ teaspoon pepper
1 teaspoon garlic powder
1 teaspoon onion powder
2 ounces blue cheese
2 large buns or rolls

Hot Sauce Mayo
½ cup mayonnaise
3 tablespoons hot sauce

For hot sauce mayo:

In a bowl, combine mayonnaise and hot sauce. Mix until smooth.
Set aside.

For blue cheese burgers:

In a bowl, combine all ingredients except the blue cheese. Form
ground beef mixture into 4 equal patties.

Place 1 ounce of blue cheese on top of one of the patties. Top the
patty and cheese with another patty. Pinch the edges closed and seal
the cheese inside. Be sure to firmly press edges closed while molding
the burger. Repeat with remaining patties.

Grill burgers 6-7 minutes per side. (As an alternative, heat skillet on
medium-high heat and add burgers. Cook burgers about 6-7 minutes
per side for well done.)

Serve with hot sauce mayo

Makes 2 servings

CRAB CAKES WITH TANGY MIXED SALAD GREENS

Crab Cakes
   8 ounces lump crabmeat (drained, picked for shells and rinsed)
   2 tablespoons breadcrumbs
   2 tablespoons chopped fresh parsley
   3 tablespoons mayonnaise
   2 tablespoons brown mustard
   1 tablespoon lemon juice
   ½ teaspoon salt
   ½ teaspoon garlic powder
   2 tablespoons olive oil for sautéing

Tangy Dressing
   1 avocado
   ¾ cup white wine vinegar
   ⅓ cup olive oil
   4 tablespoons creamy horseradish
   1 teaspoon salt

Salad
   6 cups mixed salad greens

For dressing:
   Cut avocado in half and remove the pit. Scoop avocado flesh into blender. Add vinegar, olive oil, horseradish and salt. Blend until smooth (as an alternative, add avocado to a bowl and mash. Add remaining ingredients and combine with an electric hand mixer until smooth).

   Yields 1½ – 2 cups.

For salad:
   In a large bowl toss mixed greens with ¾ cup tangy dressing.

For crab cakes:
   Add crab meat to a bowl. Gently fold in remaining ingredients (except olive oil). Form into 4 cakes.

In a sauté pan, heat 2 tablespoons olive oil over medium-high heat. Add crab cakes and sauté until golden brown; approximately 3 minutes on each side, turning carefully.

For crab cake salad:
Plate salad. Place one or two crab cakes on top of tangy mixed greens.

Serves 2-4

TOMATO & SHRIMP BRUSCHETTA

Shrimp
  1 pound large shrimp, peeled and deveined
  ½ teaspoon salt
  ½ teaspoon onion powder
  ½ teaspoon garlic
  1 teaspoon olive oil

Tomatoes
  6 medium-sized tomatoes
  1½ teaspoon salt
  ½ teaspoon fresh minced garlic
  ½ teaspoon dried oregano
  1 teaspoon dried basil
  1 teaspoon garlic powder
  1 teaspoon onion powder
  2 teaspoons apple cider vinegar
  ½ cup olive oil

Bread
  1 loaf of Italian bread
  Garlic clove
  Olive oil for brushing on bread

Place shrimp in a bowl and add salt, onion and garlic powder, olive oil and mix. Refrigerate until ready to grill.

Prepare the barbecue grill. Shrimp should be cooked on medium-high heat. Coals are ready when they turn white with an orange glow; about 30-40 minutes. Alternatively shrimp can be broiled in the oven under the flame.

Prepare tomatoes while waiting for the grill. Cut tomatoes into quarters and spoon out seeds. Cut tomato quarters into strips lengthwise, then cut across and dice. Add tomatoes to a bowl, add remaining ingredients and mix. Set aside.

Grill shrimp until cooked through; about 4 minutes per side. Shrimp should have light grill marks (if broiling in oven, broil until shrimp begins to lightly brown, turning once). Remove from grill and let cool. While shrimp cool, prepare bread.

Cut bread into ½ inch-thick slices and brush one side with olive oil. Grill bread, olive oil side down, or broil in the oven olive oil side up, until lightly golden. Remove from heat and rub toasted side with cut garlic clove.

Chop shrimp and stir into tomato mixture. Place tomatoes into a serving bowl and place bread on a platter. Spoon a generous portion of tomatoes and shrimp on top of toasts.

Makes 6 servings

SHRIMP PUFFS

1 cup chopped uncooked shrimp, peeled and deveined
1½ cup all-purpose flour
1¼ cup milk
1 stick salted butter plus 1 tablespoon
6 eggs
1 cup shredded parmesan cheese
1 minced garlic clove
2 tablespoon chopped fresh thyme
2 teaspoons chopped fresh rosemary
1 teaspoon salt
½ teaspoon black pepper

In a sauté pan over medium heat, melt 1 tablespoon of butter. Add garlic, rosemary and thyme and sauté one minute. Add shrimp and sauté until cooked; approximately 5 minutes. Remove from heat and set aside.

In a saucepan, boil milk and butter together. Turn heat to low and add flour, stirring continuously until the dough comes together. Remove from heat and let cool.

Preheat oven to 450 degrees.

Once the dough is cool, add eggs one at a time and stir with a wooden spoon. Dough will be stiff.

After incorporating the eggs, add the shrimp and mix. Stir in the cheese.

Spray a mini-muffin pan with nonstick spray.

Drop a tablespoon of batter into each muffin cup. Bake for 15 minutes.

Remove shrimp puffs from pan and serve immediately.

Yields 48 puffs

PAN SEARED SALMON

4 half-inch thick salmon steaks
2 teaspoons garlic powder
2 teaspoons onion powder
1 teaspoon salt
1 teaspoon paprika
2 packets Sazon Goya con Azafron
20 garlic cloves peeled and smashed
3 tablespoons olive oil

Rinse and pat dry salmon steaks. In a small bowl mix garlic powder, onion powder, salt, paprika and Sazon Goya. Season salmon thoroughly on both sides with spice mixture. Set aside for 15 minutes (or salmon can marinate for 4 hours in refrigerator).

In a large nonstick frying pan, heat olive oil over medium-high heat. Add garlic cloves and sauté 2-3 minutes. Move garlic to the side of pan, being careful not to burn it. Add two salmon steaks to the pan. Sear on one side for five minutes, then using a spatula gently turn over, being careful not to break salmon steak apart, and sear other side for five minutes.

Remove garlic from pan and set aside; it should be light golden brown. Turn salmon over again and cover pan with lid. Lower heat to medium. Allow salmon to cook for an additional ten minutes, turning again after five minutes, until cooked completely through. Remove salmon from pan and keep warm in oven. Return pan to medium-high heat and cook remaining two steaks in the same manner.

Place salmon on a serving platter and garnish top with cooked smashed garlic cloves.

Makes 4 servings

SALMON CROQUETTES

2 15-ounce cans pink salmon
½ cup finely chopped onion
½ cup finely chopped green pepper
¼ cup finely chopped red pepper
½ cup finely chopped celery
1 teaspoon salt
1 teaspoon black pepper
½ teaspoon oregano
1 teaspoon hot pepper sauce
2 tablespoons butter
2 eggs
½ cup of bread crumbs
Oil for cooking

Drain salmon and remove skin, large bones and round cartilage.

Heat skillet over medium heat and melt butter. Add onion, peppers, and celery to butter. Sauté vegetables until tender; about 10 minutes. Remove from heat and cool.

In a large bowl, mix salmon, vegetables and remaining ingredients. Shape into oblong croquettes.

Fry in a pan lightly coated with oil.

Makes 16 croquettes

POACHED SEA BASS IN CHAMPAGNE SAUCE

2 sea bass fillets
2 cups dry champagne
4 tablespoons salted butter
3 minced garlic cloves
¼ cup diced shallots
4 tablespoons chopped fresh dill
¼ teaspoon salt for fish and ½ teaspoon for sauce
⅛ teaspoon black pepper

Rinse fish and pat dry. Season fillets with ¼ teaspoon salt and pepper.

In a sauté pan over medium-high heat, add champagne, garlic, shallots, dill and ½ teaspoon salt. Simmer for 5 minutes uncovered. Stir in butter.

Add sea bass fillets to pan and cover. Poach fish for 10 minutes.

Serve fish and sauce over white or jasmine rice.

Makes 2 servings.

GRILLED SHRIMP WITH SPICED COCONUT SAUCE

2 pounds of jumbo shrimp peeled, deveined and butterflied
6-8 metal or bamboo skewers

Marinade
    1½ teaspoons salt
    2 teaspoons curry powder
    3 garlic cloves, minced
    1 tablespoon olive oil
    1 13-ounce can coconut milk

Spiced Coconut Sauce
    8 ounces cream of coconut
    ¼ teaspoon nutmeg
    1 teaspoon red pepper

Place shrimp in a plastic Ziploc bag. In a bowl, whisk together the marinade ingredients until thoroughly incorporated. Immediately pour over shrimp. Close the bag and distribute the marinade evenly over the shrimp. Lay flat in a dish and refrigerate for 6 hours.

To prepare spiced coconut sauce
Mix cream of coconut, nutmeg and red pepper in a small bowl. Cover and let sit.

To prepare skewers
If using bamboo skewers, first soak in water for 30 minutes then drain. Using a slotted spoon, remove shrimp from marinade. Add 4 shrimp to each metal skewer, starting from the tail and sliding up through the middle so shrimp remains butterflied on the skewer. Lay on a platter until all shrimp are skewered.

Prepare the barbecue grill. Shrimp should be cooked on medium-high heat. Coals are ready when they turn white with an orange glow; about 30 minutes.

Grill shrimp until cooked through, turning once, about 4 minutes per side. Shrimp should have light grill marks. Brush generously with spiced coconut sauce. Turn and brush other side with sauce. Repeat. Continue to baste with coconut sauce until shrimp are nicely glazed and golden. Turn frequently, careful not to dry shrimp out.

Makes 4-6 servings

BARBECUE SHRIMP

2 pounds jumbo shrimp
4 garlic cloves
1 tablespoon olive oil
1½ teaspoons salt
1 teaspoon onion powder
1 cup barbecue sauce*

Mash garlic cloves and olive oil into a paste. Season shrimp with salt and onion powder. Using your hands, mix in garlic paste. Refrigerate for 4 hours.

Prepare the barbecue grill. Shrimp should be cooked on medium-high heat. Coals are ready when they turn white with an orange glow; about 30 minutes.

Place shrimp on seafood rack for grill. Grill shrimp until cooked through, turning once, about 4 minutes per side. Shrimp should have light grill marks. Brush generously with barbecue sauce. Turn and brush other side with sauce. Repeat. Continue to baste with sauce until shrimp are nicely glazed.

Makes 4-6 servings

* See pg 328 for barbecue sauce recipe

BARBECUE RIBS

3 pounds baby back ribs
1½ teaspoons salt
½ teaspoon black pepper
1 teaspoon garlic powder
1 teaspoon onion powder
½ teaspoon paprika
1 cup of barbecue sauce*

Rinse ribs and pat dry. Rub dry ingredients on both sides of ribs.

On the grill:
Prepare the barbecue grill. Ribs should be cooked on medium-high heat. Coals are ready when they turn white with an orange glow; about 30 minutes. Place ribs on the grill rack. Turn ribs over, rotate and baste generously with barbecue sauce every 10 minutes until tender and browned; about 40 minutes.

In the oven:
Put oven rack in middle position. Preheat oven to 400 degrees. Place ribs on a baking pan lined with heavy duty foil. Tent foil over baking sheet and tightly seal around edges of pan. Bake 1¼ hours. Remove ribs from oven and baste with barbecue sauce. Re-tent foil and return to oven for additional 30 minutes, basting with sauce every 10 minutes.

Makes 3-4 servings

* See pg 328 for barbecue sauce recipe

BBQ SAUCE

18 ounces tomato paste
1 tablespoon olive oil
2 cloves chopped garlic
½ cup chopped onion
3 chopped chipotle peppers in adobo sauce (in can)
1 cup dark brown sugar
1 teaspoon salt
½ cup orange juice
1 cup water

Add olive oil to medium-sized sauce pan over medium-high heat. Add garlic, onion, chipotle peppers, and sauté 3 minutes.

Reduce heat to medium and add tomato paste, salt and brown sugar. Stir until brown sugar dissolves. Cover and simmer 10 minutes.

Add orange juice and water to the saucepan, stirring frequently. Simmer on medium-low for 50 minutes, stirring periodically.

Yields 4 cups of sauce.

CHICKEN WITH ARTICHOKES AND ROASTED RED PEPPERS

1 pound chicken tenderloins
1 12-ounce jar quartered and marinated artichoke hearts, drained
1 roasted red pepper (in jar)
1 egg
1 cup flour
¾ cup olive oil for frying
1 teaspoon water
½ teaspoon salt
¼ teaspoon black pepper
½ teaspoon onion powder
½ teaspoon garlic powder
¼ teaspoon paprika
½ teaspoon dried oregano
1 egg

Season chicken with salt, pepper, onion powder, garlic powder and paprika. Beat egg and water in a medium-sized bowl. In another bowl add cup of flour.

One at a time, dredge tenderloins in flour then dip in egg wash. Return tenderloin to flour to coat. Shake off excess flour. Place on a platter and continue process with rest of the chicken.

Heat olive oil over medium-high heat. Working in batches, add chicken to the oil. Lightly brown chicken; about 3 minutes on each side.

Remove from oil and place in a single layer in a covered casserole dish. Cut roasted pepper into ½ inch strips. Layer roasted pepper and artichoke hearts on top of chicken. Drizzle with olive oil and sprinkle with oregano.

Cover dish and bake in 350-degree oven for 1 hour.

Makes 2-4 servings

MACARONI SALAD

1 pound box macaroni
1½ cups mayonnaise
¼ cup finely chopped onion
6 hard boiled eggs, chopped
1 cup chopped tomato
1 cup broccoli florets, finely chopped
1 teaspoon dried dill
2 teaspoons salt
1 teaspoon garlic powder
1 teaspoon onion powder
½ teaspoon black pepper
3 tablespoons olive oil

Prepare pasta as directed on package, adding a teaspoon of salt and a tablespoon of olive oil to the water. Boil pasta until tender and drain in strainer. Immediately mix 2 tablespoons of olive oil in pasta before running under cold water. Cool pasta with cold water then allow water to completely drain.

In a large bowl, mix pasta with remaining ingredients, adding additional mayonnaise and salt to taste if necessary. Serve immediately or refrigerate until chilled.

Makes 8 servings

FRESH HERB PASTA SALAD

1 pound box of mini penne pasta
  (such as Barilla brand or use your favorite pasta)
2 tablespoons fresh chopped chives
3 tablespoons fresh chopped dill
1 tablespoon fresh chopped tarragon
3 tablespoons fresh chopped parsley
2 teaspoons minced garlic
2 teaspoons salt
1 teaspoon onion powder
½ teaspoon black pepper
1 cup mayonnaise
¼ cup dijon mustard
2 tablespoons olive oil

Prepare pasta as directed on package, adding a teaspoon of salt and a tablespoon of olive oil to the water. Boil pasta until tender and drain in strainer. Immediately mix 2 tablespoons of olive oil in pasta before running under cold water. Cool pasta with cold water then allow water to completely drain.

In a small bowl, mix together mayonnaise, dijon mustard, fresh herbs, minced garlic, salt, onion powder and black pepper.

Pour drained pasta into a large bowl. Add herb sauce and mix well. Can be served immediately or chilled.

Makes 8 servings

GARLIC PARMESAN GRITS

1¼ cups grits
4 cups water
8 cloves garlic, peeled and smashed
1 cup freshly grated parmesan cheese
¾ cup light cream
1 tablespoon salt
½ teaspoon black pepper

Place garlic cloves on a cutting board. Use the side of a large butcher knife to smash garlic. (Lay the knife flat on the clove and press down until the clove breaks open.) Set aside.

Add grits to a pot and rinse with cold water. Drain slowly; careful not to pour grits out of the pot. Repeat until water runs clear.

Add 4 cups of water, salt, pepper and garlic cloves to grits. Bring to a boil over high heat, stirring frequently. Reduce heat to low and add cream; stir grits. Cover and simmer grits, stirring periodically, until thick and creamy; about 45 minutes.

Remove grits from heat and stir in parmesan cheese. Serve immediately.

Makes 6 servings

PLANTAINS

4 large ripe plantains
1½ cups vegetable oil for frying

Peel plantains. Cut plantain in half, widthwise, then slice each half lengthwise in thin slices. Approximately 4-5 slices per half.

Heat oil in large cast-iron pan on medium-high heat. Add plantains to the oil, cooking in batches, careful not to crowd in the pan. Cook until golden brown. Remove from oil and transfer to warm platter.

Makes 4 servings

MANGO RICE

½ cup chopped onion
2 cups chopped ripe mango
3 cups long grain rice (rinsed and drained)
3 tablespoons olive oil
2 teaspoons ginger
3 teaspoons salt
3 cups of water

In a 3-quart pot, heat olive oil over medium-high heat. Add chopped onion and sauté until softened. Add mango, ginger and salt and continue to sauté, stirring frequently to prevent sticking; about 3 minutes.

Add rice to ingredients in pot and sauté another 2 minutes. Add water and stir. Bring to a boil, scraping any bits from bottom of the pot. Turn heat to medium-low and cover; do not stir. Cook rice until liquid is absorbed and rice is tender; approximately 20-25 minutes.

Remove from heat and let rice stand for 5 minutes. Spoon rice into a serving bowl, mix and serve.

Makes 6-8 servings

BANANA CHEESECAKE WITH RUM SAUCE

For filling:
   3 8-ounce packages of cream cheese, softened
   1½ cups sugar
   2 teaspoons cinnamon
   5 eggs
   ½ cup sour cream
   1½ cups mashed ripe bananas
   2 teaspoons vanilla extract
   3 tablespoons all-purpose flour

For crust:
   1½ cups vanilla wafer cookie crumbs
   1 stick unsalted butter, melted
   ½ teaspoon cinnamon
   ⅛ teaspoon nutmeg

For sauce:
   ¼ cup dark rum
   1 cup water
   ½ cup dark brown sugar

Preheat oven to 375 degrees.

In a bowl, mix together cookie crumbs, cinnamon and nutmeg. Add melted butter to cookie crumbs and mix until all crumbs are coated.

Press crumb mixture into the bottom of a 9-inch springform pan. Set aside.

In a large bowl, combine cream cheese, sugar, flour, vanilla extract, cinnamon and eggs with an electric hand mixer on low speed at first, then increasing to medium. Mix ingredients until smooth.

Add banana and sour cream and mix on low until incorporated. Pour batter into prepared pan. Place springform pan on top of cookie sheet and place in preheated oven. Bake for 1 hour and 15 minutes.

Cool cheesecake on wire rack for 30 minutes. Loosen springform pan and cool for additional 30 minutes. Refrigerate at least 6 hours before serving.

In a small saucepan, bring rum to a boil. Add water and brown sugar, stirring until sugar dissolves. Simmer on low until sauce thickens to a syrup consistency. Drizzle on cheesecake slices.

Serves 12

PEANUT BUTTER AND JAM MUFFINS

1½ cups all-purpose flour
3 teaspoons baking powder
½ teaspoon salt
1 cup of sugar
2 eggs
½ cup vegetable oil
¾ cup of milk
½ cup of peanut butter
1 teaspoon of your desired flavor of jam (such as grape or
    strawberry) per muffin

Preheat oven to 350 degrees.

In a large mixing bowl, stir together dry ingredients. Add eggs, oil, milk and peanut butter. Mix ingredients with an electric hand mixer on low speed at first, then increasing to medium. Mix ingredients until smooth.

Spray a nonstick 12-cup muffin pan with vegetable spray. Divide batter evenly among the cups. Place a level teaspoon of jam in the center of each muffin, gently pressing down into the center of the batter until the jam is almost covered.

Place muffin pan on middle oven rack. Bake for 35 minutes. Cool in pan on wire rack for 10 minutes. Remove muffins from pan and continue to cool on wire rack.

Yields 12 muffins

S'MORES MUFFINS

1½ cups all-purpose flour
3 teaspoons baking powder
½ teaspoon salt
¾ cup of sugar
2 eggs
½ cup vegetable oil
¾ cup of milk
1 cup mini marshmallows
1 cup chocolate chips
1 cup coarsely crushed graham crackers (approximately 5 sheets)

Preheat oven to 350 degrees.

Crush graham crackers in a sealed sandwich bag.

In a large mixing bowl, stir together dry ingredients, excluding graham crackers. Add eggs, oil and milk. Mix ingredients with an electric hand mixer on low speed at first, then increasing speed to medium. Mix ingredients until smooth.

With a large spoon, stir in chocolate chips, marshmallows and graham crackers.

Spray a nonstick 12-cup muffin pan with vegetable spray. Divide batter evenly among the cups.

Place muffin pan on middle oven rack. Bake for 25 minutes. Cool in pan on wire rack for 10 minutes. Remove muffins from pan and continue to cool on wire rack.

Yields 12 muffins

STRAWBERRIES-N-CREAM MUFFINS

1½ cups all-purpose flour
3 teaspoons baking powder
½ teaspoon salt
¾ cup sugar
2 eggs
½ cup vegetable oil
1 teaspoon vanilla extract
¾ cup milk
½ cup heavy cream
1 cup chopped fresh strawberries

Preheat oven to 350 degrees.

In a large mixing bowl, stir together dry ingredients. Add eggs, oil, milk, heavy cream and vanilla extract. Mix ingredients with an electric hand mixer on low speed at first, then increasing to medium. Mix ingredients until smooth.

With a large spoon, stir in fresh strawberries.

Spray a nonstick 12-cup muffin pan with vegetable spray. Divide batter evenly among the cups.

Place muffin pan on middle oven rack. Bake for 25 minutes. Cool in pan on wire rack for 10 minutes. Remove muffins from pan and continue to cool on wire rack.

Yields 12 muffins

CARAMEL APPLE MUFFINS

1½ cups all-purpose flour
3 teaspoons baking powder
½ teaspoon salt
¾ cup sugar
2 eggs
½ cup vegetable oil
¾ cup milk
1 cup chopped golden delicious apples (peeled & cored)
½ cup prepared caramel topping (such as Hersheys)

Preheat oven to 350 degrees.

In a large mixing bowl, stir together dry ingredients. Add eggs, oil, milk and caramel topping. Mix ingredients with an electric hand mixer on low speed at first, then increasing to medium. Mix ingredients until smooth.

With a large spoon, stir in chopped apples.

Spray a nonstick 12-cup muffin pan with vegetable spray. Divide batter evenly among the cups.

Place muffin pan on middle oven rack. Bake for 25 minutes. Cool in pan on wire rack for 10 minutes. Remove muffins from pan and continue to cool on wire rack.

Yields 12 muffins

MELON SALAD WITH RASPBERRY-MINT COULIS

1 cantaloupe (seeded)
1 honeydew (seeded)
1 small seedless watermelon (about the size of a honeydew)
12 ounces raspberries
10 fresh mint leaves
1 cup sugar
1 cup water

Using a melon baller, scoop melon flesh into balls. Mix melon balls in a large bowl and set aside.

Rinse and drain raspberries. Place raspberries, mint, sugar and water in a medium saucepan. Bring to a boil over medium heat, stirring. Reduce heat to low, cover saucepan and simmer. Stir raspberries periodically. Be careful not to let simmering fruit boil over.

Simmer raspberries for 25 minutes. Let cool. Puree fruit in a food processor or blender until smooth. Place fine mesh sieve over a bowl. Strain raspberries through sieve to remove seeds and mint. Makes 2 cups sauce.

Spoon 1 cup melon salad into each serving bowl. Drizzle each serving with ¼ cup raspberry-mint sauce.

Yields 8 servings

PINK PLUSH CAKE

For cake:
   2½ cups cake flour
   1 teaspoon baking soda
   1 teaspoon salt
   1¾ cups sugar
   1 cup sour cream
   2 eggs
   1½ cups vegetable oil
   ½ cup freshly squeezed lemon juice with pulp (from 3-4 lemons, seeds removed)
   2 teaspoons lemon extract
   ½ teaspoon red food coloring

For frosting:
   2 8-ounce packages cream cheese (softened)
   4 sticks unsalted butter (softened)
   4 cups confectioners sugar
   2 tablespoons lemon extract
   3 to 4 drops red food coloring (adding additional coloring one drop at a time, if necessary)

   2 nonstick 9-inch round cake pans

For cake:
Preheat oven to 350 degrees.

In a mixing bowl stir together dry ingredients. Add eggs, sour cream, oil, lemon juice and lemon extract. Mix ingredients with an electric hand mixer on low at first, then increasing speed to medium. Mix ingredients until smooth. Add ½ teaspoon red food coloring. Mix on low until incorporated, turning batter pink.

Spray cake pans with nonstick spray. Divide cake batter evenly among the pans. Place pans on middle oven rack. Bake for 35 minutes.

Prepare frosting while cake bakes.

For frosting:

Place cream cheese and butter in a large mixing bowl. Add lemon extract. Beat on medium speed with a hand mixer until combined. Add half of the confectioners sugar and mix until incorporated. Add remaining confectioners sugar until well blended. Add 3 drops of food coloring; mix on low. Frosting should be a soft pink, a few shades lighter than the cake batter. If necessary, add additional food coloring one drop at a time, mixing frosting after each drop. Set aside.

Cool cake in pan on wire rack for 10 minutes. Run a thin knife around the edges of the pans to loosen cakes. Invert cakes onto wire racks. Cool completely.

Assembling the cake:

Place one cake layer upside down on cake platter. Using a frosting spatula, spread with frosting. Top with other layer, right side up. Spread frosting over top and sides.

Refrigerate two hours before serving.

Serves 12-14